MURDER AT CHRISTMAS

ALAN MOODY

A CATHERINE FORRESTER STORY

GREAT CHARACTERS.

TWISTS THAT CHANGE STORIES.

Copyright © 2025 Alan Moody
All rights reserved.

No part of this book may be reproduced, stored in a retrieval system, or transmitted in any form or by any means — electronic, mechanical, photocopying, recording, or otherwise — without the prior written permission of the publisher, except for brief quotations used in reviews or scholarly works.

This is a work of fiction. Names, characters, places, and events are either the product of the author's imagination or used fictitiously. Any resemblance to actual persons, living or dead, or actual events is purely coincidental.

First published in Great Britain by Alan Moody
Cover design by Alan Moody

For more books by Alan Moody, visit: www.alanmoodymystery.com, alanmoody1234@gmail.com.

To Jack, the brightest, kindest person I have ever met.

If you enjoy this book, please head back to Amazon and put on a positive review, this will help me keep on writing.

Character List

The Forrester Family

Catherine Forrester (née Price)
Now mistress of the Price Mansion, Catherine is intelligent, composed, and determined. A woman of sharp observation and deep compassion, she has endured more tragedy than most. Her father's murder and mother's death have shaped her resolve.

David Forrester
Catherine's husband. Loyal, steady, and quietly protective, David balances Catherine's assertiveness with patience and warmth. Though wary of reopening old wounds by returning to the mansion, he supports her decision and becomes an anchor amid the chaos that follows.

Peter Price
Catherine's younger brother. Charming but impulsive, Peter hides his insecurities behind bravado. His strained relationship with Catherine remains unresolved, and his involvement with the family's finances continues to raise questions.

Aunt Frances Price
Catherine and Peter's aunt, a widow of sharp tongue and firmer opinions. Once the family matriarch after Marion's death, Frances has returned for Christmas to offer her unsolicited

advice and to remind everyone of their obligations to the Price name.

Tulip
Catherine's faithful dog, the spirited Jack Russell.

Guests at the Price Mansion
Philip Marsh
Reginald Price's former business partner and an old friend of the family. Suave and self-assured, Philip has a gift for persuasion and a dangerous streak of arrogance.

Clara Finch
An old friend of Catherines father. Someone who likes to stir the pot.

Sally Peterson
Nervous and impressionable, Sally is haunted by the feeling that something is terribly wrong. Met Catherine in a case in Greece.

Martin Hale
A reserved, enigmatic man invited by Peter as a business associate.

Enid Bascombe
Eccentric and unpredictable, Enid lives nearby and has been both friend and thorn to Catherine. Renowned for her bizarre hobbies and riddling speech, she arrives to offer "help" and

perhaps a warning. Her sharp mind and unnerving insights make her both ally and enigma.

Holly Chamberlin

Old friend of Catherine who wants to write a book on her to revive her fortunes.

Simon Stephens

University friend of Peters

Mr. James Keene

Uninvited guest that arrives

The Household

Henshaw

The loyal butler of the Price Mansion. Punctual, discreet, and unfailingly polite, Henshaw has served the family through triumph and tragedy alike. Beneath his calm exterior, he notices more than he lets on and keeps certain truths locked behind his measured silence.

Others Mentioned or Recalled

Reginald Price (Deceased)

Catherine and Peter's late father, murdered years earlier in the mansion's study. His portrait still dominates the drawing room, a haunting reminder of the secrets that began everything.

Marion Price (Deceased)

Catherine's mother, who died of cancer earlier that year. Her absence lingers over the Christmas gathering, her quiet gentleness contrasting the storms that now rage through her family.

Matthew Askew (Deceased)

A suspect in a Greece murder enquiry. He was found dead in a lift shaft

Chapter 1: The Guests

The air was the kind that stung the throat with every breath. Crisp, metallic, carrying with it the faint tang of woodsmoke from distant chimneys and the sharper bite of frost that had settled over the countryside during the night. It was 1989, the twenty-third of December the eve of Christmas Eve and the Price Mansion stood in its winter dress, stone walls and turrets outlined in white where the frost clung stubbornly, as though nature herself had dusted the old house with icing sugar.

"Well," David said after a pause, his breath clouding in the frozen air, "It's done now. Three Geese ordered, nine guests expected, and enough puddings to feed the village choir. There'll be no escaping for four days."

Catherine turned her gaze on him, eyes sharp in the moonlight. "Peace of mind, David. That's all I want. I wonder if I'll find any during these next days."

"You will," he replied evenly, that calm tone she found both infuriating and reassuring. He had a knack for easing her edges. Tonight, she let it work.

He blew on his hands, the frost whitening his breath. "So," he said, smiling faintly, "who exactly is your brother bringing again?"

"Some dreary programmer slash business partner from America, Martin Hale." Her tone carried its usual brisk authority. "Brilliant, apparently, with his computers and wires and little boxes no one understands. I expect he'll bore me to tears. Then there's Simon Stevens, Peter's old friend from university. I've met him twice. Nice enough, but terribly young, just like Peter. I'll feel as though I'm hosting a sixth form gathering."

David's laugh rose warm in the cold. "Better that than your father's business cronies. At least these two won't fill the place with cigar smoke and boast about interest rates."

Catherine's mouth softened into a small smile. "Perhaps." She looked toward the mansion, its fairy lights blinking against the stone like patient little stars. "And then there's Clara Finch. I couldn't very well leave her out. Father always invited her, so she thinks it her right to descend upon us. She's opinionated, gets her own way, and never realises when she's insulted people. Perfect for the Price family Christmas."

"Something to look forward to then," David said lightly.

"She told me on the telephone she has a family secret to reveal." Catherine gave a short laugh. "Imagine announcing that in advance. I don't know whether to dread it or look forward to the spectacle. Either way, she'll have the stage."

"Knowing Clara, she'll thrive on keeping everyone on edge," David said. "And she'll relish every second."

Catherine tugged her scarf tighter. "Quite. Then there's Aunt Frances. She has nowhere else to go, and though she's painfully old-fashioned, she deserves her place by the fire. She'll tell us what Christmas was like before the war and knit in the corner while the rest of us argue. A welcome relief, in her way."

"She'll bring tradition," David said. "Someone has to remind the rest of us what the season's for."

Catherine shot him a sideways look. "Do you think I need reminding?"

He smiled. "Not you. But the others might. You'll carry the spirit of it as you always do."

She didn't answer at once. The compliment, quietly spoken, pleased her more than she'd admit. She looked toward the entrance again, the frost-capped lions flanking the stair like powdered sentinels.

"And Philip will come," she said at last. "Father's old partner. Almost part of the family, really. He was with Mother when she died. He was good to her. I'm glad she had someone. The cancer came so suddenly."

David's voice lowered. "Do you think your father knew about their affair?"

Catherine drew a long breath, the air biting her throat. "Perhaps," she said. "But whether he did or not, it matters little now. Philip's been decent to us since. That counts for more."

Silence stretched. Far off, an owl called across the fields, and from the valley drifted faint church-bells probably rehearsal for tomorrow's carol service. The sound threaded the still night like an old memory refusing to fade.

"Peter's friend Simon," she continued, "writes letters full of jokes and plans and wild optimism. He thinks life's a series of adventures waiting to be arranged. I rather envy that."

"You always admire what you've already outgrown," David teased.

She nudged his arm. "I'm not that old. But he'll fill the place with chatter. I just hope he remembers to wipe his shoes before he bounds in."

"I'll post myself by the mat," David said. "Sergeant Forrester, guardian of carpets."

Catherine smiled. "Excellent. Because Martin Hale strikes me as the sort who'll arrive with gadgets and jargon, convinced we're all Neanderthals. If he starts talking about circuits over dinner, Aunt Frances will faint."

"Then you'll revive her with brandy."

"Exactly."

"So that's the family invites, well I call them family, then there are the 'friends'" said Catherine.

She turned when David cleared his throat.

"You invited that nutty woman from Hollow Marrow," David said at last, his voice dry but touched with fond amusement. "Enid, isn't it? I do hope she doesn't bring her taxidermied animals with her."

The corners of Catherine's mouth twitched, though she held his gaze with her usual composure. "Enid Bascombe," she corrected. "And she isn't nutty just eccentric. You remember, she was of great help in that Hollow Marrow affair in autumn. If not for her peculiar eye for detail, I might never have realised what had been happening."

David gave a sceptical snort. "Help, yes, but at a price. If she turns up here with one of those glass-eyed foxes, I'm taking Tulip and sleeping in the stable."

As if on cue, Tulip scratched impatiently at the kitchen door and burst in, claws skittering on the flagstones. She barked once sharp, insistent and wagged her tail so vigorously her whole body seemed to wriggle.

"David," Catherine said with affectionate authority, "give her a bit of your toast. You know she'll never rest until she gets it."

With a sigh that was mostly for effect, David tore off a corner of toast and crouched. Tulip snatched it neatly, then trotted to the hearth and began crunching with relish, growling softly as though defending her prize from invisible rivals.

"Hopeless creature," David muttered.

"She's only hopeless because you encourage her," Catherine said, bending to smooth the dog's head. Tulip looked up, eyes bright, tail thumping the tiles like a drumbeat of joy.

David glanced at his wife. "And as if Enid weren't enough, you've invited that journalist fellow and his wife the Petersons, wasn't it?"

Catherine smiled faintly. "Adrian Peterson, yes. He wrote that piece for *The Times* about the case in Greece. Quite flattering to you, if I recall."

"To me?" David arched an eyebrow. "He called me 'the most reluctant detective since Maigret on a Sunday.' That's hardly flattering."

"It sold rather a lot of papers, though," she said, teasing. "And it reminded the public that you solved the impossible without ever raising your voice."

He gave a non-committal hum. "Flattery through insult, perhaps. Still, I suppose he earned his Christmas invitation." He paused. "Remind me about his wife. Sally, isn't it? Quiet sort, follows his lead?"

Catherine's tone softened. "Well Adrian isn't coming he has to write a piece on the climate. She's the gentler of the two, yes. A journalist as well, but of a different kind. Where Adrian likes the noise of things the headlines, the arguments Sally listens. She notices the pauses. It was her questions that uncovered the truth in Greece."

David grimaced at the memory. "How could I forget Greece? Heat like an oven, arguments in every corner, and those infernal olives. I still can't look at a jar without feeling accused."

Catherine's laugh rang bright. "She wrote to me, you know. Said she'd found something new, something connected to that time. She wants to talk face-to-face."

He groaned. "You do realise you're incapable of saying no to anyone with a mystery. You collect them like other women collect china."

"It's Christmas," she said serenely. "One ought to open one's doors, especially to those still troubled."

"This is Christmas, not a therapy session."

Catherine poured herself more tea. "Perhaps it's both. Isn't that what the season's for forgiveness, reflection, second chances?"

He smiled over the rim of his cup. "You make it sound almost religious."

"Almost?" Her eyes glinted. "You'll be in chapel with me tonight, I trust."

"Only if Tulip behaves better than last time," he said. "She barked through the Gloria."

Tulip pricked her ears at her name, then settled again by the fire, sighing as though in agreement.

The door opened then, and Henshaw appeared with his characteristic quiet dignity tall, silver-haired, immaculate even before breakfast. He seemed carved from restraint.

"Madam," he said, bowing slightly. "Preparations are complete. The dining room is laid, the chapel candles placed for evening prayers, and the wreaths hung along the staircase. The village carol singers will arrive at seven, as arranged."

"Excellent, Henshaw." Catherine's tone combined command and warmth. "And Mrs Wilton?"

Henshaw's mouth twitched a rare event. "She remains devoted to her puddings, madam. She has requested to be left entirely alone until they are steamed."

Catherine laughed. "Then we shall obey. The last person to interrupt Grace in her kitchen nearly lost a finger."

David raised his cup in mock salute. "To Grace, the silent general of the household army."

Tulip barked once, as if endorsing the toast. David sighed and surrendered another crust.

"One more thing, madam," Henshaw added. "Mrs Chamberlain telephoned. She was supposed to be arriving earlier than the others, but she has car trouble and will arriving at the same time, she will need to go to the Garage first."

"It is fantastic that she is coming" Catherine said, pleasure lighting her features. "Holly Chamberlain and I were inseparable at school. We used to laugh through the entire Latin class until they separated us."

"Is she the one who made you act in that detective play?" David asked, his smile teasing. "You said she insisted you had 'the voice of authority.'"

Catherine chuckled. "She did. I suspect she only wanted the prettier costume. But she has the warmest heart clever, kind, impossible to take offence. I've not seen her in ten years."

"I imagine she hasn't changed," David said. "She always struck you as the type who could make friends with a thunderstorm."

"Precisely." Catherine's gaze softened. "She'll bring life to this place."

"Between her laughter, Enid's stuffed menagerie, and Aunt Frances being Aunt Frances" David said, "we'll have quite the carnival."

"Better that than silence," Catherine said firmly. "This house has had too much silence of late."

He studied her across the table. "You've carried too much of its weight."

She didn't answer, only smiled faintly the smile that meant *enough*. Henshaw bowed himself from the room, closing the door with the gentleness of a man accustomed to ghosts.

Chapter 2: More Preparations

The fire cracked; pine sap hissed. The clock chimed ten. Frost feathered the windowpanes, softening the light. Tulip dozed, one paw twitching as if she chased imaginary rabbits through her dreams.

"Every detail just as I planned," she murmured. "I wanted it perfect before anyone arrives."

"It is perfect. It looks alive again."

"Alive and expectant," she said. "I can almost hear the walls sighing with relief."

They moved toward the fire. The carved nativity scene above the mantel glowed in the flame-light Mary, Joseph, the infant Christ surrounded by small wooden animals. Catherine touched the little manger with reverence.

"Mother used to polish this herself," she said. "Said no servant's hand should dust the holy family."

"She had good taste," David said quietly.

Catherine turned. "Tomorrow we'll take Aunt Frances to the carol service. She insists on it every year. We'll freeze solid, but she'll call it character-building."

"I'll bring a flask," David offered.

"With tea?"

"With something that keeps the soul warmer than tea," he said.

She gave a delighted laugh. "You think of everything."

She stepped back to admire her handiwork. "Three Geese," she repeated with satisfaction. "I hope they all carve properly."

"They will if we keep the knives sharp."

She looked up at him, amused. "A house like this ought to come with a manual. 'On the care of relatives and the carving of birds.'"

"Yours would sell," he said.

They wandered on into the drawing room. Logs crackled, shadows dancing on the walls. The radio now played *In Dulci Jubilo* in the distance. Catherine ran her fingers over the piano lid.

"Mother played every Christmas morning," she said. "Even when Father grumbled. She'd have us all sing until the maids joined in."

"You'll play tomorrow?"

"Perhaps," she said. "If Peter dares to accompany me. He always misses the high notes."

"Then I shall cover my ears gallantly."

She smiled. "You'll do no such thing."

David picked up a small ornament from the mantel an old glass angel with one wing cracked. "You kept this."

"Of course. It's lucky. Mother said every Christmas tree needs one imperfection, or it's tempting fate."

He replaced it carefully. "Then our luck's secure."

They sat by the fire, the heat turning their cheeks pink.

"So tell me again," David said, stretching his legs toward the hearth. "Which guest worries you most?"

She considered. "Clara Finch, without question. She thrives on drama. If she doesn't find one, she invents it. She'll wear something scandalously bright scarlet, probably and criticise the pudding as though auditioning for a column in *The Telegraph*."

"And yet you sound almost fond of her."

"I am, in a perverse way. She reminds me of my father never content unless she's stirring something."

"And Philip?"

"Philip's... complicated," she said. "He brings civility. He'll charm everyone, and he'll mean most of it. But part of him will always belong to the past to my Mother."

David nodded. "Still, he's coming for the right reasons."

"He said he wouldn't miss it," she murmured. "I think he wants to be sure I'm all right."

"You are," David said. "More than all right."

She smiled at that.

For a while they listened to the wind moving faintly through the chimneys, the gentle pop of sap in the logs.

"Aunt Frances," Catherine said at last, "will love this fire. She'll set up her knitting bag right there, between the hearth and the armchair, and narrate her pattern aloud so no one forgets she's working."

"She'll complain about drafts," David said.

"She'll complain about everything," Catherine replied, laughing. "But she means no harm. She's a good heart under all that starch."

"Come," Catherine said at last, standing. "I want to see the garlands in the hall."

David followed her through the doorway into the grand corridor. Price Mansion revealed itself room by room oak panels gleaming, stair rails wound with red ribbon, candles waiting in silver sconces. A smell of beeswax, fir, and polish hung in the stillness.

They stood a moment longer. From somewhere beyond the windows came the faint echo of church bells the children rehearsing carols down in the valley. The notes drifted up the hill, pure and tentative, like snowflakes that might melt if listened to too intently.

Tulip padded forward, sniffed at the base of the portrait, then sat, head tilted.

"Even she feels the weight of family," Catherine murmured.

"Or the smell of Henshaw's polish," David said, and she laughed, the sound easing the air.

"I placed the old fairy on top," Catherine said. "It belonged to my mother's first Christmas here."

David tilted his head to admire it a silver dressed doll slightly bent. "Perfectly imperfect," he said. "Rather like its owner."

"Careful," she warned with a smile. "I still have lists for you."

He groaned. "Assignments?"

"Tasks," she corrected. "More civilised. You're to fetch the spare heaters from the outbuilding, or the carol singers will turn blue before the second verse."

"I thought frostbite was part of the tradition."

"The tradition," she said, tapping his sleeve, "is hospitality. You will fetch the heaters."

"Yes, Captain," he said obediently, earning himself an approving glance.

They moved through the house together, the rhythm of long familiarity between them, he reaching for doors before she did, she pausing to straighten a bow on a garland or adjust a candle that had leaned too far. When they passed the study, Catherine paused, glancing in at the large oak desk where her father had once kept accounts and secrets alike.

"Do you miss them?" David asked gently.

"Every day," she said. "But I've learned to live with ghosts. They keep me sensible."

He squeezed her hand. "Then may these new guests prove the living kind of ghosts loud, inconvenient, and warm-blooded."

She laughed softly. "I shall drink to that."

In the service corridor the air cooled. Children from the village had hung paper chains along the wall, bright loops of red and green cut from old magazines. A crude cardboard angel smiled down from a nail. Someone Grace, probably had dusted the narrow windowsills with flour to imitate snow.

They fetched the heaters, brushed cobwebs from their sleeves, and returned through the chapel. The small room gleamed with readiness: brass candlesticks polished, pew cushions plumped, the scent of beeswax and evergreens serene and solemn.

Catherine checked the candles, steadying one that leaned. "Do you suppose Enid will sing?" she asked idly.

David gave a short laugh. "If she does, I only hope it isn't a duet with one of her exhibits."

"She'll surprise you," Catherine said. "Beneath all that eccentricity there's kindness."

"She's lonely," Catherine said. "People laugh at what they don't understand."

He looked at her a moment, recognising the quiet compassion behind the brisk tone. "You really do collect strays."

"Only the interesting ones, like yourself." she said, and that made him smile.

Chapter 3: Remembering the Past

Catherine Forrester drew her coat tighter around her shoulders, the dark wool crisp with cold, and stood for a long moment on the crunching gravel. The sky above was a hard, silvery grey, fading towards evening, and from the lower valley the faint bells of St. Mark's carried through the still air another early carol practice, or perhaps the vicar rehearsing the choir for the Christmas Eve service.

She looked up at the house, her house now. It loomed proudly against the pale sky, its many windows glowing with gold from the lamps within. Fairy lights looped unevenly along the gables, a tangle of gold and white blinking patiently in the dusk. Evergreen garlands trailed along the balustrades of the front steps, threaded with ribbons of red and silver. A wreath, thick with holly and ivy, berries shining like drops of blood, hung on the great oak door, its red bow stiffened by frost.

A thin plume of smoke rose from one of the tall chimneys, curling in the still air like the ghost of a forgotten Christmas.

David Forrester, standing a little behind her, stamped his feet on the icy gravel. He was not built for standing still. His breath came in white bursts. "It looks impressive," he said at last, tone dry but not unkind. "Positively aristocratic. You could charge admission."

Catherine smiled faintly, her gloved hand brushing a lock of hair from her cheek. "It deserves to be seen. For years it stood half-empty shutters closed, damp creeping into the corners. Now, at last, it feels awake again."

David's eyes travelled over the frost-tipped stonework. "You've certainly brought it back to life. The decorators must have adored you. That much holly could bankrupt a florist."

"Nothing wrong with a little extravagance," she replied, chin high. "It's Christmas."

He gave a small laugh, breath fogging the air. "I think you've singlehandedly kept the Maidstone haberdashers in business."

She ignored the tease, stepping forward a few paces. "It was my parents' pride and joy. They entertained half the county here in the sixties. I used to watch from the landing the dresses, the music, the smell of sherry and pine. I thought it all magic."

David followed her gaze to the upper windows where candlelight trembled faintly behind the frost. "And now it's yours," he said quietly. "A bit of magic reclaimed."

She turned to him, her eyes bright. "Exactly. I wanted people to see it again as it should be not some dreary monument to a past scandal, but a home. My father would never have let it fall to ruin."

"Your father," David began with care, "wasn't always right about what should or shouldn't be done."

She smiled tightly. "He was rarely wrong either."

They stood together for a moment, side by side, the silence stretching comfortably between them. The fields beyond the drive shimmered under frost, the hedgerows stiff and white, the pond a sheet of pale glass. Somewhere in the distance a robin sang, quick and bright against the hush.

"Come," Catherine said at last. "We'll freeze to death admiring it from here."

They climbed the steps, boots crunching on frost. David ran a gloved hand along the stone balustrade. "Feels like walking into a postcard," he murmured. "You could almost hear Bing Crosby."

Catherine laughed, soft and genuine. "Mrs Henshaw's probably playing him in the kitchen. She's had the wireless on since dawn. Said it helps her baste the goose with feeling."

Inside, she could already smell the faint sweetness of roasting cinnamon, orange peel, and something savoury that hinted at goose fat.

At the top of the steps, she hesitated. The brass knocker shaped like a stag's head gleamed through the frost. She brushed it with her gloved fingers, a gesture almost ceremonial, and then pushed open the heavy oak door.

Warmth rushed out, scented with pine and polish and burning wood.

The entrance hall took her breath, even now. Garlands of fir and laurel looped along the banisters; the needles dusted with artificial snow. Candles flickered in sconces, their flames reflecting in the polished marble floor. A great Christmas tree, tall enough to touch the upper landing, stood in the corner, decked in glass baubles and silver ribbons. Beneath it, parcels wrapped in brown paper and red ribbon were arranged with military precision Henshaw's doing, no doubt.

Catherine removed her gloves slowly, eyes moving over every detail as though inspecting her own work. "I wanted to keep the old look," she said. "Nothing garish, nothing new money. Mother always said Christmas should smell of wax and fir, not plastic."

David smiled. "She was right. It feels like stepping into another time."

"That's the idea." She reached out to adjust a sprig of holly that had come loose on the banister, then turned toward the great hearth at the far end of the hall. A fire roared there, bright and lively

Catherine crossed to it, her boots quiet on the floor, and touched the little manger. "Mother used to let me set this up," she said softly. "Every year I'd put the angel in a different place, and she'd pretend not to notice. I think she liked that I made it mine."

David joined her. "You've done the same with the house."

"Yes," she said. "It's my turn."

He rested a hand on her shoulder. "And you've done it beautifully."

They lingered there, side by side, the firelight playing across their faces. In the distance, a clock chimed six.

"Let's go up," Catherine said at last. "There's something I want to see"

She led him to the staircase, her hand brushing the polished banister as they climbed. The portraits that lined the wall watched them ascend stern faces, powdered wigs, men in uniforms, women in silks. But halfway up hung the portrait that mattered most: Reginald and Marion Price, painted together in the winter of 1964.

Reginald in his dark suit, proud and unsmiling, eyes as sharp as a hawk's. Marian serene beside him, her pale hands folded on her lap, her expression a mixture of gentleness and quiet defiance.

Catherine stopped before it. "There they are, the parents" she said softly.

The flicker of the hall lamps made the paint seem alive. David looked from the portrait to Catherine and back again. "You have her eyes," he said.

"Everyone says that."

"It's true."

Catherine studied the painting for a long time. "I wonder what Father would have made of everything?" she murmured.

David's mouth curved. "He would have shouted and stormed off at most of the decisions you made."

She laughed a clear, low sound that seemed to warm the cold marble around them. "Yes. He would have hated my independence, my insistence on selling the shares, on hiring decorators from London, on replacing his precious study wallpaper. But he would have admired the result, even if he never admitted it."

"And your mother?"

Catherine's eyes softened. "She'd have approved of everything. She told me once that the house only truly lived when it was full of warmth. I think she meant laughter, not central heating."

David smiled faintly. "Both help."

Catherine's gloved hand brushed the banister, her fingers tracing the grain of the wood. "I miss them. Not with grief anymore not sharp just a kind of quiet missing. As though they've gone on a long journey."

David slipped an arm around her waist, drawing her gently against him. "They'd be proud. You've carried the name, the legacy, and made something new of it. That's all any parent hopes for."

She leaned against him for a moment, resting her head on his shoulder. "You always know what to say."

"Only because you do most of the thinking for us both," he teased.

"Don't be ridiculous," she said, though her lips curved. "Come along. Let's look at the dining room. I had the ceiling repainted, and if Henshaw's set the table as I asked, it should look fit for a magazine."

The dining room was a picture of old-fashioned splendour. A long oak table ran the length of the chamber, gleaming under the glow of two crystal chandeliers. The silverware sparkled; the crystal glasses caught the light like captured frost. Down the centre of the table ran a garland of holly, ivy, and mistletoe threaded with red ribbon. Two tall candles stood at either end beside bowls of oranges studded with cloves.

Catherine stood at the threshold, surveying the scene like a general inspecting a parade. "Perfect," she said.

David slipped his hands into his pockets. "You've outdone yourself. Even the Queen might approve."

"It is fit for royalty" Catherine said briskly.

He watched her move about the room, straightening a fork here, a sprig there. Her movements were brisk, confident, graceful. "You're pleased," he said softly.

"I am," she admitted, turning to him. "And you?"

He hesitated. "It's magnificent. But part of me wonders whether it will ever feel entirely… ours."

Catherine tilted her head, studying him. "You mean mine."

He smiled ruefully. "Perhaps."

She crossed to him, the faint scent of her perfume mingling with pine. "You'll get used to it. Give it time. Houses like this don't surrender easily they need to be won over."

"And have you?"

"I think so." Her smile was small but certain. "It's begun to trust me."

He chuckled. "Only you could say that about a house."

"Only because you've never owned one like this."

She looped her arm through his, resting her head briefly on his shoulder. "You'll see. When everyone's here, when the laughter fills the halls again, it'll feel like it used to. Before the arguments, before the illness. I want this Christmas to be different calm, warm, remembered for the right reasons."

He looked down at her fondly. "It will be, if you have anything to do with it."

"Then it's settled," she said lightly. "Now, come and see the drawing room. I've moved Mother's piano nearer the fire. We'll need it for carols tomorrow evening."

They wandered through the corridor where the scent of baking drifted faintly from the kitchen, brandy, spice and butter. Somewhere below, Mrs Henshaw barked orders at a younger maid, the sound reassuring in its familiarity.

The drawing room was aglow. Logs crackled in the hearth, and above the mantel hung a sprig of mistletoe, a touch that made Catherine roll her eyes when she noticed David glance up at it.

"Don't start," she said, amused.

He raised his hands in mock innocence. "Wouldn't dream of it."

"Liar."

He grinned, and she smiled back despite herself. "You do make it all rather bearable," she said softly.

"That's the aim."

She crossed to the piano, brushing her fingers along its polished lid. "Mother played carols every Christmas morning," she said. "She'd make us sing, even Father. He'd pretend to grumble, but he loved it really."

She struck a tentative chord. The sound was slightly flat, but warm, resonant, alive.

David came to stand behind her, resting a hand on her shoulder. "It's going to be good to hear music in this room again," he said.

Catherine turned her head, her eyes meeting his. "You do realise, David, you sound almost sentimental."

He smiled. "Must be the season."

"Or the company," she said, rising.

"Possibly both."

They stood close, her hand finding his. For a brief moment, the world outside, the frost, the memories, the weight of the house fell away. Only the warmth of the fire, the faint murmur of a carol from the radio, and the quiet rhythm of their breathing filled the space.

"Well," she said at last, her voice softer, "if this is to be our Christmas, it's off to a fine start."

David kissed her temple gently. "A perfect start."

"Tomorrow The Guests arrive" Catherine mused "Tonight the house is ours.".

They stood together before the fire as the frost frosted outside, the house warm and alive around them. And in the hall, high on the staircase, Reginald and Marian Price gazed out from their portrait the past and present joined for a quiet winter's moment in the glow of Christmas.

Chapter 4: Christmas Eve

The frost clung thickly to the hedgerows, glittering under the moon like shards of broken glass. Beyond the iron gates, the long drive curved toward Price Manor, its gravel frozen hard and crisp under the glow of lanterns Catherine had insisted be lit all along the path. Real candles burned in them, flames trembling bravely in the night wind. Catherine would never have tolerated those cheap electric fairy lights townsfolk were starting to string in shop windows. Not when tradition mattered. Not when the house was hers to present.

Tulip, the little Jack Russell, stood at the window with her paws pressed against the sill, her wiry tail flicking like a metronome. Her ears twitched at every crunch of gravel, and a low growl vibrated in her chest before she gave a sharp bark. Catherine glanced over from where she was adjusting a candle on the sideboard. The tiny flame trembled in its glass holder, throwing a golden shimmer over the polished wood.

She turned to the window just as a pair of headlights appeared through the trees at the far end of the drive. Snow still lay in uneven drifts across the lawn, the edges faintly silver in the moonlight.

"A flash car," she said, brushing a stray fleck of dust from her skirt. "That'll be Peter. Always has to show off."

David, standing by the fireplace and adjusting his tie with less conviction than usual, gave a small grunt. "It wouldn't be Peter otherwise."

Catherine smiled faintly. "He'll have the car waxed even if it's snowing."

David's eyes twinkled. "Waxed, polished, and probably blessed by a mechanic in a three-piece suit."

The sound of tyres on gravel grew louder. The sleek Mercedes drew up smoothly, its engine humming like a well-fed beast. Headlights cut through the falling snow before dimming to a soft glow. Out stepped Peter Price tall, confident, every movement deliberate. His dark coat swung open to reveal an expensive suit beneath. Even his gloves looked tailored.

He smiled, his breath clouding in the sharp air, and opened the rear door with a flourish, as though there were an audience watching.

"David!" he called. "Good to see you, old man."

David moved forward, shoulders square but expression guarded. Catherine watched him, noting the faint line between his brows that appeared whenever Peter was near. Peter had that knack, she thought, for turning even a family visit into a stage performance.

From the car emerged another man, spectacles catching the lantern light. He moved with smooth confidence, his hand extended immediately, his tone easy.

"This is my business partner, Martin Hale," Peter said.

"Hello, David," Martin said, smiling warmly. "You probably don't remember me, but I came once to see Reginald. I was trying to interest him in a business venture, computers. He wasn't inclined, of course. I don't think they were his thing."

Catherine gave a sharp laugh. "Reginald thought the abacus was a dangerous gadget."

Peter chuckled, though Catherine noticed he hadn't thought of the line himself. David shook Martin's hand firmly.

Martin's grip was cool, professional. "It's hard to believe people actually live somewhere this grand."

"Not grand," Catherine said briskly. "Just large enough for too many opinions under one roof."

Peter smirked. "And perfectly run, I'm sure."

Before Catherine could answer, another figure emerged from the car a lean man with a scarf wrapped high around his neck, cap pulled low against the wind. His eyes, sharp yet kind, found David's instantly.

"This is Simon Stevens," Peter added lightly, as though presenting a curiosity. "Though I believe you know him."

David's face broke into warmth. "Simon! Good heavens, it's been years. Good to see you again."

Simon nodded, his smile quiet and genuine. "Time flies," he said. "Let's hope tonight slows it down."

"Come in out of the cold," Catherine urged, her tone practical but kind. "You'll freeze if you linger. And Tulip will bark herself hoarse."

At the mention of her name, the terrier gave an emphatic yap, nose pressed to the glass.

Before further greetings could be exchanged, another sound carried up the drive, the rattle and cough of a cab. It pulled to a halt in a splutter of steam, the driver muttering as he leaned to open the passenger door. Out tumbled Enid Bascombe, bundled in layer upon layer of scarves. Her hat sat askew, a feather bobbing like an exclamation point every time she moved.

She stumbled once, caught herself, then peered owlishly about as if taking inventory of the night.

"Enid," Catherine called, striding forward into the glow of the porch lantern.

Enid's eyes darted to the group, then landed squarely on Martin. She pointed suddenly, her finger stiff as a rod. "And who is this?" she demanded.

Martin blinked, caught mid-step. "Martin Hale," he said carefully. "A pleasure."

"Never heard of you," Enid declared. "But I know the type, city hands, no calluses. You wouldn't last a week gutting a pheasant."

"Enid," Catherine said crisply, "I see you've found your google-eyed robin jumper."

Enid looked down at the monstrous knit a bright red robin with bulging felt eyes and sniffed. "It's festive," she replied defensively.

"Festive and alarming," Catherine murmured.

From her pocket, Enid drew a small jar, popped the lid with a faint pop, and, without ceremony, speared a pickled onion onto a cocktail stick. The sharp scent drifted instantly.

Tulip barked furiously and came outside.

"Oh hush, creature," Enid muttered, shoving the onion into her mouth. She chewed noisily, then fumbled again in her pocket, producing a packet of Rich Tea biscuits. She waved one toward the dog. "Would she like one?"

"She'd love one," Catherine said dryly, "though perhaps not soaked in onion brine. Enid this is Tulip, named after your Tulip."

Tulip, oblivious to culinary nuance, snatched the biscuit with delight when it came her way, tail wagging madly. Enid chuckled with satisfaction.

"She even looks like my Tulip and she has her appetite."

Catherine rolled her eyes but smiled. "Come inside before you freeze solid, Enid. You can't be eating onions in the snow."

"Let them look," Enid said stoutly. "I'm not the one driving a peacock's car." She nodded toward Peter's Mercedes.

Peter grinned, unoffended. "You'd prefer a tractor, no doubt."

"At least you can see where you're going in one," she shot back.

David chuckled softly, and Catherine caught the flicker of amusement in his eyes. She squeezed his arm as they moved back toward the house.

Even as Enid shuffled through the doorway, another cab pulled in, headlights scattering across the drive. The driver climbed out, opened the door, and out stepped Aunt Frances tall, angular, and so precise in movement that even the snowflakes seemed to hesitate around her. Her fox-fur collar was pulled snug, her expression pinched by both the cold and her natural disapproval of everything within a ten-mile radius.

"Thank you for inviting me, Catherine," she said primly, her lips forming each syllable as though it might be inspected. "I do hope the company is suitable. I only like our type of people."

Catherine planted her hands on her hips, one eyebrow lifting. "Aunt Frances, look around you. These people are my kind of people. Which means tonight, they're yours too. Now come in before you turn to ice. There's tea waiting and sherry for the truly weary."

Frances gave the faintest sniff, her eyes sliding past Peter, then Enid, whom she viewed as though she might shed feathers. But she swept inside without argument, pausing only to dab the corner of her coat with a gloved hand where a snowflake dared to rest.

David leaned close to Catherine as they followed. "She's mellowing with age," he whispered.

Catherine smiled tightly. "That's what you call it, is it?"

Moments later, the cheerful splutter of a Citroën 2CV bounced into the drive, its headlights bobbing. It parked at a jaunty angle. The door flew open, and out hopped Holly her scarf trailing, notebook clutched beneath one arm. Her cheeks were flushed pink, her grin irrepressible.

"Thank you for inviting me," she said with a grin. "Though really, Catherine, there's always a murder where you are. I thought I'd best bring my notebook."

David gave a groan of good humour. "Don't encourage her."

Catherine laughed, clear and unshaken. "It's Christmas. Even death takes a holiday."

"I'll believe it when I see it," Holly replied, eyebrows arching as she tucked a strand of hair behind her ear.

"Come in and meet David," Catherine said firmly, her tone half hostess, half command. "He's been wanting to meet you, thinks most of my guests are hangers-on."

"And I'm not?" Holly asked, mock-offended, though she was already brushing snow off her coat.

"You're at least entertaining," Catherine shot back. "Now hurry before the sherry vanishes. It has a habit of evaporating when Peter's near."

Peter looked over, hand on his chest in mock indignation. "Slander, sister dear."

"Observation," she corrected.

As Holly stepped past, she muttered, "To go and meet the other weirdos, you mean?"

"Exactly," Catherine answered briskly, her eyes gleaming with amusement.

Tulip barked again, racing in delighted circles. The hall swallowed them in warmth and light. The scent of pine was strong fresh and earthy from the great tree in the drawing room beyond.

A fire crackled in the grate, logs hissing softly. Somewhere a record player spun, the King's College Choir drifting through the house pure treble voices rising and falling like snow over rooftops.

Coats were shrugged off, scarves unwound, boots thudded onto the tiled floor in a chorus of arrivals. The air filled with the scent of wet wool and perfume, the mixture curiously comforting.

Tulip darted between legs, barking at each new arrival as though announcing them all in turn.

"Mind the dog," David warned mildly, stooping to ruffle her fur. Tulip looked up adoringly, eyes bright. Catherine smiled at the sight; David's gentle patience with the little terrier always softened her heart.

Enid was first to comment. "The tree's lopsided," she announced, tilting her head critically. "You've got too many baubles on the left."

"It's twelve feet tall," Catherine replied. "If it leans a little who cares, so do most of us after a glass of sherry."

Martin Hale laughed politely, that careful, polished laugh of a man who never risked offending anyone. Peter gave him an approving glance, as though humour were part of his quarterly report.

Simon Stevens, meanwhile, lingered near the fire, rubbing his hands together. The glow lit the side of his face, accentuating the fine lines around his eyes. "Feels like the Christmases I remember as a boy," he said softly. "Proper cold."

Catherine nodded, her expression softening. "That's the idea," she said. "A proper Christmas. cold outside, warmth inside, and a few sharp tongues to keep everyone honest."

Chapter 5: More Arrivals

The crunch of tyres on frosted gravel announced the arrival of the next guest. The sound broke the hush of the early evening, echoing faintly across the frost-stiff lawns and through the dark shapes of the trees that ringed the drive. A fine layer of ice dusted the branches. Soft white bulbs traced the line of the bare beeches and oaks like fallen stars, a quiet rebellion against the gloom of December.

Now, she turned toward the window beside the front door, her reflection merging with the glimmering glass. ""That will be Carla. Look at the shine on that paintwork. No one else could arrive so determined to be noticed."

David, straightening the lapels of his jacket, gave a quiet snort. "Trust Carla to make an entrance. You'd think she was pulling up at a premiere, not a Christmas gathering."

The car rolled to a smooth halt. A faint hiss of cold air followed the click of the driver's door. Out stepped a woman wrapped in fur and self-importance, her heels sinking slightly into the gravel. Even the wind seemed to pause as she surveyed the house, her chin lifted, her eyes sweeping across the façade as though measuring it for worth.

Catherine watched in silence, one hand resting on the doorframe. Carla had always had that rare talent of filling a space before she even entered it.

"Carla!" David called, striding forward into the drive, his voice carrying its usual polite amusement. "I trust the journey wasn't too unbearable?"

"Barely tolerable," Carla replied, closing the door with an exaggerated sigh. "The M20 was appalling, and honestly, David, one would think Maidstone were a frozen outpost of civilisation."

David chuckled, though there was no warmth behind it. "We prefer to think of it as rural charm."

Carla tilted her head, eyeing the manor again. "Charm, yes, if one overlooks the drafts. I do hope I have my usual room this time. You remember what happened two years ago at Christmas? I was tucked away like an afterthought beside the servants' stairs. In the box room, My luggage hardly fit."

David's smile tightened. "That 'box room' is one of our medium doubles, as it happens. Perfectly comfortable by anyone's standards. But..." he bowed slightly, "as requested, your usual room awaits. No one has claimed it."

Tulip, the little Jack Russell, had already bounded forward, her nose quivering with excitement. The faint rustle of paper and the sweet scent of biscuits had reached her, and she danced on her paws, staring up at Carla's glossy bag.

"Really, Catherine," Carla said, shifting the bag protectively behind her leg. "This dog has no manners. She's quite spoiled."

Catherine descended the last step and came to stand in the doorway, her figure framed by the light spilling out from the hall. Her tone, calm but iron-edged, left no room for debate. "Tulip remembers everyone, Carla especially those with food. You'd do well to guard that bag, unless you fancy sharing."

David smothered a grin. Carla pursed her lips, her expression souring for a moment before she composed herself into a smile too bright to be real.

"Catherine," she said, lowering her voice suddenly. "There's something I must speak to you about privately. I've discovered certain things about people in this house. It's quite urgent."

Catherine's eyes narrowed slightly. There was always something with Carla always a secret or a scandal waiting to be told, always just on the edge of propriety. Catherine let a small silence linger before answering. "We'll talk later," she said, evenly. "Inside, when you've thawed and I've a moment to listen properly. Right now, it's too cold to stand about whispering."

Without waiting for assent, Catherine crouched and pulled half a sausage from her coat pocket one she'd slipped from the kitchen earlier. Tulip's ears twitched. Catherine broke it in two and handed the smaller piece to the eager dog, who settled obediently at her feet, tail wagging contentedly.

"See?" Catherine said with a faint smile. "Bribery. Works wonders."

Carla gave a brittle laugh, but before she could reply, the sound of another engine reached them. Headlights swept the frosted hedgerows and glinted off the icy gravel. The second car that pulled up was an older model solid, practical, the kind of motor that spoke of steadiness rather than display.

Philip stepped out, buttoning his plain overcoat against the biting wind. The shadows of age and fatigue clung to him more heavily than they had last year. Catherine's expression softened.

"Philip," she said warmly, moving to greet him. "I'm so pleased you came. I know how hard it's been since Mother passed. You shouldn't spend Christmas alone."

He managed a tired smile. "Thank you, Catherine. I wasn't sure I'd manage it. The roads nearly defeated me." His breath misted in the air. "But it's good to see familiar faces."

"Then come in," Catherine said briskly. "The fire's roaring, the tree's lit, and there's mulled wine enough to drown the chill."

David stepped forward to shake Philip's hand, his tone respectful. "Good to have you with us. You're just in time; the evening's only beginning."

Before they could turn inside, the low growl of a third engine broke across the drive. The headlights were dimmer this time, the car older a boxy saloon dusted white from salt and frost.

A young woman climbed out, bundled tightly in her coat, her scarf wound high about her chin. She hesitated before closing the door, glancing back as though checking the darkened road behind her.

"Sally," Catherine murmured. "She looks frozen."

Sally spotted her and hurried forward, boots crunching through the thin ice. "Oh, Catherine," she said breathlessly, "I'm worried. Truly. There have been sightings again. People are talking."

Catherine's frown deepened. "Sightings?"

Sally nodded, voice trembling. "Yes. Of those we shouldn't name"

Catherine raised a hand gently but firmly. "Later. We'll talk later. Not here, in the dark. Come inside all of you. The cold will turn us to statues if we linger."

Her voice carried command without sharpness; even Carla obeyed. She ushered them through the grand oak doors.

Warmth enveloped them immediately. The air inside was fragrant with pine and spice garlands twisted with crimson ribbon hung along the banisters, and the faint crackle of logs filled the hall.

The nativity scene stood pride of place beneath the sweeping staircase: hand-carved figures of Mary, Joseph, and the Child, their wooden faces lit by a soft halo of fairy lights. Catherine paused beside it for a moment, her expression tender.

"It grounds the season," she said quietly. "Reminds us what we're meant to celebrate."

David brushed her arm, his smile gentle. "Even in this house, you find meaning in everything."

Tulip scampered ahead into the drawing room, claws clicking on the parquet. The scent of roasting Goose and sugared biscuits drifted from the kitchen. Somewhere deeper in the house, faint music played instrumental carols from the wireless.

Carla shed her fur coat in one dramatic movement, revealing a clinging silk dress that caught the light like fire. She moved straight to the mirror above the mantelpiece, touching her hair and turning to catch her reflection from several angles.

"Well," she said finally, "at least the decorations are tasteful this year. Last time, those paper chains looked as if a school fête had exploded in the hall."

David's eyes flicked toward Catherine, who didn't flinch. "The children made those chains," she said evenly. "They were proud of them."

The silence that followed was sharp but brief. Carla coloured faintly and pretended to study the tree instead.

Philip hung his coat neatly on the stand, his movements slow, deliberate. His gaze lingered on the nativity; eyes shadowed with something unspoken. Catherine noticed and touched his arm lightly. "It reminds us of what Christmas is truly about," she said softly.

"Yes," Philip murmured. "Hope. Even in the darkest night."

Sally, meanwhile, hovered near the door, still wrapped tightly in her scarf as if the warmth hadn't yet convinced her, it was real. Catherine guided her closer to the fire, where David was pouring steaming glasses of mulled wine.

"Come, Sally. Warm yourself. You look half frozen."

"Thank you," she said faintly, clutching the cup as if it were a lifeline. "The roads were dreadful. Ice all the way past the church."

David passed another cup to Catherine, brushing her fingers briefly with his. "To Christmas Eve," he said quietly, and she met his gaze with a small, knowing smile.

The room filled with low chatter as the guests settled. The fire crackled, throwing soft light over their faces. For a while, the talk was easy, roads, weather, the state of the world. Philip spoke of the market in town, of the wreaths strung across the shops. Carla reminisced about Christmases abroad "In Nice, we had fireworks over the water. You've never seen such a thing."

David chuckled. "You'd have missed the frost though. A Christmas without cold isn't a Christmas at all."

"Spoken like a man who's never had to chip ice from his windscreen in heels," Carla said tartly, though a smile touched her lips.

Sally laughed softly for the first time that evening. "I'd take frost over fireworks any day," she murmured. "At least frost doesn't argue back."

Catherine looked between them, content for the moment to let conversation flow. The tension she'd felt earlier still hummed beneath the surface, but warmth and wine were beginning to ease its grip.

Carla, of course, couldn't stay idle for long. "I hope," she said to David, "that the menu has improved this year. Last Christmas's pudding was almost inedible."

David smiled politely. "The pudding was traditional. You simply dislike raisins."

"I like refinement," Carla countered. "And too much suet ruins refinement."

"Then eat the custard," Catherine said crisply from across the hearth. "No one forced you to finish your slice last year, and no one will this year. But you'll not insult the cook in my house."

Carla blinked, startled, then laughed lightly as though it were a harmless jest. Philip's lips twitched; Sally looked down to hide a smile.

David leaned closer to Catherine, murmuring, "I think that counts as the first battle of Christmas won."

Catherine's tone softened. "I prefer to call it maintaining order."

Tulip, curled on the hearth rug, gave a small snuffle of contentment. The firelight gleamed on her smooth coat.

Sally turned toward Catherine. "Do you think the carollers will still come tonight?"

"Yes," Catherine said with certainty. "They'll sing outside later. I've arranged for hot punch for them in the porch. You'll hear them from the windows if you prefer to stay in."

David smiled. "And if I know you, you'll be out there leading them yourself."

Catherine's eyes sparked. "If needs be. Tradition matters, David."

He raised his glass. "To tradition, then."

"To warmth," Philip added quietly.

"And to better pudding," Carla murmured, earning another glance from Catherine that silenced her for good.

Laughter broke the tension. Conversation flowed once more gentler now, interwoven with the crackle of firewood and the faint music from the music system.

The house seemed, for a rare moment, at peace.

The wind sighed around the house, but inside all was golden and still. The fire glowed, the garlands swayed faintly in the draft, and Tulip, ever loyal, slept on, guarding the hearth.

Catherine looked around the room at Philip staring into the flames, at Sally thawing slowly into a smile, at Carla inspecting her reflection in a bauble and allowed herself, just for a moment, to feel content.

The ghosts of the past still lingered, but tonight, she thought, they could wait.

Christmas had come to Price Manor.

Chapter 6: Christmas morning

It was Christmas morning, and the world outside had been transformed overnight. Catherine stood at the bedroom window, her breath fogging faintly on the cold glass as she pulled back the heavy curtains. The scene that met her eyes seemed almost painted, snowflakes drifted thick and fast from a sky the colour of pewter, settling on the lawns and trees until every branch and hedge bowed under its weight.

"Merry Christmas, Catherine," David said from behind her, his voice low and warm, still rough with sleep. He leaned against the doorframe, hair slightly dishevelled, his dressing gown loosely tied.

She turned, her expression softening as her eyes found him. "Merry Christmas, Mr. F."

He smiled faintly. "I wonder if Tulip's ever seen the snow."

Almost on cue, Tulip's sharp bark echoed from the corridor. Another bark answered from somewhere outside one of the estate dogs, perhaps from the cottages. Tulip gave an impatient whine and scratched at the door, nails clicking excitedly against the polished boards.

Catherine already tying her robe with brisk precision said "I'm going down to let her out. I want to see what she makes of it."

David stretched, yawning. "Don't let her vanish after a rabbit. We'll never see her again till the thaw."

Catherine laughed softly, one hand brushing against his as she passed. "Then you'd have to come looking for her and for me."

"Tempting," he said, his smile lingering as she slipped out.

The house was hushed, wrapped in that peculiar stillness of early Christmas morning.. Their scent mingled with wax polish and the faint lingering smoke from the fireplaces below. The great clock on the landing chimed seven, echoing through the quiet halls.

As Catherine descended, she caught her own reflection briefly in the gilt-framed mirror by the stairwell: her robe cinched neatly, her hair loose around her shoulders, her face calm but alert.

She crossed the hall and pushed open the drawing room door, expecting emptiness, perhaps the faint glow of dying embers. Instead, she halted.

Slumped in the high-backed chair by the hearth sat Clara, head tilted at an unnatural angle, her hair dishevelled, her gown creased. One hand dangled loosely, still clutching a half-full wine glass. The fire had burned to embers; the candles from the night before were nothing but wax pools along the mantel.

"Clara?" Catherine's voice was quiet but edged with command. She stepped forward, crossing the rug in three swift strides. The silence in the room was thick only the faint hiss of cooling coals broke it.

"Clara." She called out.

From behind the Christmas tree, a voice piped up, startling her.

"She's gone," Enid declared, matter of fact and unconcerned. She stepped out from behind the branches, clutching a small jar of pickled onions. Her jumper, patterned with snowflakes and a reindeer that had lost one antler to age, hung loosely at the cuffs. "Dead as a doornail. I know that look. I helped out as a nurse during the war."

Catherine turned sharply. "Enid! What on earth are you doing behind the tree?"

"Looking for the biscuits," Enid said, perfectly calm. "And hiding from Philip's snoring. Sounds like a bandsaw through a foghorn. I found these instead." She popped an onion into her mouth with a crunch. "Anyway, no need to call for a doctor. She's well past help."

Catherine drew in a steadying breath. "We'll do this properly," she said, voice firm. "I'll ring the police station."

"I already tried," Enid replied cheerfully, dabbing her fingers on a handkerchief pulled from her sleeve. "Spoke to some young lad barely old enough to shave. Says they've no chance of getting out here till the roads clear. All the lanes from Maidstone are blocked. Might be hours, maybe all day."

Catherine's brow tightened, but she remained composed. Enid took the wine glass from Claras hand and passed it to Catherine, who brought it to her nose.

"Well," she said at last, setting the glass down on the mantelpiece with deliberate care, "it's murder."

Enid froze mid-crunch. "Murder?" she said faintly. "Are you certain?"

Catherine's reply was calm, measured. "Quite certain. I can smell the poison."

Enid's face puckered, but fascination soon overtook horror. "Well, I never. On Christmas morning, too. Some people have no sense of occasion."

Before Catherine could answer, Tulip began barking frantically from the hall. Catherine moved to the door and unlatched it. The little dog bounded out ahead of her, nails skittering on the tiles, tail a blur of excitement.

The cold hit Catherine's face as she opened the outer door a sudden slap of winter. The snow lay deep across the lawns, pure and untouched, softening every shape. Tulip plunged into it with enthusiasm, then stopped, confused, pawing at the strange softness beneath her.

Catherine smiled despite herself. "She doesn't know what to make of it."

Tulip barked, leapt, then turned back in a flurry of snow, bounding to Catherine's feet. Catherine stooped and ran a hand along the little dog's back before ushering her inside.

"Good girl. That's enough adventure." She shut the door firmly, the latch clicking.

Enid watched from her post by the hearth, her jar of onions now half-empty. "Snow on Christmas morning," she mused. "Almost biblical, isn't it? Shepherds and angels, all that. Only we've got murder instead of a miracle."

"Less poetry, Enid," Catherine said briskly. "More sense. Tell me exactly what happened when you came down."

Enid looked thoughtful, tapping a finger against the jar. "I woke early. Couldn't sleep with all that racket from Philip. Came down for a look at the tree still pretty, even with half the lights gone out. Then I saw her. Thought she was dozing at first. Called her name, but nothing. So, I checked her pulse stone cold."

"You didn't move anything?"

"Just her hand. It was hanging funny, and I thought it'd drip wine on the carpet. Lovely carpet, this."

Catherine's mouth tightened. "Try not to touch anything else."

Enid sighed. "You always were the serious one."

"And you," Catherine said evenly, "were always incapable of taking direction."

Enid chuckled. "Takes all sorts to make a village."

Catherine was about to retort when she heard the faint sound of footsteps overhead. The rest of the house was waking.

"Then we'll prepare ourselves," she said quietly. "And I'll need you to keep calm, Enid."

"Calm? I'm as calm as a cucumber." Enid said, tapping her jar.

Moments later, the sound of slippers on the stairs drew nearer. David appeared in the doorway, fastening his dressing gown. His eyes swept the scene the motionless figure in the chair, Catherine's stance, Enid's wide-eyed composure and his expression hardened.

"Catherine?"

"She's dead," Catherine said simply. "Poisoned, I believe."

David's shoulders sagged, his face tightening with weary understanding. "Then it begins again."

Enid interjected before Catherine could answer. "She's right, you know. You can smell it plain as day."

David gave her a steady look. "Smelling isn't evidence, Enid."

"Well, neither are onions," she replied, undeterred. "But I've got those."

Catherine exhaled through her nose, a flicker of humour crossing her face. "David, could you fetch Philip and Holly? They should know."

He nodded and disappeared up the stairs.

Enid wandered to the window, peering out at the drifting snow. "The police will never get through from the village. We're quite cut off."

Catherine didn't answer at once. She stood by the hearth, studying the scene: Clara slumped, glass on the mantel, the faint shimmer of tinsel above her head. It all looked perversely serene.

The quiet was broken by the murmur of voices in the hall. Philip entered first, dressing gown belted tightly, Holly close behind him, rubbing her arms.

"Good heavens," Philip said when he saw Clara. "What's happened?"

"She's gone," Enid said helpfully, still holding her jar. "And Catherine says it's murder."

Holly gasped, pressing a hand to her mouth. "Murder? But who would…?"

Catherine cut in gently but firmly. "We'll find out in time. For now, I need everyone calm. No one leaves the house."

Enid nodded sagely. "I told the lad on the telephone we had a death, but I didn't say murder. Didn't want a fuss."

"Fuss is precisely what we have now," Catherine said quietly.

Philip sank into a chair, rubbing his temple. "She was drinking late," he murmured. "I passed by about midnight she said she couldn't sleep. I told her to go to bed."

"She didn't," Catherine said. "Mugwort takes a few hours to work so she could have had the poison earlier in the evening."

A small silence followed. The clock on the mantel ticked steadily. Outside, snow brushed against the windows like whispers.

"Well," Enid said eventually, "if we're snowed in, we may as well have tea. Nobody solves anything on an empty stomach."

"Enid," Catherine said warningly.

But Enid only shrugged. "Suit yourself. I'll put the kettle on anyway. Dead or alive, people need warming up."

David caught Catherine's eye. "Let her. Keeping busy might help."

Catherine hesitated, then gave a brief nod. "Very well. But no one goes far."

Enid shuffled off toward the kitchen, humming *Good King Wenceslas* under her breath.

Left in the drawing room, the others spoke in low, uncertain tones. Holly stood close to the tree, her fingers absently adjusting an ornament. "She was laughing last night," she said softly. "Talking about summer plans. How can someone just...?"

"It happens quickly," Philip murmured. "Quicker than you think."

David moved to Catherine's side. "Are you alright?" he asked quietly.

She met his gaze, steady and clear. "I'm fine. Shocked, but fine."

He touched her arm briefly, a gesture of solidarity. "You always keep your head."

"I have to," she said. "Someone must."

Behind them, Holly turned back to the fire. "Should we cover her face? It seems wrong to leave her like that."

"Not yet," Catherine said softly we will need to move her.

Philip rose, crossing slowly to the mantel. "What kind of poison, did you say?"

"Mugwart" Catherine replied.

He inhaled lightly, frowned

A silence settled again, fragile and heavy.

Tulip, restless, padded back into the room, sniffing the air. She circled the chair once, then sat at Catherine's feet with a soft whine.

David knelt to stroke her. "Even the dog knows something's wrong."

"She always does," Catherine said. "She feels things before we do."

From the kitchen came the faint whistle of a kettle and Enid's voice calling cheerfully, "Tea for the living!"

Despite everything, David almost smiled. "Only Enid could say that at a time like this."

"She has her uses," Catherine said dryly. "Mostly as comic relief."

Holly returned to her chair, still pale. "Do you think it could have been an accident?"

"No," Catherine said, without hesitation. "Clara didn't strike me as the careless sort."

"Nor the suicidal," Philip added grimly.

"Exactly," Catherine said. "So, until proven otherwise, we proceed on the assumption that someone killed her."

David leaned back, crossing his arms. "You mean we're trapped here, with a murderer?"

Catherine's eyes met his. "Yes."

Another silence fell. This one deeper.

Outside, the snow thickened, blurring the windows to opaque white. Inside, the fire cracked softly, the room heavy with warmth and unease.

Catherine straightened her shoulders, taking command once more. "Until the police arrive," she said, her tone calm but final, "I'll take charge. No one leaves. No one touches anything. We'll keep our heads and our tempers. And we'll find out what happened."

Enid reappeared then, carrying a mismatched tray of cups and the teapot balanced perilously beside her jar. "Tea's up," she said cheerfully, setting it down. "Murder or not, it's still Christmas."

Catherine didn't quite smile, but her tone softened. "Quite right. We'll need our strength."

They sat, awkwardly, the clink of china sounding almost obscene in the silence.

Outside, the church bells began to toll for morning service, their sound softened by the storm. Inside, the guests and family sat gathered in uneasy fellowship, eyes shifting from Catherine to the still figure by the hearth.

Christmas had come to Price Mansion bright, cold, and terrible and Catherine Forrester, calm as ever, stood at its heart, already thinking, already piecing together the truth.

Chapter 7: Christmas Conversations

The previous evening.

"It grows grander every year," Aunt Frances said, standing with her sherry glass held just below her chin. Her voice, rich with memory and self-importance, carried easily across the drawing room. "I remember when we had to make do with those pitiful tabletop trees during the war. Do you recall, Philip? Bits of tinsel scrounged from old sweet wrappers. And the oranges in our stockings miracles, they seemed. Candle ends clipped on crookedly and dripping wax all over the place. Still, we thought it marvellous then."

"Oranges still find their way into stockings in this house," Catherine replied firmly. She stood near the fire, one hand resting on the mantel, the glow outlining her profile in amber. "Some traditions ought never to be abandoned. My father insisted upon them, and so do I."

Frances tilted her head, indulgent but faintly teasing. "Ever the guardian of custom, Catherine. Your father would have approved. He used to say a proper Christmas was a test of discipline."

"And patience," David murmured, earning a few chuckles.

"And the candles," Clara added, her tone silky, drifting in like perfume. "You're very daring, Catherine, to still use real flame. I suppose you're confident enough to keep watch or is that David's duty?"

Catherine's lips curved slightly, though her eyes stayed steady. "Electric lights are too cold. Christmas needs warmth. Besides, I've a jug of water ready if disaster strikes."

She gestured toward the hearth, where Tulip lay curled on the rug, the dog's ear flicking as though in lazy agreement.

"Even Tulip approves," David said, smiling. "She has the good sense to keep to the warmest spot."

The company laughed, and for a while the talk remained light debate over decorations, endless and cheerful.

"Red and gold are timeless," Aunt Frances declared, swirling her sherry. "Multicoloured baubles are a vulgarity of the seventies. All that glitter!"

"Glitter's fun," Holly argued. "Children love sparkle."

"Children love noise," Carla countered, stretching her legs elegantly toward the fire. "And broken baubles, sticky fingers, crumbs in the carpet no thank you. A tree should look sophisticated."

Catherine raised an eyebrow. "I'll take joy over sophistication any day. Christmas isn't a showroom."

Sally, seated close to the window, had been silent through it all. Her eyes were fixed somewhere beyond the frosted panes, as though watching ghosts move across the lawn.

Clara noticed the stillness. She slipped off one glove, laying it deliberately across the arm of her chair, and said in her smooth, carrying voice, "I've been coming here for years, haven't I? Practically part of the furniture." She smiled, but her gaze locked on Catherine, waiting for acknowledgment.

"It wouldn't be Christmas without you, Clara," Catherine said evenly. There was warmth enough in her tone to please the others, but everyone recognised the undertone of authority that always reminded them who truly presided over the Price gatherings.

Clara's smile deepened a performer taking a cue. "Exactly. And, being part of the furniture, I know all the family secrets." Her eyes glinted like the rim of her glass. "Some even you don't know, Catherine."

"Oh, I think I know more than most," Aunt Frances cut in crisply. "I've been here longest, after all." She lowered herself into an armchair with a rustle of skirts that sounded like punctuation. "Secrets that go back before the war, when some of you were not yet born. I could tell you things about this family that would make your hair curl."

"Then perhaps don't," David said lightly, topping up her glass. "Let's keep our hair where it belongs."

Laughter flickered round the room nervous, brief.

Carla sniffed. "Reginald was obsessed with me. Until he wasn't."

A faint, uncomfortable shifting went round the room. Catherine set her glass down and spoke with measured calm. "Reginald isn't here to speak for himself, and I won't have his ghost dominate the evening. Christmas is for the living."

Her voice had a finality that no one wished to challenge.

"That's our Catherine," David said, half-smiling. "Always keeping order."

"Someone must," she replied, and though she didn't look at him, the brief curl of her mouth betrayed affection.

Across the room, in a quieter corner, Martin had begun explaining something to Peter, his American accent cutting cleanly through the soft murmur of resumed talk. "I've got this remote computer," he was saying, hands shaping his words. "You hook the phone line to a modem, type a few commands, and you can send programs straight from my machine to yours. Instant. No post, no couriers just data flying through wires."

Peter lifted a sceptical eyebrow, swirling the ice in his glass. "I think people want a computer they can see and trust.

Something solid on their desk. Not this invisible nonsense of lines and signals."

Martin laughed. "You'll change your mind when you see it in action."

Sally stirred, her voice small but clear. "I agree with Peter. I wouldn't want anyone seeing what's on my computer. I've just written a report on those murders in Greece."

That caught several ears. Heads turned.

"That was where I met Catherine," she added quickly, a flush creeping to her cheeks.

"Oh yes, the business abroad," Aunt Frances said, ever curious. "You never did tell us all the details."

Catherine raised a hand lightly. "There's no need to revisit it tonight. Greece was solved, and that's that."

"But it was fascinating!" Enid interjected, leaning forward eagerly from her seat on the sofa, her robin-embroidered jumper bright in the firelight. "I saved every newspaper clipping. Every one! I said it at the time nothing is ever as it seems."

"You always say that, Enid," David teased.

"Because it's true," Enid insisted, beaming. "Appearances deceive. Even Christmas pudding looks innocent until you find the coin."

The laughter that followed eased the tension again. Catherine allowed it, smiling faintly.

"Luckily," she said, "I solved it within the week. Which left David and me another week to sit on the beach instead of chasing suspects." She glanced at Sally. "That second week was much improved, wasn't it?"

Sally nodded, colour returning to her face. "Much better," she said softly. "Quieter."

"Ah," Clara said with mock wistfulness, "a mystery and a holiday romance. Some people have all the luck."

"Hardly romance," Catherine replied dryly, though her glance at David betrayed affection. "More a partnership of endurance. He followed me through half of Athens in the heat."

"And would again," David murmured, just loud enough for her to hear.

From the other sofa, Holly laughed brightly. "See what I mean? It's not even safe to be around you, Catherine. Murders and mysteries follow you like a curse."

"Or a calling," Philip said softly.

"Either way," Holly went on, "I vote for less murder and more wine. Where's that decanter?"

"Here," David said, rising with a host's practiced grace. He moved to the sideboard where bottles of claret, port, and sherry gleamed beside the cut-glass decanter of whisky. "A toast then.

To Catherine who keeps us all in line and somehow manages to make us come back year after year."

Glasses lifted, laughter circling once more.

"To Catherine!" came the chorus.

She inclined her head, expression composed but eyes bright. "And to Christmas," she said. "To hope, to goodwill and to honesty. Let's try to keep that in mind this time."

There was a ripple of knowing smiles. Glasses clinked.

Outside, faint church bells drifted through the cold air, mingling with the fire's crackle. Someone, Holly again, began to hum *O Come, All Ye Faithful*.

The melody softened the edges of conversation. For a time, the talk wandered through memories rather than arguments.

Aunt Frances spoke of blackout curtains and ration books. "Even on Christmas Eve, the sirens wailed," she said, eyes distant. "But we sang *Silent Night* down in the shelter. The echo under those brick arches it sounded like heaven."

Clara countered with tales of London in the sixties parties on rooftops, champagne served from bathtubs. "We thought we'd invented joy," she said with a laugh. "And perhaps we had, for a little while."

Enid seized the lull. "My robins began in those days. I carved the first from driftwood. Since then, one every

Christmas. Thirty of them now. I line them up on the mantel my little choir."

"Do they sing?" David asked.

"They would," she said with perfect seriousness, "if people only listened properly."

More laughter gentle this time.

Sally, drawn out again by questions, began to speak of her writing. "It was delicate to report on Greece," she said. "I wanted truth without cruelty. Catherine deserves the credit. She saw what no one else did."

Catherine shook her head. "You wrote it beautifully. You understood the people involved. That matters more than deduction."

"Bah, modesty," Enid said. "Ink lasts longer than memory, Sally. You've written yourself into history."

Clara smiled behind her glass. "We could all use a little rewriting, don't you think? Erase a few unfortunate chapters."

"Speak for yourself," Aunt Frances retorted. "I'm perfectly content with my history."

David leaned toward Catherine, voice low. "Do you ever tire of refereeing?"

"Never," she said, eyes glinting. "It gives me purpose."

Across the hearth, Carla caught the murmur and called lightly, "What are you two conspiring about?"

"Peace," Catherine answered. "An endangered species in this family."

"Well, you won't find it by talking," Carla quipped. "Pour me another sherry and I'll demonstrate."

David obliged, the motion easy, practised.

Philip, quiet until now, lifted his glass. "To Reginald," he said softly. "For all his faults, he gave us this place and the means to quarrel in comfort."

The room fell briefly still. Catherine's eyes met his grateful, measured. "To Reginald," she agreed. "And to what remains."

They drank. The silence that followed was not heavy, only thoughtful.

Tulip stirred on the rug, gave a soft huff, and settled again.

Holly broke the hush. "You know what this house needs? Music. Where's that old record player?"

"In the study," David said. "But we'd have to brave the corridor to fetch it."

"Then sing," Enid urged. "Voices are better than machines."

Aunt Frances cleared her throat and launched, surprisingly tuneful, into *The Holly and the Ivy*. Enid joined in; Holly clapped time. The others followed, half-hearted but smiling. Even Clara's laugh softened.

When the last note faded, Catherine looked round the room the glowing tree, the fire, the mixture of faces, some dear, some difficult and felt the ache of love that came with keeping everything together.

David's hand brushed hers as he passed her a replenished glass. "Still holding the fort," he murmured.

"Always," she replied.

He smiled. "Then here's to you, Commander-in-Chief."

She raised her glass slightly, eyes amused. "Just remember, David, even commanders need loyal lieutenants."

"Then I'm well-placed."

Chapter 8: Evening turned to night

The previous evening turned to night.

Clara, who had made herself conspicuous from the moment she arrived, set down her glass with a deliberate click. The sound seemed to travel across the drawing room like the crack of a whip. Conversation dwindled; only the soft pop of the fire and the faint rustle of tinsel remained.

She leaned forward, her earrings swinging in the candlelight. "Now," she began, her voice cutting through the lull, "one of the reasons I came to see you all apart from catching up with my favourite family, of course is this."

The chatter died entirely. Even Enid's constant fidgeting stilled.

"When Reginald and I were close," Clara continued, drawing out the word *close* just enough to provoke, "I used to do his books. I had another look recently and it isn't just a few thousand missing, but *millions* gone from the accounts."

A sharp intake of breath passed through the room like a draught. Even the fire seemed to hesitate.

"I know he was a drama queen," Clara said, her painted lips curling into a smile that didn't reach her eyes, "and yes, he had several women to pay off no denying that but there's no way he could have haemorrhaged that much money, even with a monkey in charge."

Her gaze slid toward Philip, gleaming with challenge. "Now, Philip, I'm not calling you a monkey," she said sweetly. "I'm saying you'd have had more left if you'd truly been in control."

Philip stiffened, fingers tightening around his glass until the stem looked ready to snap. The flicker of the firelight cast hollows along his jaw.

"That's a very large accusation," he said evenly. "Do you have proof or just your usual gossip?"

Clara's smile widened. "Oh, I have proof. Pages of it, darling. But I thought I'd save the performance for an audience."

A few uneasy chuckles surfaced, but Catherine did not join them. Sitting upright beside the hearth, her expression composed, she spoke with calm precision. "We were lucky we didn't leave it all to that new bit of his Belinda."

That name Belinda fluttered through the company like a ghost.

Carla, who had been silently adjusting her skirt, seized the opening. "Well, I was very close to your father, Catherine. We probably all know about *the affair*."

Her tone was slyly sympathetic, as if offering an olive branch dipped in poison.

Catherine's eyes fixed on her, cool and steady. "Well, I didn't know," she said evenly. "But I do now."

The words landed with a quiet finality.

An uncomfortable pause followed broken only by the tick of the mantel clock and the distant whistle of the wind at the eaves. Aunt Frances gave a small harrumph of disapproval, while Enid whispered something inaudible to Tulip at her feet.

Then Clara leaned in again, her perfume heavy and floral cutting through the scent of pine and smoke. "One of you," she declared, lowering her voice just enough to make everyone lean closer, "Catherine, David, Peter, Philip took those millions. And I'm here to find out who took it."

A collective stir rippled through the room.

Peter, flushed with sudden colour, sat forward. "Father didn't understand new business procedure. He was bleeding money long before anyone touched his accounts. Anyone could see it."

"Bleeding money?" Clara echoed, feigning surprise. "A colourful choice of words."

Philip snapped before Catherine could intervene. "If I hadn't taken charge, Price Enterprises would have collapsed completely. There would be *nothing* left to argue about now. You should be thanking me."

"Thanking you?" Peter shot back. "You drained it dry. You kept Father in the dark while you shifted funds around like a magician with a pack of cards."

"Stop it," Catherine said sharply, her voice slicing through the noise. The men froze at once; even Clara blinked.

Her tone softened but remained firm. "It's Christmas Eve. This is not the hour to quarrel like schoolboys over the ashes of the past. If there is truth in what you say, Clara, it will come out in time. But not by shouting across my drawing room."

Her command stilled the room completely.

David, lounging on the sofa, tilted his glass with a faint smile. "I, for one, am glad I'm out of all this. I was never good with investments. I've got my new life now; Catherine and I have the house back. That's worth more than any lost fortune."

Catherine glanced at him, the faintest glimmer of affection crossing her features. His words, casual though they sounded, grounded the moment, drawing breath back into the room.

"Well," Aunt Frances muttered, breaking the silence, "I think we could all do with fewer fortunes and more common sense."

"Common sense doesn't pay the bills," Clara replied sweetly.

"No," Catherine said, lifting her glass with quiet authority, "but it keeps you from behaving like fools."

The tension loosened slightly; a few nervous laughs fluttered around the room.

On the other side, Sally was perched at the edge of her chair, whispering to Enid. "I think there's a killer in the house," she said, eyes darting toward the quarrelling group. "Some people aren't what they seem."

Enid, untroubled, was slipping pieces of sausage to Tulip beneath the table. "You're right there," she said in her brisk, singsong voice. "More evil about than anyone realises. But I've seen it too the slip of a word, the look that doesn't fit. Well, we must all keep our wits."

Sally frowned. "You make it sound normal."

"Oh, nothing's normal at Christmas," Enid said cheerfully. "Never has been. Too much food, too much family, and everyone pretending they like one another."

Sally gave a small, nervous laugh. "You make it sound rather bleak."

"Bleak? No, just honest." Enid dusted crumbs from her lap. "Still, you're right to be wary. I'd keep your eyes open."

She rose then, muttering to herself. "Now, where are you, Mr Whittaker? I definitely brought you with me. You were in the basket."

Several heads turned.

Catherine frowned faintly. "Mr Whittaker?"

Enid waved a hand vaguely. "My cat. He's gone missing."

No one spoke; a few exchanged puzzled glances.

Across the room, Simon had cornered Holly near the drinks table. His grin was wide but hollow. "Could I come visit you in the night?"

Holly froze, glass halfway to her lips. "Simon," she said, forcing a brittle laugh, "that was a one-off and only because my husband spent all our savings on that ridiculous computer. Don't imagine it will happen again."

"Come on, Holly," Simon murmured, leaning closer. "It'll be fun."

Her smile vanished. "Not tonight," she said sharply, and crossed the room in a rush, cheeks flushed pink.

She went straight to where Martin stood nursing his drink, his posture neat and self-contained. "So, Martin," she began, her tone suddenly bright, "do you know Peter well? I've never seen you here before."

Martin smiled, a touch too smoothly. "I knew his father. Peter represents the future, though. He understands where the world's heading computers, technology. It's all changing."

Holly arched a brow. "Everywhere, you say. You make it sound like they'll walk among us."

Martin chuckled. "Not quite. But one day, perhaps, everyone will have one. Small enough to sit on a desk maybe even smaller. We'll talk through them, work through them, live through them."

"Live through them?" Aunt Frances repeated from her chair, looking baffled. "What on earth does that mean?"

"It means," Martin explained patiently, "that one day, people will rely on computers for everything. Communication, records, business"

"Good grief," Frances interrupted, "I hope I'm gone before that day arrives."

David laughed quietly. "Don't worry, Aunt. We'll keep you safely in the world of pen and paper."

"Thank you," she said primly. "I've managed perfectly well without machines that think for me."

Catherine smiled faintly. "A sound philosophy, Aunt Frances. Machines may change, but human foolishness does not."

That earned another ripple of laughter, easing the tension once more. Even Clara allowed herself a sip of wine and a thin smile.

The door opened then, and Henshaw entered with the solemn grace of a man who had served generations. A polished tray rested on his arm, bottles gleaming like jewels in the candlelight. "Wine is served," he announced.

David rose, taking one of the bottles reverently. "One of Reginald's old favourites," he said, turning it toward the light. "He never drank it just let it gather dust in the cellar. I think it's time it saw the light of day."

Glasses clinked as he poured, the deep red liquid catching the flicker of flame.

"To family," Clara declared, raising her glass.

"To survival," Philip muttered under his breath.

Catherine heard it but chose not to respond.

The wine worked its usual magic, loosening tongues and smoothing edges. Talk grew livelier, if no less barbed. Enid recounted how she once fell asleep in a church pew on Christmas Eve and woke up during the sermon. Aunt Frances countered with a story about rationing gone wrong "We once had to make Christmas pudding with turnips, you know."

Even Sally managed a smile. "Did you really?"

"Oh yes," Frances said proudly. "We were resourceful. Nobody died of it though one guest pretended to."

Laughter bubbled again. The fire flared, golden light dancing across polished furniture and glass. For a fleeting moment, it almost felt like peace.

Then the lights flickered.

A collective murmur swept through the room. Candles wavered, shadows jumped. In the next instant, the electricity failed altogether.

Gasps. A thud. Someone bumped the Christmas tree; baubles chimed faintly as they swayed.

"Keep calm," Catherine's voice rang out, firm and commanding. "No one move suddenly."

"I'll find the torch," Peter said, already crossing the room. A moment later, a beam of light sliced through the dark. "Fuse has blown," he announced.

For several tense minutes, only the creak of floorboards and the soft hiss of candle flames filled the air. Then, just as suddenly, the lights returned.

Applause half relief, half nervous laughter.

"Well done, Peter," Clara said, smiling too brightly.

But Peter didn't join the laughter. "The fuse was tampered with," he said quietly, holding it up. "Someone's been meddling."

The laughter died. People exchanged wary glances.

Catherine stood, her face composed but her eyes sharp. "Then we'll be careful. No one touches anything electrical without speaking to me first. Understood?"

A murmur of assent.

The chatter began again, but it was softer now, filled with little pauses. Glasses clinked, the fire crackled, and unease hung like mist.

Enid, bustling past Catherine's chair, managed to knock her elbow against the armrest, sending a splash of wine across the rug.

"Oh, drat it," Enid said, fishing for her handkerchief. "Sorry, Catherine. I should be more careful. But so should you. You shouldn't drink wine left lying about. I've seen what happens."

Catherine gave her a look that silenced the room. "Thank you for your advice, Enid. I'll take it under consideration."

Enid blinked, then nodded solemnly. "Just saying. These things have a way of sneaking up on you."

"Indeed," Catherine said dryly, rising to her full height. "Now, you all know it's been a long day. It's Christmas tomorrow. I'm retiring. You may carry on if you wish but I expect everyone at breakfast at eight sharp."

Her words were not a request but a verdict.

The company murmured polite assent. Some looked relieved, others, uneasy.

As Catherine moved toward the door, Tulip fell into step beside her, tail wagging faintly. David rose, kissed her hand lightly. "I'll be up shortly," he murmured.

"I'll hold you to that," she replied with a faint smile, before leaving the room.

Behind her, the conversation rose again low, uncertain, like the sound of a sea tide after a storm. The Christmas tree sparkled; the snow pressed thick against the windows; and through the polished glass, the dark night seemed to watch back.

The household would not sleep easily.

Chapter 9: The Briefing

The breakfast room was bright with winter light, though the heavy curtains kept most of it at bay. Outside the windows, the snow still came down in soft sheets, coating the gardens in silence. The bells from the parish church rang faintly through the storm, muffled as if wrapped in wool. On the long sideboard, platters of ham, rashers of bacon, eggs in silver dishes, and baskets of toast had been laid out by Henshaw. But little was eaten. The clatter of cutlery was half-hearted, the voices subdued. Everyone's eyes seemed to dart, nervously, from one to another.

Catherine entered the room with her usual composure, though her gaze was sharper than ever. Her steps carried the firmness of decision. She paused by the head of the table and let her eyes sweep across the company. Some looked back at her, others dropped their gaze to their plates.

"You've probably heard already," she began, her voice carrying clearly over the stillness, "Carla has been murdered."

The words expected, yet suddenly cold as the frost on the panes sent a ripple of unease along the breakfast table. Someone dropped a fork with a clatter; someone else coughed into a napkin as if to muffle a startled sound. Henshaw, hovering near the sideboard with a pot of coffee, paused mid-pour and lowered the pot to its tray with the gravity of a parish clerk closing a ledger.

"Due to the snow," Catherine continued, "the police are not coming. The roads are closed, and it may be some time before they can reach us. In the meantime, I will investigate this murder myself. I will have to interview each of you. As far as Christmas goes, we carry on. You all play games and sing. When we have finished the interviews, we will have Christmas dinner, followed by presents."

At the far end of the table, David let out a long sigh and rubbed his temples with the heels of his hands. "Here we go again," he muttered not without bitterness, but not without weary affection either.

A few nervous smiles ghosted across faces; most people stared at the tablecloth pattern as though it might provide an answer. Catherine shot David a look firm, not unkind; a look that said *steady yourself*. "Right let's get on with it."

She didn't raise her voice; she didn't need to. Even the clock on the mantelshelf seemed to tick more quietly for her.

Enid had been fussing with a plate of toast cut into perfect triangles, rearranging them into little fan-shapes as though constructing a model of a cathedral. At Catherine's announcement, she looked up brightly, as if the conversation concerned nothing more serious than the weather. "Well, that settles whether we go to church," she said in her crisp, practical way. "We shan't."

"Enid," Catherine said, "my Aunt Frances is not here. Would you go and find her?"

"As long as I can take Tulip with me," Enid replied, brushing crumbs from her snowflake jumper. "She's more useful than most people in this house. Have you seen my cat, Mr. Whittaker? I definitely brought him." She peered beneath the table as if the missing creature might have disguised himself as a shoe.

"You can take Tulip," Catherine said crisply. "As for your cat, I haven't seen him."

"He's about somewhere," Enid muttered, rising and patting her pockets. "He always turns up when there's ham." She gave a little whistle, and Tulip, who had been sitting very straight by Catherine's chair as if trying to look like a responsible dog, bounded down with a hopeful yip. Together they shuffled out into the corridor Enid mumbling about robins and ham, Tulip's nails ticking on the parquet.

The room breathed out and then in again. A chair squeaked. The silver covers over the kippers and bacon breathed a faint mist of warmth into the cold bright room. Outside, snow clung to the windows like nets of lace, and beyond that, a world of white and hush.

Catherine turned back to the table. "David and Sally if you'd come with me. We'll use the study for privacy."

.

The rest of the company pretended to busy themselves: Philip re-folded his napkin with military precision, Holly poured a little too much tea and dabbed at the spill, Peter reached for the marmalade he didn't want. Simon murmured something about the cold in the pipes. Martin looked down at his watch, then up again and smiled at no one.

They crossed the corridor. The study was warm and smelled faintly of pipe smoke and leather. Holly wreaths framed the mirror, and the fire in the grate glowed low, orange as a banked coal. On the mantel, a pair of brass candlesticks stood at attention; on the desk lay the orderly detritus of a life spent reading and deciding blotter, letter knife, fountain pen, the little wooden tray with elastic bands and paperclips as neat as regimental lines.

Catherine shut the door behind them. "Sit, Sally." She took the chair opposite; David leaned against the desk, arms folded, his weight on one hip, the stance of a man who intended to keep vigil as long as necessary.

"The reason I've picked you first," Catherine said, "is so we can have a little chat about what you wanted to discuss with me yesterday." She kept her voice level, but her eyes were incisive. "But first things first. We believe Carla was poisoned. I inspected the wine glass. It looks like the poison was added after the wine was poured. Did either of you see anything suspicious?"

Sally's fingers worried at the edge of her cardigan sleeve. She stared at the hearth as if the answer might be written in the coals. "Well… Henshaw definitely handed out the glasses. He gave one to everyone. But Peter I noticed Peter he took three glasses. One for Martin, Simon, and himself." She glanced up, anxious to be precise. "I thought it odd, but then the lights went out. Everyone was close together. Someone could have slipped something in then."

"All that business with the fuse," David muttered, his voice the low growl of a man who had learned to distrust coincidence. "A perfect moment for mischief."

Catherine inclined her head once acknowledgment without speculation. Then she leaned forward slightly, elbows on the chair arms, fingertips together. "Look at me, Sally. Why did you come here? Why do you look so frightened?"

Sally's throat moved. She tried to smile and couldn't. "This is what I wanted to talk to you about." Her voice shrank to a thread. "You know, in Greece… Matthew was murdered." The next words slipped out like a confession into a church. "What if he wasn't?"

David straightened away from the desk.

But Sally pressed on, as if the words had gathered momentum and would no longer be contained. "They found the remains of his parents in their flat. And in the paper I saw a photo of some businessmen in London. One of them looked like Matthew. I thought what if he's still alive? What if he's coming after us? Or after you, Catherine?"

Catherine's face didn't change much, but David, watching her as he always did, saw the muscle jump once in her cheek. She didn't look away. "We found him dead, Sally. We saw him. He can't come back from that."

Sally swallowed. "I don't know what to believe anymore."

There was a pause. In the pause a log in the grate shifted; the fire released a small sigh; the brass on the fender flickered.

"The poison in the glass," Catherine said then, steering the conversation back with deliberate firmness, "was mugwort." She didn't soften the word. "Have you ever used it?"

Sally nodded, hesitant and ashamed in equal measure. "Yes… for my nerves. It can be steeped in tea. But I don't have any with me." She twisted the cardigan hem again. "Not here."

David's eyes softened for a moment. "Nerves are allowed," he said quietly. "After the year you've had."

Sally managed a flicker of gratitude in his direction. "Thank you."

"When the lights came back on," Catherine continued, "people picked up glasses near them. Some were abandoned, some exchanged. It's possible the wrong glass was taken." She didn't look down at her notes; she remembered everything. "Are you saying you think the wrong person died?"

"I don't know," Sally whispered. "Maybe. What if it wasn't meant for Carla at all?"

Catherine didn't answer immediately. She studied Sally with that steady gaze that seemed to measure not only words but their weight and temperature. In that silence, the house spoke: a distant door closing; the faint rattle of crockery from the breakfast room; the muted squeal of Tulip greeting someone in the hall.

"We'll talk about this again another time," Catherine said briskly at last. "Thank you, Sally. You may go. Please send Peter in."

Sally rose too quickly; the chair legs scraped, and she winced as if she had stepped on someone's toes. "I'm sorry," she said at once, as if apology might balance the scales of the last twenty-four hours. "I'll, I'll find Peter." At the door she turned back, suddenly a child asking for permission she knew she already had. "Do you think I should keep to my room?"

Catherine's tone softened a fraction. "No. Keep to the public rooms. Stay where there are people. Eat something. That's an order."

Sally nodded, almost smiled, and slipped out. Her footsteps clicked across the corridor and faded.

David expelled a breath he seemed to have been holding since Greece. He dragged a hand through his hair, leaving it untidier than before. "She'll send herself mad if she keeps on like that," he said, not unkindly. "She looks as if she hasn't slept in days."

Catherine stood and smoothed her skirt a small, practical gesture that had the curious power to reset the room. "Mad or not, she's seen something. And if she's right about the glasses being switched, then we may all be in more danger than we realise."

"Mm." He came off the desk and crossed to the fire, prodding a log with the poker then remembering himself and setting the poker down neatly.

"Let me ask the questions." said Catherine.

"As if I'd do otherwise." He smiled sideways at her an old, private smile that belonged to a warmer world. "You're better at intimidating the living."

"And the dead?" she said lightly.

"I've seen the dead acquiesce."

She allowed herself the smallest of laughs; he watched it with the fond attention of a man who had decided long ago to count that sound among his blessings.

From somewhere distant came the faint, stubborn thrum of a carol *Hark! The Herald Angels Sing* played by fingers that knew the notes but not the joy. Someone attempting to knit the house back together with melody. The cheer of Christmas seemed very far away from the weight of the study.

Chapter 10: Where are the millions?

Peter stood by the Desk, turning a half-empty glass slowly in his hands. His expression bore that mixture of irritation and weary amusement that Catherine knew well. He looked older than his years in the shifting light, yet still somehow boyish when he smirked. His tie was slightly loosened, his hair ruffled as though he had run his hands through it in exasperation.

"Well," Peter began, his tone thick with complaint, "Carla kept hinting that we all stole Father's millions. Over and over, in that way of hers half sly joke, half accusation. Honestly, Catherine, I wish I had that money. I'd be able to fund all these great computer ideas people keep talking about. You know this thing I've heard whispers of the internet. Apparently, all knowledge could be stored on it. Imagine…" He gestured with his glass and nearly sloshed claret onto the hearthrug. "A world where you could carry the whole *Encyclopaedia Britannica* in your pocket."

David gave a low chuckle, leaning back with one arm draped along the chair. His other hand found Catherine's knee under the arm of her chair, a quiet weight she welcomed. She tipped her head an inch toward him, their eyes catching for a heartbeat before she turned back to Peter.

"Peter," Catherine said firmly though her mouth softened "you've always been full of mad ideas. But really the *Encyclopaedia* in your pocket? It would take shelves upon shelves, and even our strongest suitcases couldn't carry the weight. How could something like that ever be possible?"

Peter shrugged, the faintest grin pulling at one corner of his mouth. "Some clever people are making it happen. You'll see. We'll all live in a world where you can send letters instantly, without paper, without stamps. Whole libraries on a small machine." He sighed, the bravado flattening. "But of course without Father's millions, I'll keep tinkering with second-hand bits of kit, persuading them to do things they were never built for."

"Father's millions," David said, dry as the log on the grate, "were more myth than reality. He always lived like a man with plenty, but I never saw the money myself."

Peter leaned forward. "Carla believed it. She practically announced it. She made it sound as if we'd all hidden cash under the floorboards or in some Swiss vault. She had a way of making her voice cut through everything, didn't she? Accusations served with cranberry sauce."

Catherine's hand tightened over David's, and she straightened. "Carla had a way of provoking. That was her gift, if you can call it that. She thrived on stirring trouble. But her hints… they weren't harmless this time. Someone took them seriously enough to poison her."

Peter grimaced and set down his glass, prowling a step or two toward the Christmas tree. The fairy lights blinked their slow rhythm; a glass bauble shivered as a draught moved through the chimney. "Where do you find all these people, Catherine? Every time I come here there's someone eccentric under your roof. That woman Sally she keeps giving me odd looks, like she's adding sums. And Enid… Enid acts as if she knows exactly what's happening but insists on talking about a non-existent cat, Mr. Whittaker. Half the time I think she's mad; the other half I think she's laughing at us."

Catherine allowed herself a short breath of amusement; her face, however, remained set. "Enid sees more than she lets on. As for Sally, she's cleverer than she appears. But that's not our concern just now. Tell me about your wine glass?"

"Yes." He stopped, scratched the back of his head, disarranging already stubborn hair. "I think someone took it. I left mine on the table when I went to sort out the fuse in the hallway. When I came back, it had gone. So, I picked up another one. They were all muddled. If there's poison in one of them, Catherine well, who knows who it was meant for?"

Catherine's expression grew grim. She glanced at David an exchange of thought with no words then back to Peter. "That," she said, "is going to be the problem. If glasses were muddled, perhaps Carla wasn't meant to be the victim at all. The tangle has left us with death and no certainty."

Peter gave a mirthless laugh. "Come now, Catherine. You almost sound as if it wouldn't be Christmas in this family without a murder."

Her eyes narrowed though a ghost of a smile tugged. "It wouldn't be a family gathering for this family without one. And don't forget, Peter, you're getting free bed and board. Murder or not, that's more than some people get at Christmas."

David's thumb brushed across her fingers once, a quiet pulse of reassurance. "She's right, Peter. You may moan, but you're well looked after here. And Catherine's determination to get to the truth that's the best chance any of us have to get through the holiday with our sanity intact."

Peter put on a theatrical swoon. "Yes, yes. I bow to the great Catherine. I only wish she'd let me relax *before* dragging me into these interrogations."

Catherine's gaze sharpened. "I'll drag you in at whatever hour I please if it helps us find the killer. Lives are at stake.

And if Carla pushed too hard if her endless goading drove someone to desperation then I mean to know who."

Peter stopped pacing and leaned on the back of the visitors' chair, spinning it an inch to square it with the desk, the sort of fidget he'd always had around authority. "One thing I *will* say your friend Holly was talking to Carla in the hall not long before… well." His hand hovered, unwilling to name death. "It looked heated. Carla pointed; Holly flushed; her voice was sharp. I didn't hear the words, but it wasn't friendly."

"Thank you," Catherine said, inclining her head. Already her mind walked from the hall to the fuses to the glasses, rearranging the room like chess pieces. "That may prove useful. Now can you do something for me?"

Peter raised his brows. "Depends."

"Tell Philip to come in next. We need his account."

Peter sighed as only brothers can yet drained the last mouthful dutifully. "Very well. But don't expect him to be cooperative. He thinks I outmanoeuvred him by working with Martin. Perhaps I did. He'll hold it forever." a small, wry snort "Philip looks at him like the Devil in a decent suit."

Catherine's gaze sharpened by a degree. "We'll see how he fares under questions. Fetch him."

Peter nodded, put the empty glass down with more care than he'd taken picking it up, and moved to the door. He paused, looking back at them. The firelight threw a soft gold across his features, and in that glow he looked younger, almost wistful. "Catherine," he said softly, "be careful. You've a way of pulling truths out of people that they'd rather die than share. And in this house, tonight, that may be the case."

The latch clicked behind him. For a moment, silence and the fire's friendly murmur. A tiny jingle as a tree ornament settled. The study breathed.

"He's worried," David said, leaning nearer, voice low. "When Peter's worried, he hides behind sarcasm. You saw it."

"I did," Catherine said. She turned to him; her eyes, for all their resolve, warmed. "And I don't blame him. None of us is safe until we know the truth. But don't fret." She reached for his hand again; their fingers intertwined, warm, certain. "We've faced worse than this together."

Chapter 11: Have you got the money

Philip Marsh came into the study, which had been done up for the season with an effort that bordered on stubbornness. Beyond, the lawns had lost all contour beneath the snow save for the clipped cones of box hedges, and a blackbird batted a short, indignant route from one shrub to the next.

"Hi, Philip," Catherine said, her voice even, as she crossed to the small sofa opposite his chair. "Thank you for waiting."

"Still playing Detective Forrester then," he said, with an attempt at levity that didn't quite get off the ground.

"Not playing, as you know, I'm the real thing now." Said Catherine

He held her gaze. "I know."

He gestured to the room, as if the air itself might need an apology. "It has been a tough year. As far as Marion is concerned." His mouth moved around the name as if it were something delicate that might break if he handled it badly. "I still miss her dearly."

"I'm sorry," Catherine said, and meant it.

David took a quiet step forward. "Would you prefer tea? Something stronger? We've mulled wine coming for those who want it, though I'm not sure any of us have the stomach just now."

Philip managed a half-smile. "Coffee is doing what it can. And Marion well. She would have insisted on tea with cloves, just to make everything taste faintly of a dentist's waiting room. 'It's Christmassy, Philip,' she'd say. She was fierce about it. Traditions." He sat again, a careful lowering. "I've put all my effort into the business since. Now Price Enterprises is better than it's ever been." He glanced toward the window, as though the snow itself were the ledger he could measure success against. "Everything is better."

Catherine settled on the seat, smoothing her skirt. David stood at her shoulder, attentive without intruding. "You've worked hard."

"I know that without your father, this business would not be here," Philip said, and there was sincerity in the words, the kind that edges towards defensiveness only when once or twice they've not been believed. "But we all know that in the last few years, the business was stagnating. He… dug in." Philip's hands made a small, unsettled motion, something like opening a book you aren't ready to read. "Now everything is booming, and you and Peter are part of this. You'll have a quarter share each."

Catherine watched him, letting the words sit in the space, feeling their weight. The fire stirred, collapsed inward, and then flared as if encouraged by its own fall. "It's a generous arrangement," she said at last.

"It's a fair one," Philip replied, almost sharply, then softened. "That's why it annoys me so much when Carla waltzes in and accuses us all of stealing." He released a breath through his nose, a huff like an old bull. "Anyway, shouldn't talk ill of the dead."

"Do you know who killed her?" Catherine asked, and her tone shed the duvet of pleasantries the way a body sloughs snow at a doorway. "Or did you see anything?"

Philip's eyes moved to the nativity as if he might find something in the carver's patience that would serve him now. "She was the kind of woman who…" he stopped, shaped the sentence "who made everyone she met, even the most mild of characters, want to kill her." He lifted his coffee and put it back too hot. "From a personal point of view, she didn't implicate me on my own. I know what she's like. I was planning on ignoring her for three days, not killing her." The corners of his mouth tugged. "She always has these fancy ideas and then doesn't act on them. But the rest of the guests don't know that."

Catherine leaned forward a fraction. The tree in the hall gave a soft chime as a draught set a glass bell tapping against a strand of tinsel. David, hearing it, stepped over to push the door more firmly closed, then returned to his place near her, his hand briefly brushing her shoulder in an unconscious kiss of reassurance. She felt the warmth of his touch through wool and spine.

"What do you make of the other guests?" she asked.

"Enid," Philip said immediately, with the weary fondness reserved for mad aunts and beloved lunatics, "is as mad as a hatter and as sharp as ninepence. You'll need to keep her close, though you might want her to stop eating those pickled onions." He grimaced. "She was carrying a jar like a holy relic. It's the kind of thing that makes a man grateful this is a big house. You can always step into another room for air."

"Enid's onions," David murmured, resigned amusement touching his voice. "We may need to issue a warning."

"She means well," Catherine said, because Enid did, and because sometimes meaning well had to count for a little, even when the result was chaos. "And she sees more than she pretends."

"She sees more than she should," Philip countered, but there was no heat in it. "Sally has been looking for a murder before the murder happened. Where did you find her?"

"On holiday in Greece," Catherine said. "She does get anxious." She softened it with the tilt of her head that meant she was protective of someone, and David, catching it, smoothed his thumb absentmindedly across the crease of her sleeve.

"I've met Martin before," Philip said, his expression narrowing, the conversational equivalent of moving closer to the fire. "He was an associate of your father's. I never liked him. Whenever he was involved, dodgy things would happen. Don't get me wrong. His ideas are sound and Peter could learn a thing or two from him." He paused, pleased despite himself at the business talk; it steadied him. "But when he is around, documents went missing, people went missing, and suddenly he had money. If Carla had upset him, who knows what he might do?"

"You think him capable?" Catherine asked.

"I think him capable of whatever suits him," Philip replied. "Last year, I did think Peter could have murdered your father," he admitted, and his eyes met hers with something like apology. "But not anymore. Not unless he has the missing millions." He shifted, as though he had spoken a draught into the room. "We know Holly from years ago. I think she is going to like this murder. She's writing everything in that notebook of hers. She even brought it to dinner. Your father would have had a fit. He despised paper at table unless it was contracts, of course."

Catherine let a smile breach the barricade of her face. It came and went quickly. "Holly likes to be thorough."

"Hm." Philip tugged at his cuff. "Thorough can be a problem when you don't know where to stop."

"What do you think about the power cut?" Catherine asked. She heard, faintly, from the far rooms, a burst of laughter that felt out of place and therefore healthy. This house had always insisted on being both solemn and joyous depending on which door you opened. "Do you think someone pulled the fuse to be able to poison the wine?"

"I do," Philip said simply. "I think the timing was too convenient. I think people do things in the dark that they'd hesitate to do in the light. I think if you were going to slip something into a glass, or switch a bottle, or… anything that required a steady hand without a steady eye on you well. Darkness is a friend to cowards."

David's gaze angled to Catherine: a quick consultation the way two experienced dancers check each other's weight before the turn. She nodded almost imperceptibly. "Thank you," she said to Philip. "Without the police here, I need as much help as I can get."

Philip's mouth twisted, either at the mention of police or of their absence perhaps both. A small gold angel on the mantel tilted forward, then settled back; he reached up and righted it with a forefinger and a sigh. "Plus," he added in a tone that announced he had been waiting to say this, "if I had your father's millions, do you think I would have kept coming around to see him to get all that abuse over the years?" He spread his hands not exactly clean hands, but hands that had laboured.

"I don't suppose you could send in Holly next, could you?" Catherine replied

"I will," Philip said.

The case was getting clearer, well clearer to Catherine anyway.

Chapter 12: Can I write a book?

Holly entered the study. The heavy oak door swung shut behind them with a muffled thud, sealing out the draught from the hallway. The room was warm, alive with the glow of a roaring fire that licked the iron grate and crackled with each fresh breath of air that slipped up the chimney.

Holly sat down across the desk from Catherine and David. Her auburn hair caught the firelight, turning strands to gold. She looked perfectly at home, and yet there was a restless sparkle in her eyes that suggested her mind never ceased moving.

"How are you, Holly?" Catherine asked, her tone direct but not unkind.

Holly flashed a quick smile, a glint of mischief in it. "Well, I'm enjoying myself so far. I'm loving all the characters in this house." She lifted her glass in a half-mock toast to the fire, to the tree, to the shadows listening from the bookshelves. "As long as I don't get myself murdered, it'll all be grand."

David gave a soft laugh; the sound knocked the edge off the room for a second. Catherine didn't smile. She studied Holly as if weighing not just the answer but the angle of the answer, the way it sat in the mouth. Holly, catching the scrutiny and preferring not to notice it, sailed on.

"I've always loved this house," she said. "You've done wonders with it already. It doesn't feel gloomy anymore." She tipped her head toward the mantle where the holly wreaths hung square and green. "Look, Catherine, I want to write a book. About you. About all this." She gestured vaguely toward the door, where voices drifted like smoke; toward the tree, the fire, the glitter, the soft chime of baubles when the draught breathed. "I want to make my fortune on it. And I might even do it now that there's been a murder. Imagine the headlines. *The Lady Detective of Price Mansion.* Please endorse it."

David's eyebrows rose, amusement flickering across his face; his glance found Catherine's. She held his gaze for a fraction, then returned to Holly steady, almost stern.

"I will," Catherine said at last, "as long as you report everything properly. And none of it can be released until after the trial."

Holly blinked twice. "Trial?" The word clinked like a spoon against china. "What trial?"

"Before New Year," Catherine replied, each word laid down like a card in order, "I will have worked out who murdered Carla. There will be a trial. And the guilty will face it."

The room took in the finality as a church takes in a bell. For a few beats, only the logs cracked and the wind pressed its cold hand against the window.

"Oh, I see," Holly said at last, subdued a degree. She swirled her wine and took a deliberate gulp as if a swallow might grant courage. "Even before the murder, I'd been making notes. I can't help myself, you know it's in my nature." She tried on a grin and let it sit awkwardly. "Even though I adore Enid to bits, I noticed her after the lights went out. She was looking at one or two of the wine glasses. At first, I thought she was just finding her own, but what if she was slipping poison in?"

David shifted, leaning a hip against Catherine's chair; his hand brushed her shoulder in a casual, proprietary reassurance. "Enid?" he said, slow, sceptical. "She's eccentric, but not sly. She wears her madness openly. Poison feels too subtle for her."

"Still," Catherine said, tapping one finger once against the chair arm, "it's worth noting. People often hide things in plain sight. Go on, Holly."

"Well…" Holly leaned forward, warmed to her theme, eyes bright. "Sally seems obsessed with Peter and his friends. At first, I thought she was a rival company rep, sniffing for secrets. She listens constantly. I know she's a journalist, but she sees stories where there are none. And Martin he's so consumed with his work it's almost comical. It might suit Peter to have a partner like that. Simon, meanwhile…" She smirked, tossing her hair back with a small flourish. "Simon is obsessed with me."

Catherine's mouth curved just faintly, though her eyes stayed level. "You did encourage him a little, last time you were here."

"Perhaps I did," Holly admitted, laughing softly more for herself than for them. "I can't help it; I enjoy attention. Still, I'm married, and he ought to remember it." She lifted the glass, but the brief glance she cast into it looked like someone checking a mirror for a bruise.

"I've known Peter and Philip most of my life," Holly said, tone softening on the names. "They're the same men they've always been. It's hard to see them as suspects."

"I know what you mean," Catherine said. "They were not involved in previous murders. To me, they are family. But loyalty cannot blind us. I must keep them in my sight, just as I keep you in it, Holly."

David bent a little nearer to Catherine, his voice low for her alone. "You're too fair for your own good. You never let sentiment cloud judgement." His hand covered hers; she let her cheek tilt into his fingers for the briefest moment, then turned back.

"Peter says you were arguing with Carla in the hallway," Catherine said.

"Yes," Holly admitted. Colour crept up from her collar like heat. "She was being cruel about my... about Simon. She said she was going to tell my husband. Can you imagine?" She shook her head, a sharp little movement. "That woman never missed a chance to stir mischief. She's been whispering poison into everyone's ear, I'm sure of it. Not that they'll admit it to you."

"Carla's tongue," David said, "was sharper than any blade. If you ask me, her malice caught up with her."

"It did," Catherine said evenly. She let the quiet sit, heavy but not hostile, and then: "Holly, tell me everything. Every detail, no matter how small. A murderer depends on silence on people dismissing what they see."

Holly nodded quickly; her eagerness stumbled at the first step, then found its pace. "All right. The hallway well, it was just before the lights went out. She cornered me by the peacock umbrella stand." She flicked a glance at the corner where the old bronze bird preened. "She said I 'collected men like keyrings.' I told her she collected enemies like unpaid bills. She laughed. Not nicely. Then she said, 'I'll telephone your husband first thing Boxing Day and give him a little Christmas present.'"

"The line was down from the weather." Catherine said.

"She didn't know that." Holly said, shrugging. "Anyway, I told her she'd do no such thing. She said, 'Watch me.' And I said, 'Watch yourself.' That's it." She spread her hands and then clasped them, as if catching the words after they had flown.

"Did anyone else hear?" Catherine asked.

"I don't know. The hall was busy. Henshaw passed with the tray of glasses doing that thing where he pretends no one exists but still sees everything. Simon hovered, pretending to look at the hunting prints. Enid drifted through humming *Good King Wenceslas*. Peter... well, you know Peter; he's always somewhere he shouldn't be, but I didn't see him."

"And your glass?" Catherine asked.

"I set mine down on the little mahogany table with the lamp the one whose shade lists to the left." Holly mimed the tilt. "I didn't trust myself not to throw it in her face."

David's cheek twitched at the image. Catherine did not react. "When the lights went out, where were you?"

"In the doorway to the morning room," Holly said. "I'd taken a step back. I could feel the draft on my knees. I said 'Oh, for heaven's sake' and grabbed for the lamp, but of course that was no use."

"And when the lights returned?"

"People had shifted," Holly said. "It was like a set change in the dark. Philip was to my right, looking at his hand as if it had betrayed him. Sally was white as paper. Martin smiled into the middle distance. Simon laughed too loudly. Carla stood under the gilt mirror as if it were a spotlight. And then Peter appeared with the fuse, looking falsely heroic don't write that down." She caught herself and gave a quick, crooked grin. "Sorry. That was catty."

"Truth is allowed," Catherine said. "We'll edit later."

Holly exhaled, relieved. "All right. Then glasses were everywhere. I picked up one from where I thought I'd left mine. I don't know if it was the same. The coaster had stuck to the base made a little popping sound. I remember that. Then someone bumped the table and I apologised to the lamp as if it were a person."

"You apologised to Philip," David said mildly, "not the lamp."

Holly grimaced. "Yes, well. That too."

"Did you see *anyone* touch Carla's glass?" Catherine asked.

Holly took her time. The fire rearranged itself softly; the lights on the tree did their slow blink; upstairs, the young voice found the chorus again and missed it by a note and kept singing anyway. "No," she said finally. "I saw Carla raise her glass in that theatrical way of hers. I saw her glance sideways to see who was watching. But I can't swear to the drinking. She always drank like she was doing it for a magazine."

"Did Carla mention money to you?" Catherine asked. "Father's accounts. Missing sums."

Holly rolled her eyes. "She mentioned it to everyone within ten feet. 'Millions,' 'mysterious,' 'monkeys,' 'proof' she loved the music of a word more than its meaning.

Chapter 13: Revelation

Enid stormed into the study, her boots squeaking faintly against the polished wood as she flung the door wide. Her woollen skirt swayed heavily, and her cheeks were flushed with cold and indignation. She clutched at the doorframe as though to steady herself, though her voice rang out strong and strident.

"It's Aunt Frances," she declared breathlessly. "I've just come from her room. She's dead."

The words seemed to hang in the air like frost crystals, delicate yet terrible.

David, who had been standing by the window with his arm resting along the back of Catherine's chair, stiffened at once; his hand left the chair and hovered at Catherine's shoulder, not quite touching, then settled there as if remembering itself. Holly, perched uncomfortably on the edge of a chair with her notebook in her lap, startled upright the pencil clattered to the floor and rolled toward the hearth, where Tulip tracked it with grave concern.

"Dead?" Catherine repeated, her tone clipped but steady. "Enid, are you certain?"

Enid nodded vigorously, setting the small baubles on her robin jumper jingling. "I'm not in the habit of mistaking sleep for death, Catherine. Her hands were cold as the grave, and her lips had turned that colour. Don't argue with me I know what I've seen."

There was no room for disbelief in her manner, though Catherine's keen eyes searched her face nonetheless, measuring agitation against accuracy.

"Very well," Catherine said. "We'll go to her room."

The three of them David, Catherine, and Holly rose together. Tulip looked from one to the other, sprang to her feet, then sat again, uncertain whom to guard. David placed his hand lightly at the small of Catherine's back as they moved toward the door, a gesture of support as much as guidance. Catherine straightened her shoulders; grief would not master her, not now.

"Come on, Tulip," David murmured, and the little dog padded out with them, nails ticking softly on the floor.

In the corridor the air held the faint strains of carols from the distant drawing room; the tree lights glowed dimly through a crack in the door, a constellation of obedient stars.

"Where was she when you found her?" Catherine asked as they climbed, not hurrying but wasting no step.

"In bed," Enid said shortly. "Where else would a person be, given the hour and the weather? I took her a little something a slice of the cake that no one is eating because they are all too nervous to be human and she didn't stir. I thought she was ignoring me on purpose. Then I touched her hand. Cold as fish."

"Cake?" Holly repeated faintly, as though the word didn't belong with the others.

"People die and people still need cake," Enid replied. "The world doesn't stop just because hearts do."

Holly said nothing. David's hand pressed, once, at Catherine's back; she glanced up at him, quick and grateful.

"Did you move anything?" Catherine asked.

"I straightened the sheet," Enid said, and then, with defiance, "and I closed her mouth. She wasn't going to be left gaping at the ceiling like a landed trout. And I pulled the curtains a touch because there was a draught. That's all."

"Thank you," Catherine said, in a tone that made gratitude an instruction as well as a courtesy. "Don't touch anything else."

"Wouldn't dream of it," Enid muttered. "I'm not an idiot, Catherine. I know you like your evidence sitting neatly where you left it."

They reached the landing. The carpet here was thick and pale; the snow light made it glow with a faint, wintry sheen. Catherine paused outside Aunt Frances's door; her hand rested on the handle for a moment, familiar with the weight of this, then she pressed it down.

The room felt colder, heavier. The curtains were half-drawn, letting in the pale gleam of snow-reflected sky. A small nativity stood on the dresser: wooden figures arranged with prim exactness. A sprig of holly pinned above the mirror had shed two scarlet berries on the dressing table and left a dot of red that looked, from a distance, like punctuation. On the bedside table, a bowl of satsumas lent their sharp, clean scent to the air.

And on the bed lay Aunt Frances. Her features were composed as though in sleep tidy even now. The stillness, though, was the wrong kind: not a pause but an end. At the bedside, a bottle and a wine glass stood in patient company, the crystal catching the candle's small flame and returning it in fragments.

Catherine moved forward, measured, as if her footfalls might bruise the silence. She lifted the glass by the stem; the fine ring of crystal against her fingernail sounded faintly. She inhaled. Beneath the wine's tart note something bitter, herbal, grimly familiar.

She closed her eyes for the briefest moment. "Just like Carla's death," she said, voice low but unwavering. "The smell of mugwort. Distinct. Unmistakable."

Holly hovered in the doorway, arms drawn tight about herself, her breath clouding faintly in the cool room. "But… why? Is someone killing at random? Did she pick up the wrong glass, or was she…" She faltered. "…targeted?"

"That is the question," Catherine replied, returning the glass to the table. Her fingertips lingered briefly on the wood as if petitioning it to tell what it knew. Then she rested her palm on the coverlet, just beside the old woman's hand, not touching, paying a kind of respect.

David stood close, close enough that when Catherine straightened, his arm could slide, light, around her waist. His thumb brushed across the curve of her hip, a comfort brief and unshowy. "I know you will miss her," he said gently. "She was a fixture, part of the fabric."

Catherine nodded once, not trusting herself to more. "She was stubborn and sharp. She loved this house in her way." A breath; she set the breath carefully down. "We will miss her."

Enid tugged at her cardigan sleeve and shook her head as if the wool had betrayed her. "Are we to leave her?" Her voice wobbled, more with outrage than grief. "Just lying there like some poor unfortunate waiting for a hearse?"

"Yes," Catherine said firmly. "For now." When Enid opened her mouth again, Catherine lifted her hand: not harsh, but absolute. "We must keep this between ourselves until I have concluded the interviews. No one must suspect a second murder has taken place. If the killer believes we are still muddled by Carla's death, they may make a mistake."

"Secrecy," Enid muttered. "Secrecy never ends well. It ties people in knots. And I like my knots where I can see them."

"Even so," Catherine said. "We'll do it properly."

Holly edged nearer to the foot of the bed, as if hoping proximity might make sense. "She looks… peaceful," she said quietly, and sounded surprised.

"She would be furious to hear you say that." David murmured. "Frances prided herself on never being peaceful. She preferred purpose."

Enid sniffed, half laugh, half sob. "Purpose and peaceful."

Catherine's eyes returned to her aunt. She let a small silence rest between them, a thin ribbon of private farewell in a room that would soon belong to statements and measurements and the business of death. "I am going to miss her," she said softly. Then her expression settled; the air around her seemed to align. She turned to Enid. "I will interview you next. Come to the study."

Enid, in a characteristic act of defiance against propriety and despair, produced a small jar from her pocket, extracted a pickled onion, and popped it into her mouth. The brine's sharp scent cut through satsuma and candle. "Very well," she said thickly as she chewed. "But don't expect me to mince words, Catherine Forrester. You'll have them as they come."

Catherine allowed the faintest flicker of a smile. "I wouldn't expect anything else."

They retraced their steps along the landing. Tulip, who had waited in the corridor with a gravity incompatible with her size, rose and fell into step beside David, brushing his calf with her shoulder. On the stairs, Enid talked not to fill the silence, exactly, but to keep it in check.

"She told me last night," Enid said, half down one flight, "that the Queen's speech had grown too long for modern attention spans. I told her that was rich coming from a woman who can talk for thirty minutes about the correct way to fold a napkin into a bishop's hat. She laughed. Imagine Frances laughed. I nearly fell over."

"She laughed more than she allowed people to notice," David said.

Chapter 14: More onions

Catherine sat in the study, her hands clasped loosely in her lap as she stared out at the courtyard beyond the tall bay window. Snow had begun again, soft flakes drifting like pale feathers onto the frost-crusted gravel. The windowpanes trembled faintly with each gust of December wind.

"Are you enjoying yourself, Enid?" she asked, her voice steady but not unkind.

Enid was perched in the armchair opposite, her robin-red jumper complete with googly eyes sewn on with cavalier stitches bright against the subdued colours of the study. She looked almost cheerful, a pickled onion speared on a cocktail stick in one hand, the other resting on her knee. Tulip, sat at her feet with a hopeful look, tail twitching each time Enid's fingers drifted vaguely near the biscuit tin on the low table.

"This is the best Christmas I've had in years," Enid said, her mouth curling in something between a smile and a grimace. "There's nothing like a good murder to keep your mind in good order and focused." She popped the onion into her mouth and chewed with gusto.

Catherine arched an eyebrow. "Two murders, Enid." Her gaze flicked to the window; for a second her reflection dark hair, steady eyes stared back at her like a ghost in the glass. "I can walk about this house and listen, and people still try to put me off. It's… like being back in the old days, before David. Before…" She caught herself, shook her head lightly, and looked back at Enid. "Never mind."

"Goodness," Enid said dryly, "don't stop for my sake. I thrive on unfinished sentences." She reached, without looking, and found a rich tea biscuit, offered it to Tulip with a queenly flourish. Tulip accepted it with delicate ceremony and retreated under the chair to crunch it to gravel.

"People are careless around me," Enid went on, dusting crumbs from her skirt. "They think I'm just another silly old woman with my cats and my pickles. But I see things. I hear things."

"I know you do," Catherine said. She leaned back and crossed her legs, posture composed. "That's why you're here with me now."

Enid's eyes brightened. "Yesterday, you saw me knock over your glass of wine?"

"Yes," Catherine said slowly. "You made quite a spectacle of it. Half the carpet still smells of claret."

"That was no accident." Enid set down her empty cocktail stick like a gauntlet thrown. "I checked. The wine had poison in it. I should have been quicker then poor Clara and Aunt Frances would still be alive."

For a heartbeat Catherine's composure faltered; a flicker of pain crossed her face, quick as a bird shadow. David, standing by the mantel with a brandy glass he wasn't drinking, reached out and brushed his fingers across her shoulder in a quiet gesture of support. She tilted her head slightly toward him, the briefest acknowledgement, before facing Enid again.

"You're certain?" she asked.

"As certain as a woman can be with only her nose and her instincts," Enid said. "Mugwort, or something like it. I smelt it before. Years ago, at Hollow Marrow. Different context, same stink."

"Mugwort," Catherine murmured, eyes narrowing. "Just like Carla's death."

"Exactly." Enid nodded vigorously, making her robin's eyes jiggle on their slack stitches. "People think poison always smells like a story almonds and villainy but most of the wickedness in this world smells like mouldy old cupboards."

The fire hissed as a log shifted. Catherine reached for her glass of water she had not touched wine since the second death and took a slow sip. "You think Clara died because of what she said about the missing millions?"

"I think your aunt just drank too much wine, wine that happened to be poisoned." Enid said bluntly. "That's the way of Christmas. But I think Clara… Clara knew something." She dabbed her lips with a paper napkin and crumpled it into a ball. "People don't like to be found out."

"Mm." Catherine set the glass down. "Do you know anything about Martin?"

Enid's brows shot up. "Martin Hale? You invited him into your home and people are getting murdered." She leaned forward, lowering her voice even though they were alone but for David and the dog. "I'll watch him. I've already been watching him. He's too smooth by half. Smiles like a shop window."

David laughed softly. "A flattering glass?"

"A lying one," Enid said. "He sells the future like it's a casserole, says it will taste better tomorrow."

"I'm hoping to find out more about him shortly," Catherine said evenly. "Peter and Philip I've known them my whole life. But nice people can do bad things.

"Don't put ideas into Enid's head," David said. He came to stand behind Catherine's chair and rested a warm hand on her shoulder. "She already thinks I'm hiding bodies in the wine cellar."

"You could be," Enid said matter-of-factly. "Wouldn't be the first time a man in a good suit turned out to be the devil himself." She popped another onion into her mouth and chewed like a person proving a point.

Catherine reached up and gave David's hand a firm, brief squeeze. "Sally has the sleuth inside her," she said, turning the conversation. "But she's taking things too seriously. She looks so stressed even before the murders."

"She's brittle," Enid agreed. "Like spun sugar. Pretty to look at but snap her and you'll have a thousand shards. Journalism does that. You spend all day catching other people's truth, and your own goes running off with the milkman."

"I'll talk to her later," Catherine murmured. "After we eat something."

Enid's expression softened unexpectedly. "Have you seen Mr. Whittaker, my cat? I don't know where he's gone off to."

Tulip's ears pricked at the name; she peered from beneath the chair as though she might be able to help if asked properly.

Catherine shook her head.

Enid got up and left whistling 'Good King Wenceslas' ats she walked.

Chapter 15: Have I seen you before?

Martin entered the study with a kind of deliberate step, his polished shoes clipping softly against the wooden floorboards. The scent of mulled wine and evergreens lingered faintly in the air the remnants of a Christmas gathering that felt more ghostly now.

"What a fantastic place you have here," he began, his voice carrying a note of admiration that might have been genuine or might simply have been the careful polish of a businessman who always knew his audience. He turned slowly, as though letting the shelves of old books, the framed maps, and the Christmas garland draped over the mantel seep into his memory. "I've been here before, you know. Years ago, when your father owned it."

The study's small tree threw off a modest halo, glass baubles blinking as if they, too, were listening.

"My father," Catherine said, her tone steady though tinged with the faintest wistfulness, "wasn't one to change easily. He liked the world the way he knew it."

Martin chuckled softly, shaking his head as though remembering an old battle. "No, indeed. He wasn't open to my ideas at all. I came here must be five years ago now full of enthusiasm, talking about the power of computers. He waved me off as if I'd been speaking in riddles. Called me a salesman of smoke." His smile tilted. "He preferred wood and iron. Things you can stub your toe on."

"Computers," David echoed, a slight smile tugging at his lips. He shifted in his chair, the firelight catching on his profile. "They're still a mystery to half the people in the country. You press one wrong key and suddenly everything vanishes. I can't say I blame your father for his doubts."

Martin held up a finger, leaning forward with contained energy. "But they will change everything. Mark my words. Machines that can do a hundred tasks in a minute. Calculations, records, predictions all at speeds we can barely imagine now. Businesses will depend on them. Families will have one in every home one day. We'll all be sitting around typing letters to each other, perhaps even seeing each other on screens without leaving our homes."

David raised his brows. "Seeing each other on screens? From different houses?" He gave Catherine's hand a gentle squeeze. "That sounds like something out of *Tomorrow's World*, doesn't it?"

Catherine allowed herself a small laugh, crisp at the edge. "I think there's a place for computers," she said, "but they'll never replace humans. Machines can be clever, but they have no heart. No conscience. And humans are far too cunning by half."

Martin tilted his head, studying her. "You're probably correct, Catherine. Machines may never outwit human scheming. But they might help reveal it."

The words sat between them, strangely apt given the shadows of death and suspicion clouding the house. A log shifted in the grate, sending a small burst of sparks up the flue. Catherine's eyes narrowed, bright as cut glass.

"Do you know anything about Carla?"

Martin's expression flickered, almost too quickly to catch. He eased nearer the fire as though to warm his hands and, perhaps, his answer. "Well," he began carefully, "she did say that one of you, one of the family had stolen some of your father's millions. She seemed to thrive on that kind of talk, didn't she? Throwing accusations. But I never saw any of that money from Peter's perspective. I think he's as much in the dark as anyone."

"Carla never understood boundaries," David muttered, his thumb brushing Catherine's knuckles absently. "She liked to stir the pot."

"If one of the family killed her," Martin continued, lowering his voice slightly, "it would certainly have shut her up. She had a way of prodding everyone's sore spots. I did think Philip looked concerned more than once." He rolled his shoulders as if shucking off a draft. "But perhaps concern is just another mask."

He paused, glancing toward the window where snowflakes drifted slowly against the glass. "Carla," he said again, softer this time, "did seem to have a bit of a death wish, upsetting everyone in turn. As if she wanted to be at the centre of danger."

Catherine leaned back, her gaze steady, evaluating every syllable. "And Sally?" she asked. "What do you make of her?"

Martin gave a small, dismissive shrug. "Sally is watching Peter, Simon, and me. Always observing, always scribbling notes in her head, I think. I don't know what her game is, but she needs to stop. There are times her gaze is more unsettling than Carla's accusations ever were."

David frowned slightly. "She's a journalist. Watching is her trade. But she's sharper than she lets on."

"And Enid?" Catherine asked, almost with a wry smile.

That drew a genuine laugh from Martin. "Enid notes everything. She may be batty an old lady with stories about imaginary cats and endless pickled onions but nothing escapes her. She is a crow perched on the edge of every conversation. Her eyes see far more than she admits."

"Crows are clever," David said lightly. "They hide what they find and remember where they hid it."

"Exactly," Martin said, half-smiling. "I imagine Enid could find a coin under a snowdrift."

The fire crackled; the scent of pine mingled with the faint spin of smoke. A glass bauble on the tree tinkled softly, jostled by a draft as the house breathed.

"Did you see anyone put anything into the wine?" Catherine's question cut across the warm domesticity like a shard of ice.

Martin hesitated. His eyes drifted toward the drinks cabinet in the corner where crystal glasses glimmered like obedient soldiers. "No," he admitted finally. "But I suspect it was done during the power cut. When the lights went out, everything shifted. Peter showed me the fuse box afterwards. It had been tampered with, you see. Not an accident. Someone wanted darkness at just that moment."

"You're certain it was tampered with?" David asked.

"As certain as a man can be with a torch and cold fingers," Martin said, allowing the smallest grin. "Peter was very proud of being useful. He likes to be the fellow who fixes things. But the screw on the panel... it had that look. Not merely loose, encouraged."

Catherine's lips pressed together, mind sorting possibilities like cards in a deck. "And you?" she said. "Where were you when the lights went?"

"In the hall, near the peacock umbrella stand admiring its absurdity," Martin said. "I reached for the lamp and discovered, like everyone, that lamps don't work without power. You see."

"You think highly of objects," Catherine said.

"Only because people disappoint me," Martin returned, pleasantly. "Objects, at least, behave according to their wiring. You see."

"People, too," Catherine said evenly. "Wiring of a different sort."

Martin's smile acknowledged the point.

"You seem familiar," she said after a moment, gaze sharpening.

Martin's smile tightened, just slightly. "As I said, I came here about five years ago. Perhaps we crossed paths then. Your memory is keener than mine, I'm sure."

"I was thinking more recent than that," Catherine replied, voice low but firm. Her hand tightened under David's where it lay over hers.

Martin glanced down, clearing his throat. "Perhaps. Or perhaps I have one of those faces."

"Do you believe in coincidence, Martin?" Catherine asked, almost idly.

"In business, it's the word people use when they're not brave enough to say 'arranged'," he said.

"And in murder?" David asked.

"In murder," Martin said, "I haven't enough experience to have a rule." He smiled, thinly. "I hope not to acquire one."

Catherine studied him, then lifted her cup and finished her tea. "You're very tidy for a nervous man," she said. "Not a crumb on your lap."

"I learned in boarding school that crumbs are invitations," he said.

"To what?" David asked.

"To punishment," Martin said, with a cheerful shrug that didn't belong to the story. "Shall I send Simon in?"

"Yes," Catherine said. "Please do."

He stood. At the door his hand lingered on the brass handle a moment longer than necessary gathering, deciding, or simply remembering to look composed and then he stepped out into the hallway.

The door closed softly, leaving Catherine and David in the quiet hum of the study. The Christmas lights on the little tree blinked on, off, on again like a silent heartbeat keeping time with their own.

David slid his hand free and rested it on the top of the chair, leaning toward her. "Well?"

"He's careful," Catherine said. "Too careful for a man who wants to present as open. He nudges props torches, coasters, conversations toward the angle that flatters him."

"You think he's dangerous?" David asked.

"I think he's prepared," she said. "Which is a cousin to dangerous." She turned her palm up so his fingertips could find it again. "But not necessarily guilty."

He lifted her hand and pressed it, not quite a kiss more an oath. "I never tire of watching you see through people."

"I never tire of being right," she said, and that made him laugh, soft, grateful.

"Ready for him?" David asked.

"I suppose so," Catherine said. She adjusted the little snowflake brooch at her shoulder and tipped her chin toward the door. "Let's see how puddles behave when the light hits them."

Chapter 16: Pleased to be invited

Simon hesitated for a heartbeat in the doorway of the study before stepping in. The heavy oak door clicked softly behind him, shutting out the low murmur of voices and the faint strains of "O Come, All Ye Faithful" drifting from the music system in the drawing room.

Catherine was seated in one of the high-backed chairs near the hearth, her posture composed but commanding, a dark green velvet dress catching the firelight at her shoulders. A strand of holly wound around the mantel above her, studded with bright red berries, and the shadows of its leaves danced faintly on the wall. David stood at her side, one hand resting lightly on the back of her chair as if anchoring her, the other cradling a glass of water. His gaze lifted at Simon's entrance; the warmth of it softened the tautness in his jaw.

"Come in, Simon," Catherine said, her voice brisk but not unkind. "Shut the door behind you. The draught from the hall will undo all the fire's work."

Simon obeyed, rubbing his palms together as if to warm them. "Thanks for inviting me," he said with a small, almost shy smile. "If you hadn't, I'd have been on my own this Christmas. My mum and dad have gone off on a cruise somewhere in the Caribbean and it felt too bleak to spend the holiday in an empty flat."

Catherine inclined her head. "No one should be alone at Christmas," she replied. "Even this Christmas." The way she said it carried a weight Simon didn't quite know how to answer.

David pulled another chair a little closer to the fire and gestured to it. "Sit down," he said. "You'll catch a chill standing there."

Simon lowered himself into the chair with a sigh. The heat from the fire licked at his shins, but his fingers were still cold, and he stretched them toward the flames.

"Very festive," Simon said, glancing around. "Feels like one of those picture postcards you know, the ones you get from relatives who never write otherwise. Snow, candles… Someone warbling carols slightly out of tune in the corridor."

"Peter's idea of keeping spirits up," David said, amused. "He conscripts anyone who can hum and sends them round like a roving choir."

"Mm." Simon gave a lopsided smile. "I can hum. I can also ruin a perfectly acceptable song, so I've stayed out of it."

"For the best," Catherine said. It wasn't unkind; it simply acknowledged the truth and moved on. "Tea?"

"I won't say no." He rubbed his hands again, as if the very idea might warm them. "The radiators in my flat clank and never actually heat. This is… better."

David rang the little brass bell on the side table one of those archaic touches the house retained because it liked its habits and the pleasant, distant scuff of Henshaw's shoes answered down the passage.

For a moment there was only the crackle of burning logs and the faint echo of laughter somewhere in the house someone telling a story perhaps or trying too hard to keep spirits from sinking. Tulip's nails ticked once across the threshold; she poked her head in, assessed Simon with the gravity of an usher, then trotted to the hearth and settled as if she'd always been there.

Catherine broke the silence. "Aunt Frances has been murdered." she said, not as a question but as a statement.

Simon's expression faltered. "No." He cleared his throat. "Your Aunt Frances, she was always good to me. Do you think it was the wine?"

"That's what I'm trying to confirm," Catherine said. Her gaze did not waver. "Did you notice anyone interfering with it? Anyone sending people to 'mess around,' as you put it, Simon?"

Simon's eyes slid to the fire, then back to Catherine. "Oh, that sweet old lady," he murmured. "I did like her. She had some really funny ways." He gave a small, rueful smile. "Over the years, I'd grown quite fond of her, actually. She used to catch me in the hall and press a biscuit into my hand like I was a schoolboy. Always said I was too thin."

"That sounds like Aunt Frances," Catherine said quietly, and the words softened in her throat.

"I didn't notice anything strange," Simon went on, "not exactly. You've got some... other really great people here." He winced at his own phrasing and corrected it. "Interesting people, I mean. I'm enjoying myself more than I expected, if I'm honest. The decorations, the carols, even the snow outside it's like stepping into a postcard." He gave a nervous laugh. "Well, except for the murders."

Henshaw appeared then with his keen, quiet timing, a tray balanced in his hands. The cups were thin porcelain with a faint gilt rim; the teapot wore a knitted cosy with a red pompom that someone, Enid, surely, had declared essential. "Tea, madam," he murmured.

"Thank you," Catherine said. "Milk, Simon?"

"A splash," he said. "No sugar." Then, because the day had taught him courtesy, he added, "Thank you, Henshaw."

Henshaw's mouth made the ghost of a smile and was gone. The door settled back into the hush.

David set his glass down and straightened, the movement drawing Simon's eyes. "Clara?" he prompted gently.

Simon's smile slipped as if someone had run a thumb across it. "Yes. Clara was… she was going around saying horrible things to everyone. Needling people, as if she got some thrill out of it. She even had a go at me for talking to Holly or spending time with her. I don't even know why. It wasn't her business."

"Clara thought everything was her business," Catherine said. She passed Simon a cup and saucer; the teaspoon chimed once against the china as he steadied it. "She liked to provoke, to stir resentment. It was one of her many talents."

Simon warmed his fingers on the cup. "She told me I was a moth. I asked what that meant and she said I flitted toward any light and singed my wings on purpose to make a story of it." He huffed a laugh that wasn't amused. "She wasn't wrong about the moth, maybe. But she was cruel with it."

"Cruelty was sport to her," David said. "She enjoyed winning games no one else knew they were playing."

"I don't know what she was saying to the others," Simon went on, "but it might be worth finding out. People are on edge enough as it is."

"We're already doing that," Catherine replied. Her eyes held a hard glint, but her voice stayed even. "Everyone's movements, everyone's words. It's all being pieced together."

Simon sipped, bought himself a second. "Right. You've made it beautiful in here."

"Christmas should still be Christmas," Catherine said. "It doesn't stop because people behave badly."

David set his hand lightly on the back of her chair again, fingers splayed as if claiming ground. "You've been holding everything together."

"Someone has to," she murmured, and the quiet gravity of it made Simon look quickly away, as if he'd stumbled into a private promise.

He cleared his throat. "I... noticed something else," he said. "I wasn't sure it mattered, but since you're asking." He leaned forward, elbows on his knees, the cup safe on the saucer. "Sally. She's been listening in on the conversations I've been having with Peter and Martin. She doesn't even pretend not to. Just drifts closer, like she's making mental notes."

"She often is," David said. "It's her work, even when she isn't working."

"I don't mind people listening," Simon said. "I object to being catalogued without consent." He made a face, recognised its adolescent quality, and smoothed it away. "Martin was getting particularly upset. I think he might… well, he might do something if she carries on. He's not as calm as he looks."

"Go on," David encouraged, tone neutral enough to keep the words flowing.

"When the lights went out earlier," Simon continued, "Sally was very close to the wine. And then, when the lights came on again, she looked… a bit sheepish. Not like someone who'd just had a fright, but like someone caught out."

The fire popped, sending a spark up the chimney. Catherine didn't move. "That's a strong observation, Simon," she said at last. "Are you sure?"

"I can't swear to it," he admitted. "Everything was confused. People were shouting, someone dropped a glass I heard the chink. But she was definitely near the wine. And then she did that thing." He pinched his fingers together as if catching a gnat. "You know. When you don't know what to do with your hands, so you touch the edge of the table and then stop, like the table might accuse you."

David bent and nudged the logs with the poker, sending a flutter of sparks into the grate. For a heartbeat the glow showed the strain carved in his mouth; then it eased as he set the poker back precisely. "And you're telling us this now because..?"

"Because I don't want to be next," Simon said simply. "And because you asked." He gave a small, helpless shrug.

"You're the only one who seems to have a handle on things, Catherine."

"I intend to keep it that way," she said. "And you'd do well to remember that, Simon."

He nodded, chastened, and then, because silence made him itch, offered, "I brought a cassette, by the way. Carols. New recording from King's. I thought well, I didn't think this was going to be.." He broke off, flustered. "Anyway. If you want it."

"Thank you," David said. "We'll put it on later."

"I've got a Walkman in my bag," Simon said, then coloured as if he'd boasted. "Well, not here obviously. In the hall. Batteries die at the worst moment, don't they? One minute you're with the choir on *Once in Royal* and the next you're in silence with your own thoughts. Less tuneful."

Catherines hand brushed the back of David's as she reached for the teapot; the contact sparked along her skin, not dramatic, simply necessary. The study felt again the way she liked it best: warm, orderly, useful. A room where truth could be asked for and, with enough patience, delivered.

Down the passage, someone struck the first chord of *In the Bleak Midwinter*. The note held, seeking the next. In the study, Catherine lifted the pot and poured.

Chapter 17: David Sums It Up

The study door was closed against the draught of the corridor, muting the hum of voices elsewhere in the house. Inside, the fire had burned down to a bed of glowing embers with only the occasional crack of a log settling.

Catherine looked across at David, her eyes sharp even in the warm glow. "What do you think, then, David?" she asked quietly.

He exhaled, leaning back a fraction. "Well," he began, "someone killed Clara for a reason. If it's about the millions that someone's stolen, it wasn't me." He gave a small, humourless laugh. "We could have gone bankrupt if this detective work hadn't taken off."

Catherine's mouth curved faintly but she said nothing.

"So," David continued, "unless you've been holding out on me" he lifted his gaze to hers, a flicker of warmth behind the tiredness "you haven't taken it either. Which means it must be either Peter or Philip. They've hidden it well, because it didn't come up in the last police investigation, and it's not as if they've been splashing money around."

Catherine tilted her head, the candlelight catching in her hair. "No," she said. "They've been discreet."

David reached for his tea, swirling it absently. "So that needs investigating. And there's Enid. She was close to the glasses when the lights went out. She also seems to know a lot about poisons."

"She does," Catherine agreed. "Her conversation at lunch about foxglove and hawthorn was hardly subtle."

David gave a wry smile. "Sally, too. She was close. We need to find out what she was doing, especially if she looked a bit sheepish. And is she plotting something of her own? She's always writing notes, listening at doors, doing this, doing that. I know you know more about that, Catherine."

Catherine leaned forward, resting her elbows on her knees. "She seems to think there's someone here who was in Greece when we were out there. She's convinced she's stumbled onto some connection." She drew a slow breath. "And the police…"

"They're not coming," David finished for her.

"No." Catherine sat back, her spine straight. "We have to solve it ourselves before someone else dies."

David rubbed his temple. "It feels like it's spiralling. First Clara, then your aunt…"

"As for the murder of my aunt," Catherine said, her voice tightening just slightly, "I wonder if it was a mistake. Poor Aunt Frances." She paused, looking at the fire. "But you've got to remember, I could have died as well if Enid hadn't stopped me from drinking the wine."

David's hand reached across the space between them and covered hers where it rested on the arm of the chair. His thumb rubbed a small circle against her knuckles. "I haven't forgotten," he said softly.

Catherine's eyes met his, steady. "We've got a lot to think about," she said. "And I think" she sat a little straighter "that Clara is the key to this. We need to go and have a look in her room, see if there are any clues before anyone else gets there."

"Agreed." he said.

For a moment they were silent, only the fire's glow and the muted carol filling the room.

Catherine reached for her tea. "Do you remember Christmases here when Father was alive?" she asked quietly.

David smiled faintly. "I do. The tree in the hall was always twice as big as it needed to be just as it is now. And the choir from the village would come to sing at the foot of the stairs."

"And Father would pretend he hated it," Catherine said, her mouth softening, "but he always slipped them a cheque afterwards."

They shared a small, wry smile.

David leaned back against the sofa. "This house is still beautiful," he said after a moment. "Even with everything going on. You've done well to bring it back to life."

Catherine's gaze flicked to the mantel where the carved nativity stood between two brass candlesticks. "Christmas should still be Christmas," she said. "No matter what people do."

David watched her for a moment, the firelight flickering over her face. "You've been holding it all together," he said softly.

"Someone has to," she replied.

He reached over and tucked a loose strand of hair behind her ear. "You're extraordinary, you know that?"

She gave a small, almost imperceptible smile. "You tell me often enough."

"Well, it's true."

Outside, bells from the village church rang faintly across the fields, carried by the wind.

Catherine set her cup down and rose, smoothing her skirt. "We should go," she said briskly. "Before someone else thinks to search her room."

David stood as well, straightening his jacket. He reached for her hand. They stood together for a heartbeat in the glow of the fire, the carved nativity watching silently from the mantel.

"Ready?" he asked.

Catherine drew a deep breath. "Ready," she said.

They left the study side by side, their footsteps muffled on the thick carpet, leaving behind the warmth of the fire and the soft echo of "Silent Night" still turning on the record player.

Chapter 18: Carla's Room

"Come on, David," Catherine said firmly, her fingers tightening around the brass handle of the guest-room door. The corridor was still alive with carols spilling faintly from the music system downstairs, mingled with the savoury scents of goose, sage and onion, and roasting chestnuts drifting up from the kitchen. "We really need to have a look. If Carla kept evidence of those missing millions anywhere, it would be here. We can't ignore it."

David gave a long sigh, brushing a piece of stray tinsel from his sleeve. "I know, love. But creeping around in a dead woman's bedroom on Christmas Day…" He shook his head slowly. "Doesn't sit right with me. Smells of goose and cloves in the air, holly on the banisters this ought to be a house of cheer, not suspicion."

Catherine shot him a look that was affectionate yet unwavering. "Proper doesn't solve murders, David. If we don't look, no one will. The police are snowed in, half the county cut off. And you know as well as I do time matters. Whoever killed her won't have stopped thinking about their next move."

She pressed down on the handle, and the latch gave way with a soft click. The door swung open, and the two stepped inside.

David paused just inside the doorway, taking in the sight with a slight frown. "Well, it hasn't been ransacked, that's one thing. But look at the bed."

The bedspread was turned back as though someone had lain there, the sheet creased and still slightly ruffled.

"Odd, isn't it?" he continued. "Carla was dead downstairs. So, who, in the name of Jesus, has been sleeping here?"

Catherine crossed to the bed, running her palm over the sheet. "Still warm," she murmured. Her eyes sharpened. "Someone lay here not long ago. Bold, very bold. Sleeping in a dead woman's bed under this roof while the rest of us gathered in the hall."

Her gaze swept the room with a detective's precision. A cut-glass goblet stood on the bedside table; the rim marked with a deep plum lipstick stain.

"Look," David said, leaning in. "That's not Carla's shade. Hers was that horrid bright pink. Certainly not yours either."

Catherine retrieved a folded handkerchief from her sleeve, ever practical, and lifted the glass carefully by the stem. "Not hers, not mine. Someone else. Careless of them to leave it here." She turned it in the light. "And see half-drunk. They lingered."

"And the fire," David added, crouching beside the hearth. The grate still glowed faintly, embers shifting under a bed of pale ash. "Fresh coals at the bottom. Someone's been warming themselves here. Used the poker too."

"Then it wasn't a quick visit." Catherine's voice was cool, steady. "They made themselves comfortable. Too comfortable."

For a moment they both fell silent, the only sound the low crackle from the hearth and faint strains of *Silent Night* from downstairs.

David rose and went to the wardrobe, pulling it open with a creak. Silk dresses, fur-trimmed coats, and blouses shimmered faintly. "All here. No sign of rummaging."

Catherine, meanwhile, opened the top drawer of the dressing table. Neat stacks of paper, envelopes, and a few photographs tied with string greeted her. She flicked through them quickly, lips pursed. Nothing unusual.

"Here it is," David said suddenly. He'd opened the bedside drawer and pulled free a notebook, its leather cover worn at the edges.

Catherine's eyes lit. "Her journal. She never went anywhere without it."

David opened it, scanning. His mouth twisted. "She's written some very nasty things about us. You especially. Says you've got your nose in everyone's business, too sharp for your own good."

Catherine gave a short, ironic laugh. "She wasn't wrong."

David turned more pages, then stopped, his tone changing. "Here listen. It's about your father's accounts."

He showed her. The ink was hurried, jagged.

"Eight million pounds is missing," David read. "She'd noticed it back when she helped with the books. Checked again recently. Same figure. Eight million, unaccounted for."

Catherine leaned closer, her hand resting lightly on his back. Her eyes moved quickly across the page.

"Eight million," she whispered. "That's no rounding error. That's a hole big enough to swallow the business whole."

David nodded grimly. "She says it didn't go to Father's side projects, either. Not the charities, not the tinkering. This was something else entirely. She was closing in on it."

He turned another page then stopped cold.

The following leaves had been torn out. Only jagged stubs of paper remained; edges ripped from hurried fingers.

Catherine took the notebook, her jaw tightening. "Someone's been here before us. Someone didn't just lie in Carla's bed and drink her wine. They stole her words. The pages that mattered most."

David looked around uneasily. "So, who was it? Who sat by her fire, warmed themselves, and tore away the very proof she died for?"

Catherine closed the book slowly, holding it to her chest. "I don't know yet. But someone is desperate enough to silence her voice twice once in life, once in ink."

The fire popped, sending a small spray of sparks up the blackened grate.

David straightened, brushing his hands together. "Love, it's almost Christmas dinner. Goose, roast potatoes, pudding… If we're gone too long, the others will wonder."

Catherine looked at him, her gaze sharp but softened by affection. "Let them wonder. We have more at stake than plum pudding."

Still, she stepped closer to him, slipping her hand into his. His palm was warm, calloused, steadying. He bent and kissed her temple, just a brush, but enough.

"Promise me," he whispered, "we won't let this house swallow us whole. Not tonight."

Her chin lifted, eyes clear. "We won't. Not while we stand together."

They lingered in silence, hearing the faint jangle of cutlery being laid out downstairs, the rising notes of *O Come, All Ye Faithful* from the Music System.

Catherine exhaled. "We won't lock the door. If they mean to return, let them. It may be the only way to catch them."

David squeezed her hand. "Then come on. Let's face dinner. Goose and gravy… and a table full of suspects."

He reached to switch off the bedside lamp. They stepped out, closing the door softly, leaving behind warmth, lipstick on glass, and the torn silence of Carla's missing pages.

Hand in hand, they walked the corridor toward the dining hall, their shadows stretched by the twinkling tree lights in the hall. The scent of cloves and roasting chestnuts thickened, mingling with the sound of laughter that didn't quite ring true.

And Catherine thought: Christmas dinner would be served with suspicion as surely as cranberry sauce.

Chapter 19: The Mask Slips

Catherine stands in the hallway, hand resting for a moment on the banister, a neat sleight of composure. Her dress is dark, simple, with a high neckline and sleeves that show a thought to the season without overstatement. David remains a step behind her, hands in his gloves, his face the image of restraint and mild amusement. He watches the passing guests, Peter with his careless, confident strid and smiles when Tulip, the little Jack Russell, darts between his legs.

Martin is coming toward them in a way that suggests he has a plan for every footfall. He is in a country-cut coat and a scarf the colour of old gold; he looks as if he could stride straight into an advertisement for a new bank. There is that careful lightness about him, and the small tilt of head that suggests he is always measuring the size of a room in relation to himself.

"David," Catherine says, voice quiet but carrying, "I need a quick word with Martin. I'll catch you up." She gestures with the smallest of nods toward the stairs where the hush of the drawing room and the gleam of the tree catch at the eye, and David inclines his head. "Don't let them start without us," he says, half to her and half to the air, and the comment is light enough to dissolve a little of the tension.

They walk on together for a few paces in the warmer air that rises from the hall lamps, and then Catherine steps slightly aside as Martin approaches. He greets them with a smile that sits just the wrong side of sincere. David gives a formal bow of the head and slips into the crowd that is forming at the mouth of the saloon; conversation swells around them talk of the puddings, of the weather, of whether Father would have liked the new wreath.

"Catherine," Martin says at once, as if the cordial address will smooth whatever follows. "A pleasure to see you looking so... radiant. The house is splendid at this time of year."

She returns the greeting with a look that measures and keeps. "Thank you. David had a hand in the decorations, though I'm sure you'd disagree as to which of us did more."

Martin laughs, a practiced, small sound. "I'd be the last to take credit from the lady of the house," he says. "Although I do have a weakness for greenery. There's an intimacy to a properly trimmed bough, don't you find? It says someone cares."

"Martin," she says, "we'll go somewhere a little quieter. I want to hear something from you." She moves toward the reception room and he follows, swift and composed.

They close the door behind them. Immediately the hubbub of the hall becomes muted; the world contracts to the dampened velvet of the curtains, the warm lamplight, the faint smell of brandy on the air. There is a low tapestry on one wall depicting a hunting scene; the glass on the mantel reflects only a single strip of light.

Catherine sits in the armchair facing him, folded hands laid plainly on her lap. Martin perches on the edge of another chair, back straight, as if posture alone could guarantee an honest account. He crosses one leg, then uncrosses it; he fingers the seam of his glove, and the gesture is small, human, and perhaps deliberate.

"You and I met in Greece," she begins. "We met Matthew. Now we meet Martin. We met a very particular combination of manners and excuses. Tell me who are you, at your core? Martin, or Matthew?"

He smiles, a thin flash. "I am both, you see, and neither," he says, almost conversationally, as if reciting a commonplace. "When I am Martin, I'm a top businessman from America. When I am Matthew, I'm a simpleton that no one sees as a risk and people speak to me unguarded." He allows himself a shrug, and his eyes find the tree-silhouette in the reflection on the glass.

Catherine watches his face; the way his smile tightens, the small creasing at his eyes that does not reach all the way to warmth. "You speak as if this were an exercise in performance," she says. "Which is it? A costume, or something you believe?"

Martin leans back, his manner just the right measure of affected ease. "A man plays the part that brings him advantage," he says. "There is nothing wrong with that." He taps a finger against his knee. "You must understand, it has a practical application. You know a man like me you know what a sharp suit and a ready joke will buy you in conversation."

"And what of the man found in the lift shaft in Greece?" Catherine asks, not letting him shape the conversation.

"What of the man I found dead in the street? He was not a costume at that moment. I looked at him closely. You did not. By then you had solved the case in your head." Stated Martin

Catherine looks him straight in the eye "And your Parents?"

For a moment Martin's face shifts. It is just a flicker a tiny alteration of expression like the quick darkening of the sky before rain and then he smooths it away as if wiping a smear from glass. "One must be careful of headlines and the appetites of men who live by being entertained," he says. "Not everything is as it appears in the morning papers."

"Did you kill them?" Catherine counters. "You played a part. There is difference between reporting a death and making a narrative out of it deciding who it fits, who it benefits."

He draws a breath a soft, staged intake and then, unexpectedly, his voice falls a little. "You have a very particular way of looking at things. It unnerves a man sometimes." There is the faintest edge to his words. "But listen to me, Catherine. You mustn't be foolish." For the first time there is something like heat in his voice; the mask slips at the corner of his mouth.

"I'm not foolish," she replies. "I am careful. That is neither foolish nor reckless. Your worry seems to be the difference between us, not my judgment."

He laughs, quick and without mirth. "Worry is not the right word." He sets his jaw and looks at the carpet for a moment, as if the pattern there entertains him. Then he lifts his head and meets her eyes directly, and there is an intensity there that was not present before. "You should be scared, Catherine."

She does not move.

"You should be scared," Martin repeats. "I am coming for you. Not this holiday. I have nothing to do with these murders now. I said I would leave you alone. And I will, for now. But a year down the line you will realise what you have done to me. Then I will be coming for you."

Catherine's mouth is a straight line. Her hands do not tremble; her features, when they move, do so with the smoothness of something that has practised restraint. "That is a strange kind of promise," she says. "A threat dressed as a bargain." The corner of her mouth tilts faintly. "Are you sure you can keep such timelines?"

Martin's fingers curl on the chair's armrest. "I keep what I intend to keep," he replies. "And I am very deliberate."

Caterine looks at him "For now, at least, we will sit at table and be ordinary."

Chapter 20: Christmas Dinner

The dining room doors creaked open on well-oiled hinges, and Henshaw, the butler, appeared in his black suit and starched white shirt. His voice, rich and solemn, rolled into the corridor like a church bell.

"Dinner is served."

The air was warm with goose fat, cloves, and the faint, resinous sweetness of the greenery.

From the record player in the corner, Wham!'s "Last Christmas" floated out in soft, slightly scratchy tones; George Michael's melancholy voice blended oddly with the crackle of the log fire. Some guests hummed along, others winced at the modern intrusion. Above it all, the snow outside pressed itself thickly against the tall Georgian windows, coating the world in a white stillness.

Paper crackers, bright with red and gold foil, had been placed at each setting. Each plate gleamed with silver cutlery; crystal glasses caught the firelight. At the head of the table sat the great prize of the evening the Christmas goose, roasted to a golden crisp, its cavity heavy with sage and onion stuffing, surrounded by browned potatoes, parsnips glistening with honey, Brussels sprouts dotted with chestnuts, and bowls of cranberry sauce glowing like rubies. There was bread sauce in a blue bowl older than most of the people present, and a boat of gravy so glossy David murmured, half to himself, "Henshaw's standards survive every regime."

Before Catherine stepped fully into the room, she caught Enid's sleeve and pulled her aside into the shadow of the doorway. David, sensing Catherine's need, gave her hand a quick, firm squeeze and then released it, drifting to his seat with a quiet dignity that made her heart ache with gratitude.

"Enid," Catherine said low, her tone brisk but not unkind. "David and I went to Carla's room. Someone has been sleeping there. The sheets disturbed, the fire burned down, a lipstick glass left behind. You see everything. Tell me what you know."

Enid, her hair escaping from its combs in wiry curls, darted her eyes around like a bird checking for predators. "Dead women don't leave lipstick, Catherine. And yet I saw her. Saw the same thing you did. That face... no one can counterfeit that." She shuddered; the paper crown at her place flashed in her hand as she tucked it into the pocket of her cardigan for later.

"Where did you put the body?"

Enid licked her lips, lowered her voice further. "I got Martin to help me. We moved her into one of the spare bedrooms. I'll show you after dinner."

Catherine's brows knitted together. "You trust him?"

"Trust? No. But sometimes a woman has to use the help she's given." Enid winked, then slipped away to her chair, leaving Catherine with the words like a splinter under her skin.

Henshaw directed the seating with the nonchalance of a man who had arranged more complicated table plans during blackouts. Chairs scraped politely. Paper napkins unfurled. The room had the cheerful, fragile hum of people doing the right things with their hands so their minds would not falter.

The meal began in proper fashion. Henshaw carved the goose with solemn precision, the knife slicing clean through crisp skin; the plate nearest the cut filled at once with shards of gold and steam. The scent rose, heavy and comforting. Bowls of potatoes, sprouts, bread sauce, and gravy made their rounds. Wine was poured generously, a deep red that glowed like garnets.

Crackers were pulled with loud pops, paper crowns donned green, red, gold, purple. Simon flinched at the bang of his cracker and then laughed at himself; he placed a purple crown on his head with a flourish as if to make amends. David grinned when his crown tore slightly as he placed it on his; Catherine reached across discreetly, straightening it for him.

"You always look after me," he murmured.

"You need it," she replied with a smile that softened her eyes.

"Careful," Holly called lightly from down the table, catching the movement out of the corner of her eye. "We'll have scandal before pudding."

"Scandal comes after tea." Enid said crisply. "Pudding is too busy being on fire."

That earned a ripple of laughter it didn't entirely deserve; people were grateful for a sound that wasn't whispering. Henshaw, unbothered by the noise, moved with the solemn, measured grace of a man who could balance a tray through a storm.

Conversation sparked around the table like kindling. Philip, always eager to assert himself, raised his glass as if the Queen herself were present and began: "Her Majesty was steady, wasn't she? One can always rely on her to sound composed, even when the country feels like it's falling apart."

"Steady doesn't mean inspiring," Holly cut in, the half-shut notebook lurking between her cutlery and the cranberry sauce. "A writer knows a speech needs fire, not just formality. Still, perhaps the monarchy thrives on being dull."

Catherine shot her a look. "It is Christmas Day. Could you not take a break from your notepad for one meal?"

Holly flushed and shut the notebook all the way. "But this house, Catherine…" she gestured vaguely as if the cornices were complicit "it's a story in itself. Murder, snow, secrets… I could have my bestseller before the year's out."

"Then wait until the year's out," Catherine said firmly. "For now, eat your goose."

"Bossy," Holly said, but she picked up her knife and fork and did as she was told.

"Depend upon it," David muttered fondly, "if goose requires discipline, Catherine will give it a timetable."

"Someone must," Catherine said, and David's grin widened.

Peter, sitting further down, pulled his cracker with Martin. It yielded a small deck of playing cards and a joke printed on cheap paper. Martin unfolded it with mock ceremony. "What do you call a three-legged donkey?" he read, then paused. "A wonky." He looked pained. "Someone was paid to write that."

"Not much," Peter said, tapping the deck. "We can do a trick later. I've been practising faro shuffles."

"Don't practise them on my wine," Enid said. "I do not like cards near liquids. Or men near cards, come to that."

"Noted," Martin said. "I shall keep my hands to myself."

"See that you do," Enid returned.

On the sideboard, the record ran out and the arm clicked back. Henshaw who knew a room's temperature like a barometer replaced it with something safer. Bing Crosby floated in, smooth as custard. Philip hummed; Simon joined, off-key but earnest; Sally's lips shaped the words without sound, as if singing might shake loose the fear lodged between her ribs.

Catherine leaned toward Sally, who was nervously adjusting her paper crown. "I know Matthew is here, he is Martin." she whispered. "Do you think he killed Clara?"

Sally's hand trembled on her fork. "What I've read of him… in the papers, it chills me. No, Catherine, I don't think it safe that he's in this house."

"Nor do I." The words were flat, ironed, final.

Sally hesitated. "I overheard them earlier Peter and Martin. Whispering. I caught the word 'kill.' It made my skin crawl."

Catherine swallowed a mouthful of wine to steady herself. She glanced down the table, studied Martin the clever disguise, the too-polite laughter, the eyes that never quite matched the smile. He leaned in close to Peter, speaking with an intensity that looked, at a distance, like friendship but felt like something darker. Peter nodded, eager, tapping a finger on the table in time with an impatience only he could hear.

David's hand found hers under the table again, warm, grounding. "Eat," he whispered, lips brushing her temple. "We need our strength."

She smiled faintly. "You always think of me."

"Always," he said simply.

Tulip had materialised under David's chair, a white-and-tan punctuation mark against the Persian rug. On instinct, the butler had placed a saucer discreetly to one side. When a sliver of goose skin, crisp and irresistible, slid from David's plate to the saucer with all the plausible deniability of an accident, Tulip delivered a grateful sound that was not quite a bark and not quite a prayer. "Hush," Catherine murmured, amused despite herself. "Lady manners."

Across from them, Philip continued his commentary, which had drifted from the Queen to the fall of the Berlin Wall and now to inflation by way of the price of chestnuts. "They're extortionate this year. Do you know how many you have to peel to garnish a bowl of sprouts? The labour alone…"

Simon, determined to be agreeable, lifted the cranberry sauce. "Does anyone…? No. I'll just… yes." He distributed spoonfuls with exaggerated care, as if the tartness might go off in any direction if mishandled.

"What are we having instead of *The Snowman*?" Holly asked, scraping gravy through a last corner of goose as if she were digging for a moral. "With the signal as it is, the television looks like a blizzard inside a blizzard."

"We're having conversation," Catherine said. "and do your research later."

"I'm always doing research," Holly said, half-apology, half-boast. "It's a condition."

"Treat it with bread sauce," David advised. "It cures most things that don't require stitches."

"It causes some of them," Philip said, but he accepted a ladleful.

Aunt Frances would have had a comment about the bread sauce's proper texture; the thought moved through Catherine like a cold breeze behind the ribs. Enid must have felt the same; she looked at Catherine and raised her glass a fraction a tiny, private toast. Catherine returned it with the smallest nod. The dead had their place at the table, and everyone knew it, even if no one dared set a plate.

"Henshaw," Martin called over gently as the butler retreated to the sideboard, "this goose is exceptional."

"Thank you, sir," Henshaw said, the barest tilt of satisfaction adjusting his punctuation. "Mrs. Turner did the roasting." Mrs. Turner, the cook, remained in the kitchen as if the stove were the front line and she its last defence.

"I'll write her a note," Martin said.

"Do," Catherine replied before Henshaw could; her tone made the courtesy not merely an offer but a requirement.

Sally's paper crown slipped; Catherine reached across with the naturalness of a sister and righted it. "There," she said softly. "Keep it on. It helps with drafts."

Sally smiled, the expression quick and grateful. "Thank you."

"What did you write at the top of your article?" Simon ventured, sincerely curious despite himself. "About Greece, I mean."

"A sentence I've rewritten a dozen times," Sally admitted, surprising herself with the ease of saying it. "A truth should be born clean. It seldom is."

"That's good," Holly said, flicking her gaze back to the closed notebook as if it burned in her palm. "I'll quote you…later," she added, catching Catherine's look and raising her hands in surrender.

The courses flowed. More wine decanted into glinting glasses. Conversation doubled back on itself in safe loops childhood Christmases, presents more interesting in their anticipation than their reality, the taste of chocolate coins ("It's the foil that makes them," Simon declared; "It's the foil that condemns them," Philip countered), whether the carol service in the village would brave the snow.

The pudding came, brandy alight and blue flames dancing across its dark fruit surface. Guests clapped politely as

Henshaw carried it in, his expression composed against the heat. Catherine found herself thinking of the old tradition the silver sixpence hidden inside and wondered which guest might crack a tooth tonight. "If I break a molar," Peter said cheerily, "consider it a donation to the dental profession." "Consider it a moral," Enid said. "Chew with sense."

Glasses were gathered; chairs exhaled; the record player clicked, and Bing gave way to the hush that waits between songs. The candles breathed. The snow pressed its quiet face to the glass. And Catherine, with David watched the room like a general who knows the battle is not the whole story but only the part that must be done before the light returns.

Chapter 21: Presents

The doors of the dining room closed behind them with a soft thud, shutting away the clink of glasses and the last sigh of goose and gravy. The corridor beyond smelled faintly of pine, the air was cooler. Catherine's hand was already in David's, their steps in quiet rhythm as they walked together toward the drawing room.

Inside, the tree stood resplendent: twelve feet of fir dressed in gold and red baubles, with paper chains that draped in long arcs, and a scattering of candles fixed in holders that flickered and made the ornaments glimmer. Beneath, parcels of every shape and size tumbled out in cheerful disorder, their ribbons glinting in the firelight.

"Ah, here we are," Enid declared as she bustled in. "The real reason anyone likes Christmas. Presents." She dropped heavily into a high-backed chair as though she owned it, eyes already darting to the parcels.

Catherine allowed herself a small smile. For all the tension in the house, the snow pressing at the windows, and the shadow of murder still fresh, the sight of the tree, the paper, the eager faces it was Christmas. The drawing room glowed with that particular evening warmth: guttering candles trimmed back to sensible flames, the last of the day's light surrendered to a deep, velvety blue beyond the glass, and the fire gathering itself for another hour's good work. David settled beside her on the sofa, their shoulders brushing, his warmth steady against her; the tree lights winked as if agreeing with him.

Henshaw brought in a tray of brandy and set it near the hearth with the soft authority of a man who knew where trays belonged. Tulip scampered close to the parcels, nose twitching, tail a metronome for the room's anticipation.

"Patience, girl," Catherine murmured, drawing the terrier in with a gentle hand and a dignified scritch behind the ear. Tulip sat, just, and trembled with the restraint of a saint.

Henshaw coughed discreetly. "Shall we begin, madam?"

"We shall," Catherine said, and the phrase felt a touch like a blessing.

Catherine reached first for a neat parcel marked with David's handwriting. She peeled the gold paper away with care. Catherine did most things with care, even when the world encouraged hurry as though prolonging the moment might lend it more meaning. Inside, the burgundy Filofax gleamed, its leather smooth, faintly aromatic. She opened it slowly and ran her fingers over the clean pages, the neat tabs, the sensibly divided sections as if testing the spine of a future she already intended to discipline.

"Oh, David," she said, her voice touched with warmth. "You shouldn't have. I can keep all my notes together at last. Brilliant. What a lovely present."

He grinned, boyish and proud. "Better this than chasing scraps of paper across half the county. Now you can alphabetise your suspects properly."

She nudged him with her shoulder, a glancing rebuke disguised as a caress. "Careful, or you'll find yourself under 'Irritations.'"

From an armchair, Aunt-Frances's empty place echoed in the air like an old friend not yet acknowledged; even so, a small chuckle travelled the room, grateful for the permission. Catherine leaned over and brushed David's cheek with a quick kiss. The twinkle in his eye softened into tenderness; he tucked a lock of her hair behind her ear in the old, practised way.

"Your turn," she said, and handed him a square parcel wrapped in red, the corners neat enough to pass Henshaw's inspection.

David tore it open with less care than she had. David's care came in other currencies and his face lit at once. "Oh, fantastic!" He held up the compact electronic chess computer, its small screen and neat buttons gleaming like a smug little oracle. "I've been practising with the lads at the pub, but this will sharpen me up no end. No excuses now."

"Except," Catherine said, arching an eyebrow, "you'll no longer be able to claim Tulip distracted you every time you lose."

Tulip barked once, indignant at slander, and then returned to sniffing at the goose bones still cooling on a sideboard.

"Speaking of which" Enid leaned forward and pushed a small parcel with a ribboned bow toward the terrier. "For the mistress of the house."

"The house is mine," Catherine said, amused, "but the floor belongs to her." She unwrapped it for Tulip, revealing a bright red squeaky duck. Tulip took it gently, gave it a perfunctory chew that produced an indelicate squeak, then dropped it with a sigh and sat back on her haunches, eyes firmly fixed on the goose.

"She has her priorities," Philip said with a dry laugh, lifting his glass. "As should we all."

"Ungrateful beast," Enid muttered. "I'd have been delighted with that myself." She glanced pointedly at the parcels near her feet.

"Open one, then," Catherine said. "Before your commentary becomes a second tree."

Enid tore the paper from a stout, tinny shape and gave a little cry of genuine pleasure. "Biscuits!" She snapped the lid off with the skill of a professional and held the tin under her nose. "Shortbread, chocolate fingers, custard creams. Proper diplomacy." She offered it round, then helped herself, two shortbread fingers tucked beneath her thumb as if one might bolt.

The others opened there presents in turn.

At last, Sally reached for another parcel. It had appeared quietly, wrapped in plain brown paper with a piece of red string tied in a perfunctory bow. "Oh, this one must be from the post," she said, frowning. "I didn't think anything else would get through." She smiled faintly as she peeled away the wrapping, expecting some trinket, perhaps a scarf, perhaps another notebook sent by a colleague with a guilty conscience.

But when the paper fell aside, the colour drained from her cheeks.

In her hands was a sheet of paper, scrawled with harsh black letters: **Stop watching us.**

Inside the box lay a knife, its blade smeared with thick red liquid that dripped slowly onto the carpet in obscene patience.

Sally gave a strangled cry and dropped the parcel as if it had burned her. The knife clattered against the hearthrug; Tulip started, gave a small defensive bark, and then quieted at Catherine's hand. "What... what is this?" Sally's wide eyes darted around the room, frantic, desperate. "Who would do this?"

No one answered quickly enough. The room held its breath because any breath might be blamed. Sally staggered to her feet, clutching her chest as if to pin her heart in. With a sob that seemed to shame even the flames into stillness, she fled the room, her footsteps echoing up the stairs until the sound was lost.

Chapter 22: Confusions

Peter emerged from his father's study with a look that was half-pale, half-defiant. His hand shook slightly as he clutched a folded piece of paper, the crisp edges trembling against his fingers. Catherine, who was standing near the landing with Enid, immediately noticed the stiffness in his shoulders.

"Peter?" Catherine's voice was clear and commanding. "What is it? You look as though you've seen a ghost."

"As you know, I used to live here and was wondering if in one of the files there maybe something to go on.". Peter swallowed hard, eyes flicking from his sister to Enid, and then back again. "I was looking for evidence of missing money." he said, holding up the letter. "It's Father. He's written something about the accounts something isn't right. Something Philip's done. He was worried, worried enough to write this down. I don't know what to make of it."

Peter pressed his lips together, clearly torn between defending Philip, his father's old partner, and acknowledging what was in his hand. Catherine stepped closer, placing her hand briefly on her brother's arm. Her touch was firm, grounding him. "Show me," she said.

Peter handed her the letter. The paper crackled as she unfolded it. Catherine's eyes skimmed the words quickly, her sharp mind catching the essence even before she slowed to absorb the details. "There's a discrepancy in the ledgers," she said, almost to herself. "Large sums unaccounted for. Philip's name appears more than once. Father must have been suspicious enough to draft this note as a safeguard. He feared something, Peter. That much is clear."

Peter's jaw hardened; bravado tried to join the pallor in his face and found it difficult to settle. "Father knew better than to keep everything in his head," he muttered. "He always said paper doesn't forget."

Catherine folded the letter neatly and put into her pocket.

From below, faint sounds of music and laughter carried through the corridors. The piano hesitant, then more confident wandered through the opening bars of a carol. Voices rose, a clumsy chorus sung more for heart than harmony.

Enid returned from seeing Sally "She is crying and shook up, she needs a moment to compose and then she will be back.".

"Hark," Enid cocked her head. "Someone's taken to the piano. Martin, by the sound of it. He can't play to save his life, but he does bash those keys as though he's chasing away demons."

"Demons only leave if invited," Catherine said. "Best not to invite anymore." She touched Peter's sleeve. "Let's go down. Best not to arouse suspicion by lingering too long on the stairs."

Together they descended the sweeping staircase. Candlelight flickered in glass holders, casting dancing shadows across the framed family portraits. It was Christmas, yet the air was thick with unease.

As they entered the drawing room, the warmth of the fire greeted them, as did the sight of Martin seated at the grand piano. His long fingers pressed confidently against the keys, though his brow was furrowed in fastidious displeasure.

"The middle C is off," Martin announced, looking up as if the matter were of great importance. "The tone is dull. Not quite right."

"Maybe it's been overused," Enid muttered, perching herself on the arm of a sofa. "Middle C always is. Just like the middle child never quite in tune with the rest."

"Leave it, Martin," Philip advised, from an armchair where he sat turning his new silver-capped pen between his fingers. "Pianos endure a lot at Christmas. They can't be expected to be perfect. People certainly aren't."

"Nothing wrong with expecting things to be better," Martin replied. "One has to have standards."

Catherine moved closer. "Let's have a look," she said mildly.

Martin lifted the polished lid obligingly. The conversation in the room thinned; even the fire seemed to lower its crackle. There was a hush, as though everyone knew Catherine was about to uncover something, and no one dared to cough in case the truth mistook it for interference.

Inside, nestled where no one would expect it, was a crystal wine glass. The stem glinted faintly under the lamplight. The liquid was faintly amber, catching the fire as if flirting with it. Catherine's brow tightened by a precise degree.

"A glass inside the piano?" Peter whispered. "What in heaven's name..?"

Catherine reached for it, steady as ever. She lifted it carefully, bringing it close to her face. She sniffed delicately, then sharply. Her eyes hardened.

"Cyanide," she announced, her voice cutting across the carol-singers like a knife. "This is poison."

The singing faltered. A chord died awkwardly under Martin's fingers. Heads turned. The room seemed to contract around her words.

Martin frowned. "Are you certain?"

"Almonds," Catherine said, her tone brooking no contradiction. "The bitter almond smell. Cyanide." She held the glass away, her face grave. "Whoever placed this here was hiding it or saving it."

"Saving it," Enid repeated, rolling the phrase around like a boiled sweet. "Well, Merry Christmas to us all. A goblet of death tucked away with the carols. How festive."

"No one touch the keys," Catherine said crisply. "Or the glass. Simon, step back. You're hovering like a moth."

Catherine set the glass on a side table, far from stray elbows. "Keep clear." She turned, already moving. "I must see Carla again."

David was beside her without being asked. "I'm coming."

Enid slid off the sofa arm with surprising briskness. "So am I," she said. "I've been waiting to be useful all day."

"Enid," Catherine said, "you've been useful since breakfast. Try not to improve on it."

"Ha," Enid snorted, and followed anyway.

They left the murmuring behind and crossed the hall. The corridor seemed longer than before; time did that in houses, stretching where fear lived. The Christmas decorations the mistletoe sprigs and dangling stars, crimson ribbons looked suddenly like theatre props in the wrong play. Shadows flickered from the sconces, elongating their figures along the wall so that Catherine looked taller, David broader, Enid wider.

In the spare room Carla lay on the bed, covered.

A hush settled as Catherine crouched, David moving instinctively beside her. His hand touched her shoulder, steady and protective. Enid stood sentry by the door, chin up, as if daring consequence to try itself against her.

Catherine eased the covering back and leaned close to Carla's pale face. She inhaled gently; her expression didn't change much when she was right about dreadful things, only the light in her eyes cooled half a shade. She replaced the sheet and stood.

Enid looked shocked.

"Almonds," she said. "Cyanide. Carla was killed with cyanide."

David's voice was pitched for her alone. "Didn't you say earlier it was mugwort?"

"I did," Catherine replied. "Because that was what I thought I detected in the wine near her. But her breath tells a different story. Cyanide leaves a distinct trace. This changes everything." She brushed her hands together as if to shake off the residue of an idea. "We've been misled. Mugwort is deadly enough, but this… this is deliberate."

"Deliberate is your favourite word when you want to frighten people," Enid said without sarcasm, which, from Enid, was almost tenderness.

"Deliberate is the truth," Catherine said. "Come."

They returned to the drawing room with the controlled speed of people who refuse to rush merely because fear likes it. Voices were trickling back into song; Holly had found a harmony out of nothing; Peter was tapping his fingers against his thigh in a rhythm that wasn't quite the carol and wasn't quite nerves and was probably both.

Catherine lifted her hand; the room quieted by habit. "Carla died of cyanide," she said, clear as a bell. "Which means we were wrong about the wine that held the mugwort being the poison that murdered her. The mugwort we detected relates to something or someone else."

Peter looked pale again. "So Carla… cyanide. But Aunt Frances…?"

"Yes," Catherine said, turning toward the door. "I need to see her again." Her eyes found Enid and David. "With me."

They left another wave of murmurs behind and climbed the stairs. The house's age spoke in the wood underfoot a soft creak here, a low complaint there. Someone had renewed the garlands recently; the holly leaves still gleamed; the paper stars bumped one another in a draft like guests who didn't know which way they were supposed to go.

Inside Frances's room the air was thick with the scent of stale wine and that other thing rooms keep after death an eloquent silence. The small nativity on the dresser watched without blinking. Frances's hands, folded neatly, belonged to a version of her that only sat for photographs.

Catherine moved forward, her presence commanding without fuss. She bent over the body, sniffed gently, testing her instincts once more. She touched the glass at the bedside turned it, considered the meniscus, held it to the light, set it down again.

"Mugwort," she said at last. "Yes. Frances was poisoned with mugwort. And by the look of it, she drank a great deal. Her lips are stained with wine."

"Two poisons, then," Enid said, clucking her tongue. "Mugwort for Frances, cyanide for Carla. Whoever is doing this isn't just a killer they're a chemist."

"Or a coward," David said, softly but not gently. "Poison keeps one's hands clean."

"Hands always tell on us," Catherine murmured, almost to herself. "One way or another."

Catherine straightened, smoothed the coverlet not to fuss, but because she understood the grammar of rooms. She met David's eyes briefly and drew strength from the calm steadiness there. "This is getting very confusing," she admitted, voice still iron-edged. "Two different methods. Two different deaths. And yet connected."

Peter had followed them as far as the doorway and now hovered like an undecided thought. "Why would anyone use two different poisons?" he asked. He looked young again, not the man who argued about the future of computing but the boy who used to walk this house as a small child.

"That's the question," Catherine said. "Were they meant for different people? Or was one of them a mistake?" She glanced at the glass on the table again. "We must tread carefully. One thing is clear: we cannot trust appearances."

"Or glasses," Enid said. "Or pianos."

They moved back into the corridor. The carols had resumed below fainter now, as if the singers had lost confidence but not the habit. *Good King Wenceslas* limped past the door, found its step on the "feeble, fainting" line and, feeling seen, recovered. The house itself seemed to lean closer to listen, interested in whether it still could.

"Two poisons," David said quietly, when they had walked a dozen paces and the hush felt private. "Tell me what you see, not what you suppose."

"I see this," Catherine said. "Cyanide for Carla. Mugwort for Frances. I see a glass hidden in a piano why there, unless haste or panic? I see a cupboard glass with lipstick Carla's shade but not the same glass as the one by her body. I see people moving in clumps whenever the lights fail, and more glasses than we have hands. Three different types of glasses with poison in each."

"You see motives," he prompted, though the word made his mouth taste of metal.

"I see opportunities," she corrected. "Motive is tidy. Opportunity is messy. People hide their motives; they forget to hide their hands." She paused. "Peter found a letter accusing Philip by implication. Or Philip, at least, sits near the smoke."

"Peter also enjoys being the man with the extraordinary reveal," David said. "And letters like to say more than they prove."

"And we need to talk to Philip," David said.

"Yes," Catherine answered. "And to Peter again with fewer flourishes."

In the drawing room the mood had eased itself into something that wasn't comfort but resembled a cousin of it. Martin, exiled from the piano by general agreement, stood by the mantel inspecting the carved shepherds as if applying for the position. Holly had put her scarf round Sally's shoulders and was pretending not to be kind.

Inside, the room gave itself permission to be almost ordinary for a little while longer. And Catherine, with David's warmth at her side and the taste of almonds in her mind, kept watch.

Chapter 23: Catherine and David

The house lay wrapped in its own midnight silence. From the drawing room came only the faintest of sounds: a log shifting on the fire, a chair creaking as one of the guests finally gave in to sleep. The grand halls, once filled with singing, piano music, and the crackle of Christmas crackers, were now hushed, carrying only the muffled whisper of snow pressing against the tall windows.

Upstairs, Catherine and David had withdrawn to their room. A fire still burned in the hearth, though it was banked low now, shadows leaping in slow, drowsy rhythms across the ceiling.

David, his jacket draped neatly over the back of a chair, sat with his elbows on his knees, staring into the flames. Catherine, always composed even when exhausted, leaned against the wing of her chair, her hand propped under her chin, watching him with the air of someone who had seen a long day's work but knew the night was not done.

David's voice was the first to break the silence. "What is going on with two lots of different poisons," he asked, "and three glasses, two of which were hidden away?" His words were measured, but there was a note of disbelief that he couldn't hide.

Catherine straightened a little, her eyes sharp. "Maybe two different types of murder," she said, "or perhaps two different people killing people off."

He ran a hand across his hair, exhaling. "But it looks like two people, tried to kill Carla off."

"Yes," Catherine said firmly, her gaze unwavering, "but you can only die once. Whoever was behind this… or whoever thought they were, made a grave miscalculation." She paused, her voice softening. "There's something desperate about it. Clumsy, even. As if they were rushing to silence her, not thinking clearly."

David's eyes flickered toward her. "Someone has definitely been hanging out in Carla's room. The bed, the lipstick glass, the fire. I wonder if the killer lingered there, rifling through her things, bold enough to sit in her chair as if it were their own."

Catherine's mouth set in a firm line. "They took something. Something from her notebook. I felt it at once. The pages were ripped. She guarded that notebook jealously every scrap of gossip, every careless word she picked up. If something has been torn from it, it was important enough for them to risk being seen."

He nodded, his jaw tight. "Yes, we need to find those papers. And we must speak to Philip about that letter Peter found. That letter… I don't like it, Catherine. It feels like the kind of thing that turns everything upside down."

She reached out, her hand brushing across his. "I think I need to think first," she said softly. "It is late. It hasn't been the Christmas we planned, but it has been… eventful."

"Eventful." David gave a short, tired laugh. "That's one way of putting it."

Catherine's lips curved, though faintly. "And yet… most people have had a good time, in a strange sort of way. They've sung, eaten goose and pudding, exchanged presents, laughed at cracker jokes. Murder has walked among us, and still they cling to festivity. Perhaps it's the only way they know to keep fear at bay."

He leaned across, brushing his fingers along her cheek. "You've kept them steady. You always do. Even when you're carrying the weight, you never let it crush you."

Her eyes softened at his touch, though her voice stayed strong. "I do it because I must. Because if I falter, they'll see it, and fear spreads quicker than fire."

They sat for a long moment, quiet but not alone. The clock on the mantel ticked softly, marking the minutes past midnight.

At last, Catherine smiled faintly. "Do you remember last Christmas?"

David's face brightened with memory. "How could I forget? You baking mince pies that burnt around the edges because you were too busy scolding me for dozing during the Queen's Speech."

Catherine let out a short laugh, covering her mouth. "You did doze. Your head tilted back like a boy in assembly. I was mortified."

"You weren't mortified," he teased, eyes glinting. "You were secretly delighted. You enjoy telling me off."

"Perhaps," she allowed, tilting her head. "But this year… this year I thought we'd have peace. A fire, a lavish dinner, excellent company."

David chuckled. "Well, we've had a fire."

"Yes," she said dryly, "and instead of a small talk, we've had poisonings."

"And yet," he said gently, "we still have each other."

Her gaze softened. "Yes. And that's worth everything."

They let the silence fall again, but this time it was tender.

David stretched his legs out, leaning back. "Did you see the angel on the tree tonight?"

"Yes," Catherine said, amused. "Crooked from the moment the lights went on. I straightened it twice."

"And Enid crooked it again, I'll wager," David said. "She can't leave anything untouched."

Tulip yawned then turned over by the fire.

Catherine laughed softly. "The room looked beautiful, though. For all the shadows we carry, it still looked like Christmas. The holly, the tinsel, the carols. My father would have been pleased."

David reached across, took her hand, and kissed it. "He would have been proud of you, Catherine. You're stronger than he ever imagined."

She swallowed hard, blinking away tears she refused to let fall. "You give me strength," she whispered.

"Always," he said simply.

The fire sank lower, glowing embers now. Beyond the window, the snow thickened, glowing faintly gold where the lamplight touched it.

"Do you know what I kept thinking this evening?" David asked after a pause.

"What?"

"That it doesn't matter what comes. We can face it. You and I. Together."

Catherine's lips curved. "Yes," she said. "Together."

She rose, smoothing her skirt, and extended her hand to him. "Come. We both need sleep. Tomorrow will demand everything of us, and I'll be sharper for rest."

He stood, slipping his hand into hers, and drew her close. They stood by the fire, their arms wrapped around one another, breathing in woodsmoke and pine, holding fast in the midst of chaos.

"Happy Christmas, Catherine," David murmured into her hair.

"Happy Christmas, Mr. F" she whispered.

And hand in hand, they turned toward the bed. Behind them, the fire whispered its last, the snow thickened its silence, and the old house seemed, for a moment, at peace.

Chapter 24: The Snowman

Catherine stirred from sleep at precisely seven o'clock. It was an old habit, the kind that refused to break even on mornings when one longed to stay curled in warmth, away from the world. She stretched beneath the heavy quilt, her hand brushing against David's side, finding him still deep in slumber. His breathing was steady, untroubled, and she lingered for a moment, allowing herself the comfort of it before duty and curiosity dragged her elsewhere.

The room was still and faintly chilled, the sort of cold that seemed to creep in even with the thick curtains drawn. Catherine slid from the bed, careful not to disturb David, and padded barefoot across the thick rug that covered the floorboards. She reached the window, pulling back the curtain with one swift motion.

Outside, the snow was falling thick and fast, a world painted in white. She caught her breath. The new lighting meant you could see clearly in the gloom. It was that magical time of year, when every hedge and branch was laced with frost and even the most ordinary of things became enchanted under the weight of winter. Candlelit wreaths still hung from the lampposts by the drive, their holly berries a splash of scarlet against the silver.

And there in the field opposite stood a stag. Tall, regal, almost otherworldly, its antlers crowned with snow. Catherine pressed her palm to the glass, awed by its presence. For a moment, she allowed herself to imagine it had been sent as a blessing, a silent guardian watching over the house.

But then her gaze shifted. At first, she thought it was another figure, perhaps someone trudging early through the fields. A labourer, a neighbour, someone caught in the snow. She leaned forward, frowning. No, it was no person.

It was a snowman.

A tall, ungainly thing, its bulk outlined against the falling snow. Its shape was crude but unmistakable: the round head, the lumpy torso, the stick arms jutting at awkward angles. On its head, a black top hat sat askew, jaunty yet sinister. Catherine squinted. From her vantage point, she could not quite make out the details of its face it was turned away, its back stiff, almost purposeful.

And then her eyes caught on something in its hand.

At first, she thought it was just another stick, part of the careless design. But no, the longer she stared, the clearer it became. It was a knife. A kitchen knife.

Her stomach lurched. She pressed closer to the glass, her breath fogging it, but there was no mistaking it now. The snowman's stick hand gripped a blade, and from the tip of it, even at this distance, something dark seemed to drip.

Catherine's breath came shallow. Instinct screamed at her to wake David, to cry out, to rouse the whole house. But something stronger pulled at her, some fierce determination born of fear and duty. She could not simply stand here and stare.

She threw on her dressing gown, knotting the belt tight at her waist. Her slippers were nowhere to be found, so she went barefoot, her steps quick and purposeful as she hurried down the landing. The decorations of the hall flickered past garlands of pine, bows of crimson ribbon, the golden glow of fairy lights still twinkling from the night before. She barely saw them.

The front door groaned as she pulled it open. Cold rushed at her, biting her skin, sending a shiver through her bones. She stepped outside.

The snow was thick beneath her feet, soft and cruelly cold, but she hardly noticed. Each breath clouded before her, and flakes caught in her hair, clinging to her lashes. She pushed forward, her dressing gown trailing damp at the hem as she crossed the drive and entered the field.

And then she was before it.

The snowman loomed taller than she'd imagined, its bulk menacing under the greying sky. Its stick arm jutted out stiffly, and in its grasp was indeed a knife one from the kitchen, she realised with a sickening twist. Its blade was smeared, glistening red, and from it dripped blood that stained the snow at its base.

Her heart thundered. The snow at its feet was heaped strangely, uneven, and her gut knew before her mind dared to admit it. A shape. A mound. A body.

Catherine staggered forward, dread clawing at her.

"No," she whispered, voice hoarse in the cold. "Please, God, no. Don't let it be one of them. Don't let it be…"

She could not finish the thought. Her mind conjured faces Peter, David, even Enid with her sharp tongue and eccentric ways. She saw Tulip bounding across the snow, barking. She saw Christmas laughter stilled, silenced.

Her throat tightened.

"I made them all come here," she murmured, her breath uneven, catching in her chest. "I brought them into this house, into this storm, into this danger. I am responsible. If it's one of mine…"

Her legs shook, but she forced herself onward. She knelt, brushing snow away from the still form. Her fingers stung with cold, but she did not falter. She would not let fear stop her.

At last, the face was revealed.

Simon.

His eyes were closed, his features slack, rimmed in frost. She released a shuddering breath, a mix of sorrow and shamefully, guiltily relief.

A tension lifted from her shoulders.

Not Peter. Not David. Not one of the few family she still clung to. The relief was sharp, cruel even, but real. And then came the guilt, flooding in like a tide.

"I know it is bad," she whispered, her voice breaking. "I know it is wrong. But I have lost so much family already. Too much. I cannot lose another. Not yet."

Her hand trembled as she brushed more snow from Simon's chest, revealing the dark stain across his coat.

Behind her, the house loomed, windows glowing with faint golden light. Inside, warmth and life still carried on. Soon, they would stir. Soon, they would come. But here, in this field, Catherine felt alone with the horror, a sentinel at the edge of something terrible.

She bowed her head, the snow falling harder now, coating her hair, her gown, even Simon himself, as though the world sought to bury the truth beneath its blanket of white.

And for a moment, she prayed. A whispered plea into the cold morning air.

"Grant me the strength to endure this. To see it through. To protect them, all of them. For I cannot, will not, lose any more."

Chapter 25: Private chat

David stirred awake, his head heavy with the kind of half-dreams that come after restless sleep. He stretched out a hand, expecting to find the warmth of Catherine's shoulder, but the bed beside him was empty and cold.

He sat up, blinking. For a moment he thought she might be in the adjoining bathroom, but then came a sound footsteps, faint but hurried, padding down the corridor outside. David frowned, pushed back the bedclothes, and reached for his dressing gown. He tied it loosely around his waist and opened the bedroom door.

In the dim light of the corridor stood Peter, his hair tousled and his dressing gown hanging awkwardly off one shoulder. He looked as though he too had been roused from sleep.

"Peter?" David said, keeping his voice low so as not to disturb the rest of the house. "What are you doing up?"

Peter shifted, clearly uneasy. "I was going to ask you the same thing. Is Catherine in there with you?"

David rubbed his eyes. "No. She must have gone already. I was half asleep, but I think she was standing at the window a moment ago. Then well, I could swear I heard the door. She must have run outside."

The two men exchanged a glance. There was an odd mixture of concern and exasperation in David's expression. Catherine's tendency to slip away without explanation was hardly new, yet the thought of her wandering outside alone, with snow falling thickly, set his nerves on edge.

"Let's see for ourselves," Peter said, motioning to the window at the end of the corridor. The two padded across the runner carpet, their breath faintly visible in the chill air that seemed to creep through every gap in the old house.

They pressed their faces to the glass. Outside, the night garden stretched wide and pale, blanketed with snow that shimmered beneath the glow of the lanterns strung across the drive. The fir trees lining the boundary were weighed down, branches sagging, glistening like something out of a Christmas card.

And there, by the far lawn, stood Catherine. Her dressing gown clutched tightly around her, she was motionless beside the snowman.

David's breath caught. It was no ordinary snowman. Whoever had shaped it had given it an oddly human stance, too deliberate in posture. Its twig arms jutted at an angle that suggested menace rather than cheer, and from the right branch protruded something unmistakably metallic.

"Good Lord," David muttered. "Who would build a snowman like that?"

Peter gave a short, humourless laugh. "That is the kind of thing you two investigate, isn't it? Murders, mysteries, the grotesque dressed up in Christmas tinsel."

David didn't answer. His eyes stayed fixed on Catherine, who seemed transfixed by the grotesque figure. He felt an ache in his chest worry mixed with admiration for her boldness. She wasn't afraid, not outwardly at least. Catherine never was.

Peter cleared his throat and shifted awkwardly. "Anyway," he said, his voice lowering, "since it's just us here, maybe I ought to remind you of something. Back in the day, you remember what we did? We stole that million from Reginald."

David stiffened, his eyes snapping from the window to Peter. "Keep your voice down."

"There's no one about," Peter said quickly, waving a hand. "Listen I'm not saying we're international money thieves. We're not. The only reason we've not touched a penny is because it was invested, as you well know. We couldn't touch it until now. But things have changed."

David's jaw tightened. "You think I've forgotten?"

Peter stepped closer, his breath faint with last night's brandy. "Well, it has doubled in value. That's a million pounds each, David. A million. And it's right there, waiting. But

Catherine..." he paused, shaking his head "you know what a goody two-shoes she is. If she gets too close to it, if she starts sniffing around like she does, we're finished. You need to guide her away. Keep her distracted."

David's eyes narrowed. He thought of Catherine out in the snow, her sharp eyes catching details no one else would, her mind piecing together fragments until she found the truth. She had always been able to see through him, through everyone.

Peter leaned in. "And don't forget Philip. That hole in the account Reginald mentioned in that letter. Four times the amount we took. That's what you ought to focus on when you're talking to Catherine. Keep her looking at Philip, not us."

David exhaled slowly, weighing his words. "I'll try," he said at last. "But Catherine doesn't miss much. You know that. If we're interviewing Philip this morning, she'll have questions. Best thing you can do is keep your story straight."

Peter's eyes flickered nervously, but then he forced a smile. "I can manage that. What I can't manage is her temper when she smells deceit."

"Then don't lie," David said shortly.

For a moment, silence hung between them, broken only by the ticking of the grandfather clock at the far end of the corridor. Then David added, his tone softening: "Peter, about Carla..."

Peter's face darkened.

"I know she was difficult," David went on. "But did you have anything to do with her death?"

Peter bristled. "No. I know what you're thinking. But I didn't murder her. She was all bluff, David. She liked to rattle us, threaten this and that. I don't even know if she'd done anything serious. She liked the sound of her own voice, that's all."

David studied him for a moment, searching for any sign of deceit. But Peter held his gaze, steady if a little weary.

Finally, David sighed. "All right. Let's go down to breakfast before the whole house wakes."

Peter nodded, relieved. The two men moved away from the window, leaving the image of Catherine and the sinister snowman fading behind them as they descended the wide oak staircase.

The hall was dressed for Christmas in all its splendour. Holly and ivy wound around the banisters, their berries bright as drops of blood against the dark green. A large nativity set had been arranged on the sideboard, its porcelain figures glowing faintly in the lamplight. The scent of pine and polish mingled in the air.

David paused a moment at the bottom of the stairs. He had always loved the atmosphere of this house at Christmas, though this year unease sat heavy in his chest. Murder, money, secrets it was a poor companion to peace and goodwill.

Peter adjusted his robe and muttered, "At least there'll be tea."

David managed a thin smile. "Tea might just save us all."

He thought again of Catherine by the snowman, her breath misting in the cold air, her eyes sharp and unflinching. Strong, determined, unyielding. Whatever secrets they tried to keep from her, he knew she would find them in time.

And in that knowledge, he felt both pride and dread.

Chapter 26: Breakfast

The breakfast room was warm and glowing against the grey white of the world outside. Snow pressed itself to the tall windows, muting the light, so that the lamps and candles seemed brighter than usual. A spruce tree stood proudly in the corner, decked with red ribbons, glass baubles, and little straw angels that one of the maids had brought from her village. It was Christmas at the Price Mansion, but there was little peace on earth in that house.

Breakfast had been set out as though the household were expecting royalty: rashers of bacon curling at the edges, fried eggs glistening in their dishes, a mountain of sausages, black pudding sliced in neat rounds, and fresh loaves still warm from the oven. Silver pots of tea and coffee steamed beside tall pitchers of orange juice. On another table rested a Christmas ham, studded with cloves, and a tray of spiced buns dusted with sugar. The scents mingled savoury and sweet, comforting and festive.

Their voices were low, the kind of muttered talk between brothers-in-law who were close enough to share confidences but also careful to keep their tones steady in a house full of watchful ears.

"She was still out there when I looked from the landing," Peter said quietly, tugging his dressing gown tighter.

"Catherine?" David asked, his brow furrowed.

"Yes. By the snowman," Peter replied, a nervous glance at the frosted windows as they reached the breakfast room doors. "I don't like it, David. She shouldn't be alone out there. Not after…"

"She's strong," David said firmly, though a flicker of unease crossed his face. "Stronger than most men I know. Still, I'll go out after breakfast. The cold is enough to freeze the marrow out of you."

Peter gave a thin smile, but it faltered when the butler opened the door for them. Inside, voices rose and fell with polite laughter, the scrape of cutlery, and the rustle of newspapers.

The family and guests sat spread along the great mahogany table, the white linen gleaming, crystal glasses catching the light from the chandelier above. Conversation turned on the usual morning pleasantries how heavily it had snowed in the night, whether the post would arrive through such weather, What Christmas tv they were missing. Someone mentioned the Queen's Speech, and another muttered about the scarcity of petrol in the village.

"Morning, gentlemen," called Philip from his seat near the head of the table. He lifted his coffee cup with an air of ease, though his eyes were sharp. "I trust you slept well. Cold night for December. I swear the frost was thicker than the windowpanes."

David gave a polite nod, while Peter busied himself with pulling out a chair.

The maid, her white apron starched stiffly, set plates before them

The double doors burst wide with a crash that silenced every voice and stilled every hand.

Catherine stood there.

The sight of her froze the room: her dressing gown flung around her shoulders, her hair loose and clinging with melted snow, her eyes blazing with an intensity that stopped conversation on every tongue. In her right hand she held a knife, its long steel blade slick with blood, the scarlet drops pattering onto the polished floorboards.

For a moment no one breathed. Then a collective intake of breath rippled around the table, as though the entire household had gasped at once.

Peter lurched to his feet, knocking his chair back. "Catherine…"

"I'm so sorry, Peter," Catherine said, her voice steady but edged with urgency. She did not tremble, though her hand clenched the knife hard enough to whiten her knuckles. Her gaze was fixed, sharp, unflinching. "Someone has stabbed Simon to death."

A cry escaped one of the women at the table; another guest's hand flew to her mouth. Philip swore under his breath, the colour draining from his face.

The clatter of cutlery against china broke the silence, chairs scraped, but no one moved closer. Catherine's presence was commanding; she filled the room with calm control, though her words rang like a church bell.

"The police aren't coming," she continued, her tone firm, cutting through the murmurs before they could rise into panic. "The roads are still blocked with snow. We are on our own. We need to find the murderer and quickly."

She let her eyes travel across the table, meeting each face in turn: suspicion, fear, defensiveness reflected back at her. "Everyone here must stay with two others at all times. No wandering about alone, no slipping away unseen. Safety in numbers, until we know who did this. David and I will investigate."

David rose from his seat and came to stand beside her. He placed his hand on her arm gently, steadying, his touch both supportive and protective. Catherine allowed herself a brief glance at him, softening just enough that those nearest caught the flicker of intimacy between them.

"It would be best if you spent most of your time in the drawing room," Catherine went on. "Stay together. Keep calm. We will be conducting interviews in the study. "Philip…" she turned to him sharply, her voice crisp "…you first, please. After breakfast."

Philip's jaw worked, but he gave a curt nod, his usual self-assurance shaken but not entirely lost.

Silence lingered for a moment, broken only by the ticking of the longcase clock and the faint carol from the radio in the kitchen: *O Come, All Ye Faithful*, cheerful and out of step with the chill that had seized the room.

Peter finally exhaled, his voice low, strained. "God help us. On Christmas week."

"Yes," Catherine said, her tone softening, but only slightly. She held the knife aloft for all to see, then set it carefully onto the sideboard where a cloth had been laid. The blood stained through the linen instantly, a grim reminder of the reality outside the warm, festive room.

"Now," Catherine added, brushing snow from her sleeve and straightening herself, "let us have breakfast. We'll need our strength. Panic will not help us. Order will."

David drew out a chair for her, guiding her gently down with a hand at her shoulder. His fingers lingered, a quiet reassurance, before he sat beside her. He poured her a cup of tea, his hand brushing hers, the small gesture grounding both of them amid the storm that had descended upon the household.

Conversation resumed slowly, tentatively, in hushed tones. No one spoke of Simon's death directly; instead, they made clumsy remarks about the weather, the quality of the bacon, the snowfall in past Decembers. A strained small talk, as though if they spoke of normal things loudly enough, the horror might fade.

Catherine, however, remained silent as she ate, her fork precise, her eyes thoughtful. David leaned toward her, his voice low enough for her ear alone.

"You've taken charge well," he murmured. "But are you alright?"

Catherine turned her face slightly toward him, their shoulders brushing. "I'll be alright, David. There's no time to be anything else." She touched his hand briefly beneath the table, a fleeting moment of warmth. "But I'm glad you're beside me."

Always, his eyes said, though he did not speak the word.

Enid, perched on the far side of the table with her ever-watchful eyes, broke the silence first. "Well," she said briskly, dabbing her mouth with her napkin though she hadn't taken a bite. "If this isn't the oddest Christmas I've had in years. Death at breakfast. It rather puts the mince pies into perspective."

Her tone was sharp, but her eyes flicked toward Catherine with something close to admiration. Few in the room could have commanded order the way Catherine had in that moment.

"Spare us your gallows humour, Enid," muttered Philip, reaching for the coffee pot with a hand that shook slightly. He masked it by filling his cup with too much speed, spilling a dark line across the saucer.

"Humour is better than hysteria," Enid replied tartly. "Unless you'd rather we all sat here wringing our hands until the murderer decided to strike again?"

Philip's eyes narrowed, but he said nothing more.

David leaned closer to Catherine, his voice pitched for her alone. "You've got them listening. Keep it steady. They'll follow your lead."

Catherine nodded faintly, her jaw set. She allowed her gaze to travel over the table. Each face seemed sharper to her now, etched with tension their words too casual, their laughter forced, the glances they stole at one another betraying unease.

Peter pushed his plate away, untouched. He rubbed his temples with one hand. "Simon," he said at last, his voice low, ragged. "He was only here yesterday, laughing about the snow, about the carol service… How could he be…" His voice faltered, and he looked down.

"None of us are safe," Catherine said gently, though her tone carried an edge of iron. "That's why we must keep calm. If we lose our heads, we hand the murderer everything he wants."

"Or she," Enid interjected crisply.

"Yes," Catherine agreed without hesitation. "Or she."

The maid came in with a fresh pot of tea, her eyes darting nervously about the room. Catherine gave her a reassuring nod. "Thank you, Mary. Please see that everyone in the drawing room has hot drinks later. No one should be left without company."

The girl bobbed her head and hurried out, clearly eager to be away from the tense gathering.

Small talk began to flow again, brittle but present. Holly, seated near the middle, attempted a lighter note. "At least the snow makes the house look like something out of a Christmas card," she said, her voice just a touch too bright. "It's all holly and ivy in the hall, mistletoe over the door. You've done wonders with the place, Catherine. You could almost forget.". She then burst into tears "I was very fond of Simon, I can't believe he has gone."

The remark settled the table back into silence.

David poured Catherine another cup of tea. She wrapped her hands around the china, grateful for the warmth. He leaned closer again. "Eat something," he urged softly. "You'll need your strength."

"I know," she murmured. She picked up a piece of toast, spreading butter in slow, deliberate strokes, as if the act itself was a way of keeping her composure. "We'll get through this, David. Together."

She met his eyes, and despite the horror that loomed over the room, something steady passed between them love, trust, and resolve.

Across the table, Philip cleared his throat. "So, Catherine… you'll want to speak to me first." He tried to sound calm, but there was a tightness around his mouth. "Shall we get it over with?"

"After breakfast," Catherine replied firmly. "No one should be interrogated on an empty stomach. Eat."

"I've no appetite," Philip muttered.

"Force one," she said, steel in her voice. "We'll need clear heads if we're to face this properly."

Enid gave a short laugh. "She's right, you know. Catherine's the only one in this room with any sense of command. You'd all do well to follow her orders without fuss. Unless you'd prefer to end up like poor Simon?"

A murmur of unease followed, chairs shifting, forks pausing mid-air.

Peter looked up suddenly, his voice rough. "Don't, Enid. Not now. Not like that."

Enid's eyes softened, if only for a moment. "I only mean that panic helps no one."

Catherine reached across the table, placing her hand over Peter's briefly. "We'll find the truth, Peter. I promise you. Simon deserves that."

Peter swallowed hard and nodded, though his eyes glistened.

The grandfather clock chimed the half-hour, the sound carrying through the room like a reminder that time was pressing on. The carol on the radio in the kitchen shifted to *Hark! The Herald Angels Sing*, the triumphant melody at odds with the heavy air in the breakfast room.

David straightened. "Once we've eaten, I suggest we gather everyone in the drawing room. Catherine and I will speak with Philip first in the study. After that, we'll proceed one by one. No exceptions."

There were nods around the table, reluctant but resigned.

Catherine sat back in her chair; her fingers curled lightly around David's. She let her eyes roam the faces again: some pale with fear, others set with determination, a few hiding something darker. Each of them was now a suspect. Each of them had to be weighed, measured, tested.

But she would not falter. Not Catherine Forrester. Not with David by her side.

She set down her teacup and drew a steadying breath. "Finish your breakfast," she told them. "And then, let us begin."

Chapter 27: Where is the money?

The study was heavy with shadows, its dark mahogany shelves pressing in around them. Every surface seemed to bear the weight of memory: the grandfather clock ticking with solemn precision; the gleaming brass lamp casting long bars of gold across the Persian rug; the faint traces of cigar smoke that lingered in the velvet drapes

Beyond the mullioned window, the night pressed in, snowflakes swirling against the glass like pale moths. The faint echo of laughter drifted from the hall, where the others were gathering near the tree. But here, in the study, all was hushed tension.

Catherine sat in her father's chair, her back upright, her hands resting calmly on the armrests. It was a seat that lent authority, but she hardly needed it her own composure was enough. David stood close at her side, one hip leaning against the desk, his hand near hers as if ready to steady her should the moment call for it. His dressing gown was open at the throat he looked tired, but the resolve in his eyes matched hers.

Philip stood before them, arms folded at first, then letting them drop as if remembering that folded arms looked too defensive. His face was pale, whether from the cold or from irritation it was difficult to tell.

"In the study," Catherine began evenly, "someone found paperwork on you. Paperwork suggesting you stole money from my father's accounts."

Her tone was quiet but it cut through the fire's crackle.

Philip gave a mirthless laugh. "Show me the paperwork."

She slid it across the desk. The paper made a faint rasping sound as it moved. Philip snatched it up, scanning with quick, darting eyes. His mouth curled.

"This is not paperwork," he scoffed. "This is conjecture. Your father's suspicions written down in his untidy hand. You know what your father was like, Catherine. He saw shadows everywhere."

"Sometimes shadows hide something real," Catherine returned.

Philip shook his head sharply. "I did take some money, yes, legally. Half of the company is mine. Always was. I used it to invest, wisely. Unlike Reginald, I saw the markets as they were moving. And we'll all benefit. That is, if you stop chasing ghosts and start facing facts."

His eyes narrowed. "If you're looking for missing millions, I'd suggest you look closer to home. At David. At Peter. Even at yourself. Do you know what your brother has signed? Do you know what transactions he's authorised?" He tapped the paper with one finger. "Give me the accounts, Catherine, and I'll show you exactly where the rot is."

The silence stretched. Catherine's gaze didn't waver. "I will need to think about that."

Philip leaned forward on the desk, his knuckles whitening against the wood. "Catherine, this business about the snowman and the knife, ask yourself, does that sound like me?"

Catherine met his eyes without flinching. "I don't think so. But I know one thing, Philip. Desperate people do desperate things."

"I am not desperate," he snapped, straightening. Then, softening, he added, "I have a firm financial future. Can you say the same?"

David's jaw tightened. He spoke with quiet firmness. "When was the last time you saw Simon alive?"

Philip turned to him, considering. "In the dining room. He was with Peter and Martin. If Simon hadn't ended up dead, I'd have sworn they were plotting something. I heard him mutter 'we need to get rid of her.' Strange words, don't you think?"

David's eyes flicked to Catherine's, and she caught the unspoken thought: Who was the "her"?

Philip went on, warming to his theme. "Martin's a slippery one. I saw him upstairs earlier, looking guilty as sin, as if he'd been caught rifling through drawers. And Sally, that woman's nerves are in tatters. Ever since she received that... gift, she's been looking over her shoulder. She believes everyone's out to get her. Talk to her, you'll see."

He spread his hands. "As for Enid... she's cleverer than any of us give her credit for. If she's behind these deaths, I doubt you'll ever catch her. She's the sort who can step around suspicion as easily as a cat stepping round a puddle."

His lip curled faintly in amusement. "And then there's Holly, positively gleeful. You've given her permission to write her little book about you, Catherine, and now she thinks she's landed her fortune. Scribbling away, enjoying herself. Murder and mayhem suit her pen far more than Christmas pudding."

Catherine's expression didn't change, though her eyes narrowed slightly. "Thank you, Philip. I will let you know about the accounts. For now, please ask Enid to come in."

Philip hesitated, as though about to add something else, then gave a short nod. He placed the papers back on the desk with deliberate care, smoothed the creases, and turned for the door.

The latch clicked shut behind him.

For a moment, neither Catherine nor David spoke. The fire popped and settled. Somewhere down the corridor, faint notes of a piano drifted, halting and uncertain.

David moved first. He placed his hand gently on Catherine's shoulder. "Look, Catherine, if I had that money, you'd know it. We wouldn't have scraped by, counting pennies, praying your projects brought in something. You know me better than that."

She placed her hand over his, squeezing. "I know, David. I never doubted it."

He crouched a little, so their eyes met. "But you're not seriously considering letting Philip anywhere near the accounts, are you? That would be putting a fox in charge of the henhouse. He'd have doctored ledgers ready, showing Peter and me as thieves."

Catherine stood, pulling him up with her. They moved together toward the hearth. The flames cast a golden wash over their faces. She leaned briefly against him, her cheek to his chest. He bent and pressed a kiss into her hair.

It was a moment too brief, but vital of warmth amid the storm.

She lifted her head, her gaze fierce. "Philip can spin his tales, but he won't fool me. I'll uncover the truth. I've done it before. I'll do it again."

David smiled faintly, brushing his thumb along her jawline. "That's my Catherine. Fierce as fire."

She allowed herself a small smile. "Fierce enough to take on all of them, if I must."

Catherine's grip on David's hand tightened. Christmas had not been forgotten, even in this house shadowed by suspicion and death. And though the season's peace seemed a world away, she meant to cling to it for David, for herself, for the memory of her father.

The fire cracked once more, and she looked into the flames as though they held answers. But all they offered was warmth.

Chapter 28: Too Many Biscuits

Enid came into the study with Tulip trotting neatly at her heel, the Jack Russell's nails clicking on the parquet and her tail doing a small, delighted metronome. Enid was munching pickled onions from a little glass jar she must have slipped from the breakfast sideboard.

"Thank you for saving my life again," Catherine said, rising from the leather armchair by the hearth. She met Enid halfway, took the older woman's forearm with both hands, and squeezed. Her fingers were cold from where she'd been holding the lead pencil poised over her Filofax. "If not for your interference with that glass…"

"Oh, we don't call it interference, dear," Enid said airily, tapping the lid back onto the jar with a pop and then immediately removing it again to fish out another onion. "We call it Providence. Or common sense. Or an old woman who doesn't care for funerals trying to keep their number down." She grinned, the vinegar sharp on her breath, then reached into the pocket of her tweed skirt and produced a dog biscuit. "And for the young lady," she cooed, bending with the suppleness of a woman half her age to offer the treat to Tulip. "There we are, you brave girl."

Tulip accepted the biscuit with polite delicacy and carried it to the hearthrug, settled with a sigh, and began to crunch. Catherine's mouth tightened and then softened; she ran a calming hand down her own skirt, smoothing an invisible crease, and glanced at David, who was already moving to her side. Without asking, he slid a hand along the small of her back, the warmth of his palm a private reassurance. She leaned into it for a breath, just a breath, before straightening.

"You just need to be very careful," Enid said, as if continuing a thought she'd begun in the corridor. "Check everything you drink. And if it looks too festive to be true, it is. I've never trusted garnishes."

David's hand paused, and Catherine shot him a look that said No laughing. "I know you like talking in riddles," Catherine said to Enid, refusing to let the woman's nonsense turn their moment into levity. "But I really need your help in solving this case."

"It wouldn't be me without a little subterfuge," Enid said, bright with mischief. She popped another onion into her mouth, chewed, and then because she could never resist feeding someone other than herself produced a small bone from the other pocket. "For Tulip again," she said, but before she could present it, Catherine lifted a palm.

"Just the one for now," Catherine said. "She's already had a busy morning."

"Quite right," Enid conceded, putting the bone away. Tulip looked up at the rustle, hopeful, then resigned herself with a soft huff of air and placed her chin on her paws. The fire gave a cheerful crackle, sending a flurry of sparks up behind the guard. From far off, faint enough to be cosy rather than intrusive, came the ghost of music from the drawing room someone had set the radio to a Christmas station. Catherine caught three notes of "Hark! The Herald Angels Sing" before the study door shut fully and the room belonged to them.

"Well," Enid went on, strolling without invitation to the armchair opposite Catherine's and lowering herself with a theatrical old-lady sigh. "There's all this financial stuff that I don't know anything about, but I do know about people."

"Which is why I want you," Catherine said simply.

Enid twinkled. "Finally, someone says it aloud."

David's hand left Catherine's back, but only so that he could pull the bell cord near the window. "Tea," he said under his breath, leaning close to Catherine's ear as if confiding state secrets. "And something to soak up the vinegar. You'll get light-headed."

He stayed near, taking up his place at the edge of the desk, one hip against it, hands in his pockets in a posture of deceptive ease. He watched Enid the way a good detective watched a friendly witness fond, alert, unwilling to be charmed out of the details that mattered.

Enid dabbed at her lips with a handkerchief that had a snowflake embroidered in one corner. "When Carla started talking," she said, "about all that money and where it had gone, and who had had their fingers in it, I looked around the room. Philip, Peter, and you, David oh, all of you looked scared. You did," she added, almost kindly, as David opened his mouth. "Fear has a little pinch to it. Like someone squeezing a bit of skin on the inside of your elbow where no one can see. You three all felt the pinch at once."

David kept his face still. He had very good control when he chose it. "I can assure you," he said, and his voice was soft, almost rueful, "that I have no money from Reginald."

Enid gave Tulip a second biscuit despite the earlier rule and smiled while the dog crunched in secret delight. "And I can assure you that you are lying," she said, not unkindly. "Or if not lying, being economical with the truth. The difference is a matter of teaspoons."

"Enid," Catherine said, before David could stiffen at the word, "leave the teaspoons aside and tell me what you mean. What did you see, precisely? Faces, hands, posture what told you?"

Enid's eyes, an unexpectedly clear blue, grew thoughtful. She put the onion jar down on the side table and folded her hands over her skirt, the robin on her jumper bumbling as if to listen. "Philip went very still," she said. "Now, Philip is never still. Even when he's sitting, he's fiddling with a cufflink or tapping a foot. He was still. That's a man trying not to move because if he moves, he might run, and that wouldn't do at Christmas in front of the tree." She lifted a shoulder. "Peter looked not still but stiff. Like a boy who's broken a window and is waiting to see if anyone heard the smash, trying to decide whether to pretend he didn't hear it either. And David…" she turned her head, an examination rather than a reproach "David looked at you."

He didn't deny it. Catherine, caught, felt the echo of the glance Enid meant last night, the tree lit and all those faces and all that talk, and David's look.

"Looking is open," Enid said. "It's not guilt. It's loyalty. But after the look," she picked up one hand, making a small skilled gesture as if threading a needle, "he did something with his mouth. The held-back thing. I've seen men do it when they've promised to keep quiet about Christmas presents but the parcel is burning a hole in their brain."

"Perhaps it was a present," David said lightly, and it almost was light; his arm brushed Catherine's again, a small tethering movement. "Or a thing that felt like a present once and now is a nuisance. We've all had those."

Enid was unconvinced. "Sally's terrified," she continued, turning the conversation with no more effort than she expended turning a page of a book. "She's sure she's the target. She keeps putting her hand to her throat like she expects a necklace to be strangling her. And Holly well. Holly is ambitious. She'll take everything you've got if you put it within reach and turn your back. That one has a Christmas list written on your stationery and signed with your pen."

"You could be describing half the village" David said. "And the other half were too bold to write their lists down."

"Mm," Enid said. "And then there's me."

The door opened and Henshaw, solemn as a churchwarden, brought in a tray with a teapot in its padded red-and-green cosy, and a plate of mince pies dusted with sugar. The room filled instantly with the comfortable smell of shortcrust and spice. Henshaw's eyebrows flicked with almost invisible relief at the sight of Catherine alive and upright; or perhaps that was Catherine's imagination, sharpened to unreasonable points by a night of too many revelations and too much danger. He set the tray on the low table, inclined his head, and withdrew without unnecessary words.

"Thank you," Catherine called after him, because all these people did things not only because they were employed but because they were trying to hold a house together with their bare hands, "And Henshaw please will you ask Martin to come here."

"Of course, madam," Henshaw said from the hallway, a voice like a polished banister.

Catherine poured the tea, sturdy and brown in the cups, and offered sugar. Enid took one, then two, then, with an expression of guilty joy, three. "It is the season," she said. "And a tonic after vinegar." She sipped, then sighed in contentment. "Oh, that's a proper cup. Whoever first thought of putting water on leaves and trusting the result should have a statue. Perhaps they do. In Darjeeling."

David let Catherine serve him and then bent to taste the tea she handed him. She sat; knees angled toward him and let her calf rest against his for the length of a breath. It steadied her. It always had.

"When was the last time you saw Simon?" she asked, the cup cradled in her palm. The question, which she had been holding like a hot coal while they spoke around it, needed air.

Enid dabbed sugar from her lip with the snowflake handkerchief again. "It was last night," she said, "after you had all gone into the drawing room and the boys had got the lights on the tree behaving properly. Martin was talking to him in the hall you know the hall with the holly garland that's a bit too prickly,"

"The hall by the grandfather clock," David said, quietly encouraging. Quietly guarding, too.

"That's the very one. They were standing by the clock. It was chiming; I remember because it chimed the half hour and then took its time about finishing, and men always think a clock that is doing something gives them licence to raise their voices. It does not. But Simon did. He said he said, 'I need to get rid of her.'" She pursed her lips. "I don't like the words 'get rid of.' They make people disappear in your mind before they've gone from the room."

"Do you know who they were talking about?" Catherine asked. She watched Enid's face rather than her words. The muscles around the eyes. The set of her mouth.

"I have no idea," Enid said briskly.

Oh, and have you seen my Mr Whittaker?" Her face opened in sudden, fretful concern. "I've definitely brought him here, and he must have sneaked off out of the window. It's just the sort of thing he does. Always peering at the neighbours."

Catherine refused, gently, to let that become the centre of the conversation. "I'm sorry," she said. "I haven't. If I see him, I'll bring him to you."

"We need to get to the bottom of this." Said Catherine

"That's what I like to hear," Enid said, and took a triumphant bite of her mince pie. "Down to the bottom, not tapping your toes on the shallow step. People paddle, and then they say the water's cold. Of course it's cold, you goose. Dive in and be done."

Catherine set her cup down and leaned forward, the fire catching the thread of gold in her hair. "All right," she said. "Dive with me for a minute. 'Get rid of her' who might Simon have meant, if you had to guess not from gossip but from behaviour?"

Enid tilted her head, robin eyes joggling. "If you want behaviour, I'll give you behaviour. Holly prowls. That's not an insult, that's an observation. Prowling is a fine thing in a cat and a useful thing in a woman who wants a raise, but it makes men talk in corners. Sally flutters, and people mistake fluttering for innocence. Don't. Fluttering is strategy. Peter is trying very hard to be better than he feels. You can tell by the way he's overly polite to door handles. He doesn't bang anything. He's afraid of loudness. Philip is not afraid of anything except his own stillness. If he has to wait, he taps. If he can't tap, he thinks, and he does not care for what he thinks."

"And Martin?" David said.

"Ah, Martin." Enid rolled the name in her mouth like a sweet. "Martin has the kindness of a man who wants you to believe in his kindness. As you know he is acting, he is not who he says he is, everything is an act for him."

Catherine didn't change expression, but David felt it in her the slight drawing together of attention.

"I shall try asking him for honesty and see what he offers," Catherine said.

"That's your way," Enid said, approving. "And it's the right way. Ask for the thing. People think hinting is subtle. It's not subtle, it's fearful. And fear makes people clumsy. You wouldn't want a fearful carpenter. Why would you want a fearful conversation?"

The tree lights across the room blinked, held their glow, blinked again. Catherine glanced involuntarily at the door. Somewhere in the house a corridor draught was playing with the bells someone had tied to a sprig of fir, and their faint chiming made the air feel like frosted glass that had been tapped with a ringed knuckle.

"You're tired," Enid said suddenly, softly, to Catherine. "You think you hide it but it shows under the eyes. Don't let them keep you talking nonsense. If someone wants to tell you the truth, they'll do it in ten words. If they take a hundred, they're selling a story."

"I like stories," Catherine said, a wryness tugging at one corner of her mouth. "But only when I choose them. And this one" She shook her head, then found David's eyes and let herself smile perhaps more fully than she had since dawn. "This one isn't mine to enjoy."

"We'll make it yours to end," David murmured. "That's better."

"Do you ever wish to be wrong, Enid?" she asked, more idly than it sounded. "Would you like to find one day that you have misread everything, and everyone is better than you think?"

Enid lifted her cup with both hands and spoke into the steam. "I am wrong all the time," she said. "But not about the large things. I am wrong about which cousin will put the extra roast potato in his pocket and which girl will say yes to the charades when she means no. Those are sweet mistakes. The large things are different. People tell you the large things early if you listen with your eyes. That's what you do, Catherine. You look. That's why I like you."

It wasn't flattery. Catherine accepted it as she would have accepted a shawl placed around her shoulders. "And I like you," she said. "Even when you feed my dog too many biscuits."

Footsteps in the corridor, then a pause. Henshaw's discreet cough. "Madam? Mr. Martin Hale says he will be with you shortly. He is…ah…tuning the piano. He asked that you forgive the delay."

"Of course," Catherine said. "Thank you."

The footsteps receded. The radio in the drawing room found a signal and the first bar of "God Rest Ye Merry, Gentlemen" arrived like a familiar friend too loudly through the wall, then moderated.

Enid took this as her cue to rearrange herself in the chair, and in the process a small paper-wrapped parcel slid from the pocket of her cardigan and landed, by sheer luck, on her lap rather than the floor. She looked at it with exaggerated innocence.

"What's that?" David asked, his voice at once playful and wary, as if the paper might contain a live coal.

"A very small present for a very large mind," Enid said. "But it isn't for Christmas Day. It's for later. I am not a creature of delayed gratification. Chocolate should be eaten when found, not when scheduled. But this this can wait. Not because it is grand, but because it is ordinary. The present is for you Catherine, open it 'when you know'."

"Ordinary is underrated, thank you I will treasure it." Catherine said as she put the present in her pocket.

"Exactly. Extraordinary things make the papers. Ordinary things make the bed. One keeps you talking; the other keeps you alive. I am glad you have a fairy for the top of that tree, by the way. Not one of those modern plastic ones that looks like a Sindy doll. A proper fairy. A fairy should be a bit wonky. Perfection is for shop windows."

"We kept the old fairy," David said. "I got it out of the attic and spent fifteen minutes extracting it from a tangle of fairy lights, last used, in 1979."

"Ah, the Seventies," Enid said, and shuddered dramatically. "A decade that taught us all the dangers of tinsel. The Eighties taught us the dangers of everything else. And yet here we are, still alive and drinking tea."

"Some of us only just," Catherine said, and immediately regretted the turn to gallows humour; but Enid took it with a nod.

Enid rose and gathered her jar of onions with ceremonial care. Tulip hopped up, expectant, then thought better of it and curled back by the fire. Enid made it to the doorway, paused, and turned back with that bright, maddening glint that meant she'd been saving one last thing.

"Oh, Catherine have you thought about who was sleeping in Carla's room?" She tilted her head. "Isn't it obvious? It was Carla. Even if she was wearing different lipstick.".

She gave the smallest nod as if the answer had been sitting in plain sight on the side table all along and walked out, leaving the door to hush itself closed behind her.

Chapter 29: A Change of Accent

Catherine sat in the high-backed chair near the hearth, her fingers absently stroking Tulip's smooth head. The little Jack Russell dozed half on her lap, one paw twitching as if chasing a dream. David leaned against the sideboard, sleeves rolled to the elbow, his expression thoughtful but watchful the stance of a man waiting for a fuse to spark.

"Well," said Catherine after a long silence, "there's a lot to talk about there." Her tone was measured, calm, but her eyes were bright with contained energy. "I think I could talk to Enid for hours. She just has an amazing foresight of what's going on. I reckon she's solved it already."

David gave a low chuckle. "I think she knows a lot more than she lets on," he said, moving to stir the fire with the poker. "I think she might even be involved in some of it."

Catherine smiled faintly. "You'd say that about anyone who knows more than you."

"That's not true," said David, crossing to her side. "Just the ones who smile like they're sitting on a secret."

Catherine tilted her head toward him, a teasing spark in her eyes. "And what secret do you think she's sitting on?"

"Oh," said David, crouching to scratch Tulip's chin, "probably the key to the whole affair." He looked up at her. "Or maybe just the recipe for that dreadful plum pudding she insisted on bringing."

Catherine laughed, a sound that briefly warmed the cold corners of the room. "You know," she said softly, "I think she'd like you, if you weren't always trying to psychoanalyse her."

"I'm not psychoanalysing," David protested. "I'm surviving."

Before she could answer, there came a knock on the door not loud, but deliberate. Three measured taps. Tulip's head lifted at once, her little body going rigid, eyes fixed on the door.

"Come in," said Catherine, her voice steady. "Martin, sit down. Or should I call you Matthew Askew?"

His expression shifted when he saw the way Catherine was looking at him the faintest flicker of surprise, then resignation.

"Call me Martin. At least with you, I can stop faking this American accent" He spoke now in his natural voice, lower, smoother, unmistakably English. "That's a relief. It was starting to grate even on me."

David straightened from his position by the fireplace, arms folded. "At last, we see the real you."

Martin ignored him and moved towards the chair opposite Catherine. He glanced briefly around the room the fire, the tree, the wreath above the mantel before fixing his gaze on Catherine again.

"What I told you is true," he said, leaning forward slightly, "I had meetings with your father. But he was very uncompromising."

Catherine's eyes didn't leave his face. "Why are you here, Martin?"

"I'm here," said Martin, resting his clasped hands on his knee, "to make a deal with your brother. But I'm also here to retrieve something of mine. Something I left in the attic years ago. I need it back, you see."

He paused, studying their reactions. Neither Catherine nor David moved. Tulip gave a soft growl, the kind that comes from deep in a dog's throat not angry, just alert.

"I've nothing to do with these murders as I told you. If I had, I would have been long gone. And I'd have framed someone else for good measure. Let me go about my business, and I'll leave you all well alone. Start making a scene, and I'll be all over you and your family."

David stepped closer, his voice low and hard. "That sounds a lot like a threat."

Martin spread his hands. "Not a threat. A promise of mutual convenience."

Catherine rose slowly, moving to stand beside the fire. The light caught her hair and gave it a haloed edge, as though she were both angel and judge. "Simon," she said. "He told you he needed to get rid of *her*, to get her out of the way. That's what this is really about, isn't it?"

"All that," said Martin with a dismissive wave. "We're talking about *you*. Getting you out of the way so we could talk to Peter. It's only natural you'd want to speak to your brother, but we needed time for business, you see."

"Business," said David dryly. "That's what you call it."

Martin looked up at him, that same thin smile returning. "You'd be surprised what falls under that word."

He shifted in his chair, glancing briefly at the tree. "Beautiful decorations," he said. "You've kept the place as I remember it. Though your father would never have tolerated tinsel. He was a man for order, not sparkle."

Catherine's expression softened slightly, though her tone didn't. "He believed things should last, not glitter for a day and fade."

"Then he and I were opposites," said Martin, running a hand through his hair. "I've always preferred a little glitter, even if it doesn't last."

David watched him, studying the small tells the restless fingers, the darting glance toward the door, the way his left foot tapped faintly against the rug. "You seem nervous, Martin," he said. "Or is that your version of charm?"

Martin gave a small laugh. "I'm many things, Mr. Forrester, but nervous isn't one of them."

"Then stop fidgeting."

Martin chuckled softly. "It's that Sally, isn't it? She recognised me. I need her off my back, and I'll let you all be. I gave her that present as a warning."

Catherine's gaze sharpened. "You might think it was Sally that recognised you first, but it was Enid. She saw your picture in the paper. But yes, you're right Sally made a scene about it."

"Holly," Martin muttered, grimacing. "She's writing that blasted book, isn't she? I'd better only appear as Martin Hale, otherwise there'll be trouble. Truth never suits print."

David leaned his shoulder against the mantel. "Truth rarely suits men like you either."

Martin's eyes flicked up, amused. "Men like me?"

"Clever ones," said David. "Ones who think the truth can be negotiated."

Catherine turned to Martin again, voice quiet but firm. "Okay, we'll let you go if you can help us find the killer. That's the deal. No tricks. No half-truths."

Martin studied her for a long time, then nodded slowly. "You always were your father's daughter," he said.

"Uncompromising. I respected that about him, even when it drove me mad." He stood, straightened his jacket. "But understand this there are things in that attic that don't belong to any of you. Let me have them, and I'll tell you what I know."

Catherine tilted her head. "And if we say no?"

Martin smiled. "Then you'll find this Boxing Day less merry than you hope."

Tulip barked sharply, as if in protest, and Martin took a small step back.

Catherine's eyes never left his. "Try it," she said softly. "See how far you get before Tulip bites your ankle and David throws you into the snow."

For a moment, the only sound was the crackle of the fire. Then Martin laughed, a short, nervous sound. "You really are remarkable, Catherine. I can see why people follow you. Even the dog knows her orders."

Tulip wagged her tail but kept her eyes fixed on him.

"Looking back on it, I think it was your aunt that drank my wine. So maybe the killer was coming for me. I want you to catch them Catherine, I do."

Catherine sat again, unhurried, and gestured toward the door. "You can go when I say so, not before. Tell me first, what exactly did my father refuse of you?"

Martin hesitated, his confidence dimming for the first time. "He refused progress," he said finally. "He refused to see that the world was changing. I offered him opportunity he saw betrayal."

"And now?"

"Now I see ghosts," Martin said, a bitter edge to his tone. "Your father's, Carla's, perhaps my own if I stay too long."

Catherine's expression softened, almost pitying. "You can't outrun ghosts, Martin. You can only stop lying to them. What did Simon mean when said 'Get rid of her' last night"

He gave her a long, measuring look.

"Why Catherine do you think every conversation is about murder, it isn't. He just wanted a bit of space with Peter, so we could discus this deal we are putting through. If you must know it was you, he wanted out of the way. I hope that is not what got him killed. You ought to talk to Holly she was blowing hot and cold with him."

David watched him walk to the door, his footsteps soft on the old rug. "You might find," David said, "that telling the truth is easier than running from it."

Martin turned in the doorway, hand on the knob. "Easier, perhaps," he said. "But not nearly as profitable."

Then he was gone. The latch clicked shut behind him.

For a long time, Catherine and David said nothing. Tulip padded in a circle, then curled up again near the hearth. The flames hissed and shifted.

Catherine finally spoke. "He's frightened; do you think someone was trying to kill him?" she said softly. "That's what men sound like when they're cornered by their own past."

David nodded. "He's also dangerous. You saw how he spoke about your father no remorse, no warmth."

She leaned back, letting her head rest against the chair. "Yes," she murmured. "But frightened men make mistakes. And frightened men talk."

David knelt beside her, resting one hand on her knee. "So do brave women."

Catherine smiled faintly. "That's why we make a good pair."

David replied "He is great at disguise, you would never think he was the Matthew from Greece, so timid, so vulnerable"

"I did" stated Catherine.

They sat together in silence, watching the fire shrink to embers, the tree lights flickering in quiet rhythm. Outside, snow blanketed the world in calm. Inside, the air shimmered with warmth and secrets the kind that only Christmas nights in old houses ever seemed to hold.

Tulip sighed, content, her tail thudding once before sleep.

And in that stillness, Catherine whispered, almost to herself, "We're close now, David. I can feel it. The truth is in this house somewhere and before Christmas is done, we'll find it."

David smiled, his thumb brushing her wrist. "Then let's make sure we're the ones who unwrap it."

The fire crackled in quiet applause, and outside the snow kept falling.

Chapter 30: Sitting Ducks

The study was warm but shadowed, the kind of room where the flicker of the fire caught on brass frames and dark wood panelling.

Catherine stood near the desk, her arms folded but not stiff, a silver brooch glinting on the lapel of her dark dress. David was by the hearth, one hand resting on the carved mantel, the other holding a glass of brandy he hadn't yet touched. Tulip lay curled on a Persian rug between them, her head on her paws, eyes flicking from one to the other. The dog's soft snore was the only sound until Catherine spoke again.

"Lots of people think you have my father's money, David," she said, her voice low but sharp with determination. "Including Enid. She gave a very good impression that she thinks you're lying."

David straightened, his brow furrowing. "Well, I haven't got the money, have I?" His tone carried a tired edge, but he crossed to her, resting a warm hand on her shoulder. "Catherine, you know I haven't. If I had, we'd wouldn't have been so short when we started solving murders."

Her eyes softened slightly at his touch, though her mouth stayed firm. "When the snow melts and the magic of Christmas is over, I'm sure if I haven't solved the murder by then there'll be a police investigation into all of this."

He gave a dry laugh. "Well, I can hardly wait for that Christmas present."

Catherine's lips twitched but she didn't smile. "We'll crack on and find the murderer before we all die. I'm not leaving it to chance."

Tulip lifted her head at the sound of Catherine's voice, tail giving a tentative thump against the rug. Catherine bent slightly to stroke the dog's ears. "At least you're calm," she murmured. "More sense than half the people here."

David reached over, brushing a stray curl from her forehead. "You've been on edge since breakfast. Have you even eaten anything?"

"I had a piece of toast." She met his gaze with that steady, unwavering look of hers. "Don't fuss."

"I'll fuss if I like," he said lightly, his thumb brushing her cheek before he stepped back. "You're no good to anyone if you collapse."

Before she could reply, the door to the study creaked open. A draught of cold air slipped in, carrying the scent of snow and a faint echo of carols from somewhere down the hall. Sally stepped inside, hugging herself as though to ward off more than the cold. Her eyes darted around the room, lingering on the dark corners, then on David, then Catherine.

"Sorry," she said quickly. "I didn't mean to interrupt."

"You're not interrupting," Catherine said. Her tone was firm but not unkind. "Shut the door, please. It's freezing."

Sally obeyed, closing it softly before moving a few steps forward. She looked pale, her hands twisting together at her waist. The firelight caught the faint shimmer of her dress a deep red wool number that would have looked festive if not for her expression.

"Catherine," she began, her voice quivering. "Martin is Matthew Askew, as you know. He must have faked his death in Greece. He's coming for us. We're all snowed in and we have nowhere to hide."

David exhaled slowly and set his brandy glass down. "We've just had a word with Martin," he said, keeping his voice level. "If we leave him alone, I think he'll let us be."

"I don't trust him," Sally said quickly. "The body count is rising. He gave me that present I'm sure of it. That's blood on the knife. That's what he's going to do to me. We're all sitting ducks."

Catherine moved a step closer, her heels soft on the rug. She didn't raise her voice, but there was steel beneath it. "Sally, you need to relax. He knows we know. Enid knows. He would have to kill all of us, and I believe him if he says he'll leave us alone if we don't start meddling."

Sally let out a breathy laugh. "Easy for you to say." She glanced at Tulip, who wagged her tail once before settling again. "Even the dog looks calmer than I feel."

Catherine reached out, briefly resting a hand on Sally's arm. "When did you last see Simon?"

Sally blinked. "I… after we had dinner. And he's another one. He's another one who wants to kill us. I heard him say to Martin, 'we need to get her out of the way.' I think he's talking about me."

"They were talking about me, actually," Catherine said evenly. "And it's just so they can get this deal over the line."

"What deal?" Sally asked sharply.

Catherine shook her head. "Never mind that now. We're not here to trade rumours. We're here to solve a murder."

The wind howled faintly against the windows, rattling the garland hung there. David went to poke the fire, sparks leaping as he did. "Do you want a drink, Sally?" he asked over his shoulder. "Tea? Brandy? Something warm?"

Sally hesitated. "Tea, if you've got it. Milk, no sugar."

Catherine poured from the pot on the desk into a china cup trimmed with gold, part of her father's old set, she noticed absently. The smell of black tea and drifted up. She handed it to

Sally, who wrapped her hands around it as though it were a lifeline.

"Now," Catherine said, returning to stand beside David, "did you see anyone outside Clara's room? Especially after her death? It could even have been Clara?"

Sally's eyes flicked up from the cup. "You mean Clara could have been around on Saturday morning?"

"Yes."

"My bedroom is close to hers. I did hear someone inside." She paused, frowning. "I didn't think about it at the time. I thought one of you must have been in there. But thinking about it now... it wasn't one of you. That changes everything, as far as I'm concerned."

David set the poker aside and came to stand behind Catherine, resting a hand lightly on the small of her back. She leaned into him almost imperceptibly, drawing steadiness from the contact.

"Look," Catherine said gently but firmly. "You need to calm down. When you've thought about it carefully, come back and tell us what you think about Clara. I'll keep Martin off your back, but you mustn't wind him up. Just leave him alone and let us deal with him."

Sally swallowed hard and nodded. "All right. I'll try."

The fire crackled. The clock on the mantel chimed the quarter hour. From somewhere distant in the house came a faint burst of laughter, brittle and strained, then silence again.

David glanced at the window. Snowflakes were swirling like confetti under the outside lantern, sticking thick to the leaded panes. "If this keeps up, we'll be buried till New Year," he murmured.

"Then we'd better solve this before the Epiphany," Catherine replied dryly.

Sally managed a small, nervous laugh at that, setting her empty cup back on the desk. "You two sound so calm about it all. Like a pair of detectives in an Agatha Christie story."

Catherine's mouth curved faintly. "That's one way of looking at it."

Tulip stirred, padding over to Sally and sniffing at her skirt. Sally bent instinctively, scratching the dog's ears. "She's sweet," she said softly.

"She's a good judge of character," David said. "If she thought you were dangerous, she'd be barking."

Sally gave a wan smile. "That's something, I suppose."

Catherine tilted her head. "Have you slept at all?"

"Not much."

"You should. You'll think clearer after some rest."

"I don't know if I can."

David moved to the sideboard, lifting a tin of biscuits with a faded Christmas scene on the lid carol singers under a gas lamp. He offered it to Sally. "Shortbread?"

She hesitated, then took one, nibbling at it. "Thank you."

For a few moments they all stood in silence, the only sounds the fire, the wind, and the faint crunch as Sally bit into the biscuit. The atmosphere in the study seemed to ease just a fraction.

Catherine moved back to the desk, sorting a few papers without really seeing them. "Sally," she said without looking up, "I need you to be steady. There's a lot at stake, and panic won't help."

"I know," Sally said quietly. "It's just Christmas, the snow, the lights, it all feels so unreal. Like we're trapped in a snow globe and someone keeps shaking it."

Catherine did look up then, her eyes meeting Sally's. "We'll get through it. But we have to be smart."

Sally nodded again. "All right."

Catherine glanced at David. "Can you send in Peter?"

"I'll go find him," David said.

"No." Catherine held his gaze. "Stay here with me a moment. Let Sally go. She needs a walk to clear her head."

Sally set down the biscuit, wiping her fingers on a handkerchief. "I can do that. I'll tell him you want him."

Catherine softened her tone. "Thank you. And Sally don't worry. We're not sitting ducks. Not while I'm breathing."

Something flickered in Sally's expression then, not quite relief, but a spark of steadiness. "All right," she said. "I'll go."

She moved to the door, hesitated, then looked back. "Catherine?"

"Yes?"

"You really think you can keep us safe?"

Catherine's jaw set. "I know I can try."

For a heartbeat, Sally stood there, then she nodded and slipped out, closing the door softly behind her.

The study was quiet again. Tulip gave a sigh and flopped back onto the rug.

"You did well with her," he murmured.

"She's terrified," Catherine said. "We all are."

He kissed the top of her head. "You're not."

"I'm holding it together." She let out a breath. "Sometimes that's all you can do."

Outside, the snow kept falling. Inside, the fire burned, and the two of them stood together, steady against the storm.

Chapter 31: What a Waste

Through the tall leaded windows, snow fell in slow, steady flakes, each one bright against the darkening sky. The windowpanes were edged with frost, and little beads of condensation gathered at the corners like tears.

Catherine stood by the desk, her back straight, one hand resting on a pile of papers, the other wrapped around a cup of black coffee gone lukewarm. David was beside the fireplace, poking at the logs with a brass poker until a new shower of sparks danced up the chimney. Tulip lay curled on the hearthrug, paws twitching in some doggy dream, the glow of the firelight warming her fur.

They had been speaking quietly, their words a murmur beneath the steady tick of the mantel clock, when the door opened.

Peter stepped in, his face pale and drawn. Snow dusted his coat collar and clung to his hair like salt. He shut the door softly behind him, leaning against it for a moment as though steadying himself before crossing the room.

"I can't believe Simon is dead," he said. His voice cracked, and he cleared his throat, staring down at the rug. "He was my best friend. It's all happening again. We're all suspects again."

Catherine set her cup down with a soft clink. "You know why anyone would want to kill him?"

Peter shook his head, moving to stand near the window. The faintest tremor in his hand betrayed him as he brushed at the frost on the glass. "That's the thing. He is nothing to do with the family or that holiday case you had. He's not rich. He's not a threat. It just seems such a terrible waste."

The fire hissed softly as a log shifted. David straightened, brushing the ash from his hands. "Sit down, Peter," he said gently. "You're like a ghost standing there."

Peter obeyed, dropping into the leather armchair opposite Catherine's. He leaned forward, elbows on his knees, staring at the carpet pattern without really seeing it.

For a moment they sat in silence, the three of them and the dog, the only sounds the crackle of the fire and the distant carol music from the hall.

Finally, Peter spoke again, his voice quieter. "Did you confront Philip about the missing millions?"

"Yes," Catherine said. "He said the money was all legal and that you and David have swiped it."

Peter's head came up sharply. "If I took the money, I wouldn't need to ask for investment from Martin," he said hotly. "Although my business is doing well, I could do with a million-pound investment."

David gave a humourless chuckle. "Wouldn't we all. We both know Philip's a slippery customer, but the numbers don't add up."

Catherine's eyes stayed on Peter. "Be careful, Peter. Martin isn't who he says he is."

Peter frowned. "What do you mean?"

"Martin is not his name," Catherine said evenly. "He was a suspect in the murder case in Greece. He faked his death, and he's reinvented himself. He says he's got something in the attic that he needs, that he left here when our father was in charge."

Peter stared at her, blinking as though trying to take it all in. "Oh," he said finally. "Nothing is as it seems."

Catherine allowed herself a small, grim smile. "No. It never is."

Tulip stirred then, stretching and padding over to nuzzle Peter's knee. He absently scratched her behind the ears, his fingers trembling slightly.

"I just... Simon was a decent man. He loved Christmas. Every year he'd drag me to Midnight Mass even when I was half asleep. Said it wouldn't feel right without the candlelight and the carols. He even sent a card to the vicar here this year, I think. Who would want to kill him?"

Catherine's voice was gentler now. "We're not going to let his death go unanswered."

Peter looked up at her. "You sound so sure."

"I have to be," she said simply.

For a while no one spoke. The fire cracked again. Snow whispered at the windowpanes. The smell of pine and holly seemed to deepen as the room cooled with the falling evening.

Then Catherine said, "Last night several people heard Simon saying, 'we have to get rid of her' You were sitting next to Martin and Simon. You must know what the conversation was about."

Peter shifted uncomfortably in the chair. "Well... I wasn't supposed to be listening then," he admitted. "But I think they didn't want you around, Catherine. I don't think they were going to kill you."

David moved behind her again, resting both hands on her shoulders now. She reached up, briefly covering one of his hands with hers.

"All right," she said softly. "Be careful, Peter. We haven't got many family members left."

Peter's gaze dropped again, his thumb tracing an invisible pattern on the arm of the chair. "You always sound like you're the one looking after us," he murmured. "Even now."

Catherine's mouth twitched. "Someone has to."

David bent closer, murmuring near her ear, "You're doing fine."

Catherine looked at Peter, "Can you send in Holly?".

Peter rose slowly, brushing at his coat as though to clear away snow that wasn't there. He hesitated by the door. "Catherine," he said quietly. "You're the only one I trust. Don't let this house swallow you."

"I won't," she said. "Go on. Get Holly."

He nodded once, then slipped out into the corridor, closing the door behind him.

For a moment the study was silent again, save for the fire and the soft ticking of the clock. Catherine turned to David, who was still standing close, his warmth a steady presence.

"Poor Peter," she murmured. "He looks like a boy again when he's frightened."

David slid an arm around her waist. "They all do, in the end."

Outside, the snow kept falling. Inside, the wreath above the fire gleamed in the flickering light, and Tulip stretched, sighing, as though she too could feel the weight of secrets pressing in.

The latch settled with a soft metallic click. For a heartbeat the house felt as if it had inhaled and then forgotten how to exhale; even the wind outside seemed to hold itself in the eaves. David didn't move at once. He stood with one hand still lifted, almost as if he were steadying the air where Peter's shape had been.

Catherine let out a breath she hadn't realised she'd been holding. "Peter will linger in the passage and look at the family photographs first, because he always does when he's rattled. He stares at Father's portrait as if it will blink and set everything to rights." She unclasped her hands, realising she'd folded them hard enough to leave faint half-moons on her palms. "He was shivering."

"The whole house is shivering," David said, glancing at the windows. "Listen to it." The wind had resumed its quiet complaint along the guttering; snow hissed like sand on glass. Somewhere, a branch ticked against a pane in a rhythm almost like knuckles. "Come away from the draft. Sit."

"Here," David said more softly.

David reached for the woollen throw folded over the arm and shook it out. He settled the throw over both their knees.

"You were hard on Peter," he said, not accusing, merely noting.

"I had to be," she replied. "He hears what he wants and edits the rest to suit his comforts." She looked towards the fire. In the reflected flames, the silver of the little nativity on the side table seemed to breathe. "Simon is dead, and we can't afford blur."

David nodded. "He loved Simon," he said. "Sometimes grief makes people noble. More often it just makes them childish."

They heard footfalls then, faint at first the way sound moves in big houses as if it's shy then closer, unhurried. A knock, careful and decorous, sounded on the study door.

Catherine straightened, not as a soldier stands but as a woman does who is used to carrying things. She smoothed the throw, touched the edge of the Filofax to square it, lifted her chin.

"Come in," Catherine said, her voice steady as candlelight. And the next chapter of the evening began.

Chapter 32: All my Christmas's

Tulip, curled up in a wicker dog bed beside the fire, raised her head as the door opened. The faint jangle of the old brass handle was followed by a waft of cold air and the scent of someone's perfume, musky, expensive, and just a little overpowering. Holly swept in, closing the door behind her with a soft click. She was wrapped in a crimson wool dress that looked festive against her dark hair, and over one arm she carried a fur-trimmed shawl.

"Holly," Catherine said evenly, though her eyes flicked to David. "I know it's not in the Christmas spirit, but all of this murder business has ruined Christmas for us all, hasn't it?" Her tone was cool but not unkind, and her fingers pressed briefly into David's sleeve as she spoke, a small gesture of reassurance that he answered with a squeeze of her hand.

Holly laughed, a bright, almost brittle sound that clashed with the solemn quiet of the room. "You've got to be joking," she said, tossing her shawl over the back of a chair. "I feel like all my Christmases have come at once. The story you're letting me write has everything: family drama, murder, food, old suspects…" She perched on the edge of a velvet-upholstered chair, crossing one elegant leg over the other. "This book is going to be a bestseller, especially if you're going to put your name to it, Catherine."

David shifted his weight, leaning against the mantel, his gaze steady on Holly. Catherine moved a little closer to him, and he slid his arm around her waist with a protective ease that made Tulip's tail thump once in the dog bed. "But Holly," Catherine said, her voice still calm but underpinned with steel, "they could come for us next. Is the risk worth taking just to be number one on the bestseller list?"

For a moment the only sound was the hiss of a log collapsing in the fire. Holly tilted her head, her smile faltering. "You think I don't know the risk?" she said finally. "But honestly..." She spread her hands, bangles glinting in the firelight. "What's life without a story worth telling? You've got to admit, Catherine, even you must be intrigued by how this has played out. Everyone's secrets leaking out like wine on white linen..."

Catherine's lips pressed together. "Intrigued, yes. Complacent, no." She slipped free of David's arm and took a step closer to Holly. The holly wreath above the mantel cast tiny shadows over her features, but her eyes were bright, sharp. "What was going on with you and Simon?"

Holly's eyebrows lifted. "Simon?" she echoed, and then she gave a little shrug. "Well..." Her voice softened, losing some of its earlier sparkle. "I do like a young man sometimes. My husband's a little way away, and I've always had a taste for company, you know. So yes, I did take Simon to bed on Christmas Eve." She glanced down at her manicured hands. "But then he left to go to his own room. I hadn't seen him after that."

David exhaled slowly, and Catherine caught the faint furrow between his brows. She moved back to him, her fingers brushing against his as though to anchor herself. "Have you got any idea who could be behind this?" she asked.

"None," Holly said brightly, but there was a quiver under the word now. "But I can't wait for you to solve it. That's all I'm waiting for now, a good ending. Though I will tell you one thing Sally has gone loopy since getting that present, I just saw her in the hallway muttering to herself 'Carla was alive, alive' mad words if ever I heard them."

Catherine smiled faintly, but her eyes were hard. "Well, that's convenient," she said, "because I have just figured out who's done all the murders. The pieces have just come together." She straightened, her voice taking on that calm authority David loved and feared in equal measure. "We need to get everyone to the drawing room. I have solved the case."

Holly blinked, leaning forward. "Already?" she said. "You've really…" She broke off, staring at Catherine with open curiosity. "You're not just saying that, are you? Because if you are, you're a better actress than I gave you credit for."

David gave a low chuckle, though his eyes stayed on Catherine. "She's not acting," he said. "When Catherine's like this, you know she's got it all lined up in her head.".

Catherine allowed herself a small smile at him, but her focus remained on Holly. "I've had enough of secrets," she said. "I want this out in the open. But before we call everyone in, Holly, I want to be sure you've told me everything."

Holly hesitated, then shifted in her seat, her ankle swinging nervously. "Everything?" she repeated. "You think I'm hiding something?"

"I think everyone here has been hiding something," Catherine said. She walked to the window, pulling back the curtain a little. Snow still fell in lazy flakes, catching in the glow of the courtyard lanterns. Somewhere in the distance, faint strains of a carol floated from the drawing room "O Come, All Ye Faithful" the voices soft and blurred by distance. "You said you saw Simon last on Christmas Eve. What did he say to you before he left?"

Holly's eyes flicked to David as if hoping for a lighter question, but he only gave her a steady look. "He said he had to go back to his room," she murmured at last. "He seemed… distracted. Kept glancing at the clock, as though waiting for something. I thought maybe he was meeting someone else, but he didn't say who. He just kissed me and left. That's all."

Catherine turned back to her. "And you didn't follow him?"

"No." Holly's voice sharpened a little. "I'm not in the habit of chasing men down corridors. Besides, I had my notes to write up. You forget, Catherine, I'm working too."

Catherine's eyes narrowed. "So, you stayed in your room?"

"Yes." Holly held her gaze. "I never left. And before you ask, no one saw me. I know how that sounds, but it's the truth."

David shifted, picking up a sprig of holly from the mantel and twirling it absently between his fingers. "You've always liked a good story, Holly," he said mildly. "But you're in one now, and it's not fiction. You realise that?"

Holly gave him a rueful smile. "I realise," she said. "But I also know Catherine. She'll sort it out. She always does."

Catherine walked back to David, slipping her hand into his. "That's not faith in me," she murmured. "That's just you wanting a neat ending."

"Either way," he said quietly, "you're about to give her one."

Tulip stretched and yawned, the soft chime of her collar tags breaking the quiet. Holly glanced down at the dog, then back up at Catherine. "Do you ever get scared?" she asked suddenly. "You talk so calmly, but aren't you frightened? All of this murder, poison, secrets…"

Catherine's eyes softened for a moment. "Of course I'm frightened," she said. "But fear's no excuse for inaction." She glanced at David. "I'm not alone."

He smiled at her, his eyes warm. "Not ever," he said.

The fire popped, sending a spray of sparks up the chimney. Holly leaned back, crossing her arms. "Well," she said. "If you've really solved it, Catherine, I hope you'll make it dramatic. My readers like a dramatic ending."

Catherine's expression cooled again. "This isn't a performance, Holly," she said. "This is about people's lives. About justice."

Holly looked away, her gaze fixed on the holly garland above the mantel. "Sometimes," she said softly, "those are the same thing."

The clock chimed the quarter hour, a deep sound that rolled through the study. Catherine straightened, her shoulders squaring. "All right," she said. "It's time."

David moved to the door, but Catherine caught his sleeve. "Wait." She looked at Holly again. "One last question. When Simon left you that night did he take anything with him? A glass, a note, anything?"

Holly frowned, thinking. "He had his watch," she said slowly. "And a little envelope. I thought it was money at first, but he tucked it into his jacket. That's all I noticed."

Catherine's eyes gleamed. "Thank you," she said simply. "You've been more helpful than you realise."

Holly blinked. "I have?"

"Yes." Catherine moved toward the door, David at her side. "Come on. We'll do this together."

David slipped his arm around her waist as they walked "You've got that look," he murmured. "The one you get before you pull the rug out from under everyone."

Catherine gave a short laugh. "Do I?" she asked.

He bent his head close to hers. "It's why I fell in love with you," he said quietly. "That mind of yours."

She smiled up at him, a rare, unguarded smile. "You always say the right thing at the wrong time," she teased.

He kissed her temple. "I say it when you need to hear it," he said.

Behind them, Holly stood up, smoothing her dress. "Well," she said, her voice bright again but a little tremulous at the edges, "this should be interesting."

Catherine opened the door, the draught bringing with it the distant scent of mulled wine and pine needles from the drawing room. She looked back at Holly. "It will be more than interesting," she said. "It will be the truth."

Then she stepped out, David at her side, Tulip trotting ahead of them, and the snow had stopped, the sun was out, the thaw had started outside it felt as the world itself were holding its breath.

Chapter 33: The Attic

The corridor was cold, the kind of chill that came from old stone and unheated corners of great houses. Martin stood in the hallway, his breath faintly visible in the light that seeped through the stained glass above the stairs. Tinsel had been draped along the banister, its edges glinting with the last of the morning sun. From the drawing room came the muffled hum of voices, Catherine's, firm and commanding even through two closed doors, and David's lower, steadier tone, always near her, always keeping her grounded.

Martin looked up at the garland looped around the picture rail, then down at his watch. "She's calling everyone together." he said, almost to himself. "But this won't take long."

Peter appeared from the far end of the corridor, shoulders hunched, hands thrust deep into the pockets of his corduroy trousers. His face was drawn and pale; the sleepless nights of the past few days had left their trace. "Martin," he said, forcing a thin smile. "You look as though you're about to rob the place."

Martin laughed under his breath, a dry sound that echoed faintly against the plastered walls. "Nothing so dramatic, Peter. Though, perhaps, just a little of that spirit wouldn't go amiss. I need a hand, quite literally, with something upstairs."

Peter frowned. "Upstairs?"

"Yes. The attic," Martin said, lowering his voice. "I know all this hasn't turned out as you'd hoped. The holiday's been… rather more eventful than any of us imagined. But I still need your help with my computer ideas, yes and, more to the point, I need help getting my money down from the attic."

Peter blinked, uncertain whether he'd misheard. "Your… money?"

Martin nodded gravely, his expression calm but his eyes bright with urgency. "Yes. Don't look at me like that. I'm not mad. It's all up there. I had to keep it hidden, given the circumstances." He glanced toward the ceiling as though he could see through it. "I can't leave it there any longer. I'll make it worth your while. You help me, and I'll give you a bundle of cash."

Peter folded his arms, sceptical. "You realise how that sounds? Like the start of one of Catherine's mysteries."

Martin smiled faintly. "Exactly why I'm telling you quietly before she calls us all into the drawing room. If she sees what I've got, she'll have the whole thing catalogued and logged before tea."

Peter hesitated. There was something oddly persuasive about Martin's tone a mixture of confidence and desperation. "All right," he said finally. "But if this turns out to be a joke…"

"It won't," Martin assured him, already turning toward the staircase. "Bring a torch, will you? The bulb up there's gone again. Can't seem to keep the thing working in this house."

They climbed the narrow back staircase, the one that wound behind the servants' quarters. The steps creaked under their weight, and dust swirled in the shaft of light that spilled from the landing window. At the top, the air grew colder. The scent of pine from the Christmas tree below faded, replaced by the dry smell of dust and old fabric.

Martin reached for the pull-down ladder and tugged it free. "Here we are," he murmured, steadying it as it unfolded with a soft clatter. "Mind your head when you come up."

Peter followed, brushing cobwebs from his sleeve. "You could have told me to wear a coat," he muttered. "It's freezing up here."

"That's what keeps things preserved," Martin said, climbing the last rung and disappearing into the gloom. His voice came down muffled, echoing through the narrow opening. "Careful with that last step. There's a loose board."

Peter climbed after him, the torch beam cutting through the shadows. The attic stretched out before them, vast and filled with the detritus of generations, trunks, hat boxes, faded decorations, and stacks of yellowing newspapers tied with string. Dust coated everything like snow. Against one beam, a box of old baubles glimmered faintly in the torchlight, their surfaces dulled but still glinting red and gold.

"It looks like Father Christmas's graveyard," Peter said, half amused, half uneasy.

Martin chuckled. "That's one way of putting it."

He crossed the floorboards carefully, each step deliberate. At the far end, half hidden behind a draped mirror, was a large canvas bag. The sight of it made Martin's breath quicken. He crouched, pulling it forward, and the fabric rasped against the boards.

Peter raised an eyebrow. "What on earth's in there?"

Martin looked up at him. "See for yourself."

He unfastened the clasp and peeled the bag open. The torchlight hit bundles of notes thick, heavy stacks bound with rubber bands. The smell of old paper and faint damp filled the air.

Peter took a sharp breath. "Good Lord, Martin. That's…"

"Over two million," Martin said quietly. "Give or take. All legitimate, before you ask. Just… inconvenient to explain to the taxman."

Peter stared, stunned. "Why would you keep that here? Of all places?"

Martin shrugged. "Where else? You think I could keep that much in a bank and not draw attention? Besides, the attic's dry, quiet, and no one ever comes up here, well, not unless they're hiding from the chaos downstairs."

Peter crouched beside him, brushing dust from the edge of a bundle. "It's freezing cold. The notes must be like ice."

"Money keeps better in the cold," Martin replied with a small, knowing smile. "It's the heat that makes it smell. Once the temperature rises, the paper gives off this peculiar scent, like mould mixed with ink. That's why I said I have to move it before the smell melts through."

He looked toward the small attic window, where thin light pushed through the frost. "It's stopped snowing for now, but the drifts outside are too deep to get through easily. Still, I'll manage. I need to get back to the States sharpish before anyone notices I'm gone too long."

Peter straightened up, shaking his head. "You're talking like a spy in a film."

"Sometimes it feels like that," Martin said softly. "You've seen how people look at me since all this began. Every conversation's loaded. Every glance measured. But this…" he gestured toward the money, "…this could be something clean. A new start. I need someone I can trust to head up the UK branch of my computer business. And that someone, Peter, is you."

Peter blinked. "Me? You want me to…?"

Martin picked up one of the bundles and tossed it toward him. It landed softly in Peter's hands, heavier than it looked. "There's your signing bonus," Martin said. "A hundred thousand pounds, give or take. I'd say that's a decent incentive."

Peter turned the bundle over, his mouth slightly open. "Martin, this is madness. You can't just…"

"I can," Martin interrupted. "And I am. You're sharp, Peter. You've got that combination of integrity and imagination. That's what this business needs. It's the future, computers. I can feel it. People don't understand yet, but they will."

Peter hesitated, his practical mind at war with temptation. "What would Catherine say if she saw this?"

Martin gave a dry chuckle. "Catherine would have it itemised, photographed, and probably turned into evidence before the day's out. She's remarkable, but she doesn't see opportunity the way I do. Besides, she has her hands full with that murder business. I heard her calling everyone into the drawing room just now, probably another grand revelation. We've got a few minutes yet."

The attic light flickered, the single bulb swaying faintly from its wire. Peter exhaled, brushing his hands on his trousers. "You really think this business of yours will work?"

Martin's eyes glinted. "It already is. I've got contacts in New York, Los Angeles, even a few in Tokyo. Microchips, data storage, personal systems, it's the next revolution. People will have computers in every home within ten years. Mark my words."

Peter smiled faintly. "You sound like one of those salesmen."

"Maybe," Martin said, returning the smile, "but at least I believe in it."

A silence settled between them for a moment the kind that came not from discomfort, but reflection. Below, a faint sound of laughter drifted upward, Catherine's voice again, sharper now, calling out instructions. Somewhere, a carol played softly on the radio in the kitchen. The faint strains of *O Come, All Ye Faithful* rose through the floorboards.

Peter glanced around. "You know," he said quietly, "for all the madness, there's something about this house at Christmas. Even with everything that's happened the garlands, the firelight, the smell of cinnamon, it almost feels… safe."

Martin gave a small nod. "It does. Though I wonder if it's the illusion of safety that keeps us all here. Catherine's trying to hold everything together. You can hear it in her voice. That mixture of control and compassion, that's what makes her so dangerous to the truth."

Peter looked at him curiously. "Dangerous?"

"In the best way," Martin said quickly. "She won't stop until she finds what she's looking for, whatever it is. She's got that detective's mind. But you and David, she trusts you both. That counts for something."

Peter sighed. "Sometimes I think she trusts everyone and no one at the same time."

"That's her strength," Martin replied softly. "It's what makes her Catherine."

The two men began to gather the bundles, stuffing them into a smaller bag. The rustle of paper filled the quiet attic. Martin moved with efficiency, almost ritualistic precision, while Peter worked more hesitantly, as though each note weighed on his conscience.

"So, what happens next?" Peter asked. "You load this up and drive off into the snow?"

"Something like that," Martin said. "We'll carry it down, slip it into the car, then join the others before anyone suspects. Catherine's probably got the fire roaring by now. I imagine David's poured her a brandy. They're quite the pair, aren't they?"

Peter smiled faintly. "They are. You can feel it even when they're silent, that connection between them."

Martin paused, considering that. "Yes. There's something enviable about it. They fit together like two pieces from different puzzles that somehow found the same box."

Peter gave a low laugh. "That's one way to put it."

They finished loading the smaller bag. Martin zipped it shut and hoisted it over his shoulder. "Right then," he said. "Let's get this down to the car before Catherine's detective instincts send her wandering up here."

They descended carefully, the ladder creaking under their combined weight. On the landing, the warmth from below was immediate, a rush of comfort after the attic's icy air. Someone had placed a bowl of oranges on the side table, studded with cloves, filling the air with their sharp, sweet scent.

Martin paused halfway down, listening. The house was alive with the sounds of Christmas, the crackle of a fire, the faint rattle of teacups, and somewhere, Tulip's bark followed by David's familiar voice soothing her.

They reached the ground floor. Martin nodded toward the side door that led to the drive. "We'll take it out that way. Less risk of running into anyone."

Peter hesitated. "You're sure about this?"

Martin grinned. "As sure as I am about snow in December."

They stepped into the cold. The snow had stopped indeed, though the world was still blanketed in white. The trees glittered faintly under the weak winter sun, and the air smelled of smoke and pine. In the distance, the church bells of the nearby village began to toll for afternoon service, their sound carrying softly through the still air.

Together they lifted the bag into the boot of Martin's car, a dark saloon that gleamed faintly under a layer of frost. The thud of the boot closing echoed through the stillness.

Martin exhaled, his breath misting in the air. "That's that," he said quietly. "Now, let's not keep Catherine waiting. She doesn't like to be kept waiting."

Peter gave a wry smile. "No. She certainly doesn't."

They re-entered the house, stamping snow from their shoes. Warmth met them at once, the scent of mulled wine and woodsmoke wrapping around them like a blanket.

Catherine's voice floated from the drawing room: "Peter? Martin? We're starting!"

Martin straightened his coat and ran a hand through his hair. "Just in time."

As they entered, Catherine turned, her eyes bright and commanding.

"You two took your time," she said, arching an eyebrow. "I was beginning to think you'd gone missing."

Martin smiled easily. "Just a bit of unfinished business."

Catherine's eyes flicked between the two men, then softened. "Come and sit down. We've got much to discuss before dinner."

Peter nodded, his expression unreadable. Martin followed, glancing briefly toward the window, where the snow was melting fast, how long until the police turned up, how long until he could leave.

The world outside was still, hushed as though holding its breath. Inside, beneath the twinkle of the tree and the flicker of the fire, the air hummed with anticipation. The season's warmth could not quite chase away the shadows of what had passed, but for a brief moment, there was peace the kind of fragile peace that came only between storms.

Chapter 34: The Reveal

The drawing room of Price Mansion looked almost serene that evening, though every soul inside it was knotted with nerves. The Christmas tree glowed in the far corner, tall, heavy with glass baubles that caught the firelight and threw pinpricks of gold against the dark red wallpaper. The scent of pine and warm brandy mingled with the faint tang of candle wax. Someone had added another log to the fire; it crackled brightly, sending sparks up the chimney.

Outside, snow pressed thickly against the windowpanes. The holly garland along the mantelpiece drooped slightly in the warmth, and tinsel glimmered dully in the lamplight.

Everyone had gathered, as Catherine had requested, or rather, commanded. They stood or sat in a loose semicircle before her: David by her side, quiet but firm. Peter sat nearest the fire, his face pale and drawn, his fingers worrying the arm of the chair. Philip stood near the drinks cabinet, as though the proximity to sherry might steady his hands. Holly perched cross-legged on the sofa with her notebook open, though for once she wasn't scribbling. Sally sat stiffly beside her, eyes darting between Martin and Enid.

And Enid, well, Enid looked entirely at home, as though murder and revelation were part of the usual Christmas entertainment. She had Tulip on her lap, feeding her scraps of sausage, and she was crunching through another pickled onion with evident pleasure.

Catherine let the room settle before she began.

"This," she said, her voice clear and strong over the crackle of the fire, "has been a difficult case. Mainly, as Enid pointed out, because nothing was as it seemed."

Her words fell into the hush like small stones dropped into water. Everyone's eyes turned toward her. David straightened slightly beside her, his presence both anchor and encouragement.

"It all started," Catherine continued, "when Sally noticed who Martin Hale really was."

There was a ripple someone sucked in a breath; another shifted uneasily.

"She recognised him," Catherine went on, "because his face appeared in one of my past cases. A suspect named *Matthew Askew*. A simpleton, yes but a dangerously clever one beneath the act. The same man who, faked his own death in Greece."

Martin's head bowed slightly. The firelight flickered across his face, casting deep shadows beneath his eyes. He did not deny it.

"He is wanted," Catherine said evenly, "for the deaths of his own parents."

For a long moment, no one spoke. Then Philip muttered, "Good Lord…" and reached for his glass again, though his hand trembled.

Sally, who had slipped into the back of the room earlier and now leaned against the doorway, looked as though she'd been struck. "So, Sally wasn't mad after all," she whispered.

"No," Catherine said softly. "She wasn't. Sally was beside herself to think a killer was in the house under a false name. But no one would listen to her."

Catherine's gaze shifted across the room until it rested on Enid. "But *you* did, didn't you, Enid?"

Enid stopped mid-chew, blinked, and then gave a crooked smile. "Well, I wouldn't say I *listened* so much as *observed*," she said, voice as dry as kindling. "Sally could talk the legs off a donkey, but yes, I knew it to be true in fact I recognised him from my newspaper clippings. I found him too smooth for my liking. Like jelly without a mould."

A nervous laugh fluttered from Sally, quickly stifled. Catherine inclined her head in agreement.

"I say it all started when Sally recognised Martin," Catherine said, "but Enid, the all-knowing, had already put the pieces together. She recognised him from the newspaper clippings she keeps at home."

"Old habits die hard," Enid murmured, patting Tulip absently. "I keep clippings about people who give me the wrong sort of tingle. It's a hobby."

David shot her a sideways look. "A disturbing one," he murmured under his breath. Catherine almost smiled.

"She tried to calm Sally down," Catherine went on, "telling her that they weren't in danger unless Martin realised, they were on to him."

Sally, her face flushed, spoke up suddenly. "I couldn't just *sit* there, Catherine. You must understand. I heard them, Simon, Martin, and Peter whispering near the conservatory that night. I didn't catch every word, but I was certain they were plotting something dreadful. I thought…" She swallowed, twisting her hands. "I thought they were planning to kill together. That Martin or Matthew, or whatever his name is. I thought if I acted quickly, I could stop it before anyone got hurt."

David's brow furrowed. "And so you decided to…?"

"I put mugwort in three of the wine glasses," Sally said, voice trembling. "The dried kind the sort you get from garden plants. I'd read that mugwort could cause sickness, confusion I didn't mean to kill anyone. Just to stop them, to make them ill enough that the plan would fall apart. No one noticed my slight of hand dropping the poison into their three glasses."

The fire hissed softly, like it disapproved.

"You didn't reckon on Enid," Catherine said gently.

Enid grinned, wiping her fingers on a paper napkin. "Well, if you *know* there's going to be a murder," she said, "you want to stop it, don't you?"

The sentence hung there, half-comic, half-horrifying.

"I turned the lights off," Enid continued. "Pulled the fuse out. Sorry, Peter, you were most annoyed, I remember."

Peter looked up sharply. "Annoyed? I nearly fell off the ladder fixing it!"

"Exactly," said Enid serenely. "That's why it worked. Everyone put their wine glasses down while you fussed about in the dark. Then, once the lights came back, no one could remember whose was whose. I'd bought myself time."

Catherine's tone softened. "You saved Peters, Martin and Simon's lives that night."

Enid shrugged. "I did what I could. It's not often one gets to stop a murder. I rather enjoyed it." She popped another pickled onion into her mouth, crunching contentedly.

Tulip gave a small yap, and Enid fed her another bit of sausage. The sound homely, absurd punctured the tension for a moment.

"In the confusion," Catherine went on, "as I said, people picked up the wrong glasses. But Enid, you knew which ones had the poison in, didn't you?"

"I did."

"And you didn't just save three lives that night," Catherine continued, turning toward her fully. "You saved *four*."

Enid leaned back, enjoying the attention. "Oh, at least four," she said. "Probably five, if we're counting properly."

Philip's eyebrows rose. "Good heavens, woman, who else did you rescue?"

Enid's eyes twinkled. "Well, patience, dear. I like to build to my punchlines."

Catherine allowed herself a faint smile. "She's right," she said. "Because it wasn't only Martin, Simon, and Peter. Enid saved *my* life that night, too."

A ripple of surprise moved through the group. David's hand tightened slightly on Catherine's arm protective, proud.

"Thank you," Catherine said softly. "Truly, Enid."

"Oh, don't mention it, love," Enid replied. "I just knocked the glass over. Everyone thought batty old woman can't watch where she is walking. But we know different don't we Tulip. Just to clarify Peter, Martin and Simon had poison in their glasses but put them down when the lights went off. When they came on again Catherine picked up one of the glasses, so did Clara and Aunt Frances."

Catherine glanced at David, who smiled faintly. "You see, she notices *everything*."

Enid gave a satisfied nod. "So yes, I saved *five* lives that night Martin, Simon, Peter, and you Catherine."

Catherine folded her arms. "That's four but you said *five*, Enid."

The room held its breath.

Enid's grin faded into something gentler, almost solemn. "I did tell you it's not all what it seemed," she said quietly. "I saved *Carla's* life that day, too."

Silence fell. Even the fire seemed to still. Outside, a gust of wind stirred the snow into a sighing whisper.

Catherine's expression softened. "Go on," she said, her voice almost tender now.

Enid reached into her cardigan pocket and drew out a small handkerchief printed with holly leaves. She dabbed her mouth delicately, as though preparing to tell a Christmas story rather than the final piece of a tragedy.

"Well," she began, "When the lights came back on and everyone was flustered, Carla reached for the nearest glass one of *those* three. I was quicker than she was."

"You switched them," Catherine said quietly.

"I did," Enid said. "Slid hers away and handed her mine instead. She barely noticed. Too busy laughing at Peter's ridiculous Christmas jumper."

Peter blinked. "It was festive!"

"It was offensive to snowmen," Enid countered. "Anyway, that's how I saved her."

The words hung heavy in the air, shimmering like frost.

Holly finally broke the silence. "So, you saved *everyone*, Enid. Except Aunt Frances"

"...I lost sight of who took the third glass" Enid finished softly. "Yes, love. Some things you can't prevent, no matter how many fuses you pull."

Catherine looked around at them all these broken, frightened, eccentric people and felt a weight lift, even if only slightly. The truth had been tangled, but it was truth, nonetheless.

She turned to David. "You see," she said quietly, "I told you it was Enid who held the key."

Chapter 35: You Only Die Once

Catherine stood in the centre of the room, her shoulders straight, her chin lifted. A touch of tension showed in the way she held one arm across her waist, but her voice was calm and unwavering. David stood at her side. Tulip, ever faithful, sat at their feet, her white coat blending with the cream rug, ears flicking at every raised voice.

"Yes," Catherine said slowly, "it was my poor Aunt Frances that died. She had a heart condition, and this pushed her over."

Her voice caught for a fraction of a second, but she pressed on. The others shifted uncomfortably. Somewhere, in another room, a carol played faintly on an old cassette deck "O Come All Ye Faithful" its cheerful strains sounding oddly brittle against the tension.

Sally's hands trembled as she smoothed the front of her skirt. She had always been the kind of woman who looked neat even in chaos, but now her face was pale, the freckles standing out starkly on her skin. "I'm... I'm sorry for all this," she said. "I only tried to kill Martin, Simon, and Peter because I thought they were going to kill us all off." Her voice cracked on the last word. "Sorry, Catherine. You say I didn't kill Carla. So, if I didn't kill Carla, who did?"

"Enid told Carla what had happened. Then Carla thought it would be better if she remained dead. She could investigate without being worried that someone was after her." said Catherine.

The fire popped, sending up a little spray of sparks. David shifted his weight, but his hand stayed on Catherine's back, a silent reassurance. Catherine felt the warmth of his fingers even through the wool of her dress and took another slow breath.

"Enid always knew what was going on," Catherine went on, more softly now. "She always did."

"I tried to help," Enid said from her chair near the tree. Her voice, usually so sharp with wit and riddles, was low, the edge dulled. She wore a jumper with a cross-stitched nativity scene on it. "We thought it best if she remained dead. She was very good at putting on the death face and if you noticed I kept you away from 'the body'. She stayed in her room, changed lipstick but not the room. But somebody killed her. Somebody came in the room and finished her off. That was why I was so surprised when she was dead."

She shook her head, staring at the pine needles that had scattered on the carpet. "When we went into that room," she said, looking up now."I noticed your face and because of that and because of the fact that someone had been using her room that made me realise what was going on." Catherine replied.

Enid rubbed at her knuckles, the gesture strangely vulnerable. "And the different wine glasses," she murmured. "The wine glasses with the mugwort you put them in a cupboard, didn't you, Enid, so that no one drank them."

"I did," Enid said. Her voice was steadier now, but there was a faint tremor in her hands. "But that meant that I had to give Carla a different glass when she looked like she was dead. And then there was the third glass."

She gave the tiniest shake of her head. Not yet.

"I've also been looking into the finances," Catherine said. Her voice cut across the murmurs like a bell toll. "Philip, what have you been doing?"

All eyes swung to Philip. He stood near the window, the snow behind him making him look even paler. He tugged at his cufflinks, then at his tie, as though the air had grown too tight to breathe.

"Well," Philip said at last, "I noticed also that Carla's room had been used. And I saw Carla. I thought…" He hesitated, the pause stretching. "I thought if she was going to get me done for fraud. You can't kill someone who's already been killed."

A faint murmur ran around the room. David's jaw tightened. Catherine didn't move.

"You would have got away with it too," she said, her voice still level, "if you hadn't used a different poison."

Philip gave a short, almost amused huff. "Ah. The details."

"The details," Catherine echoed. "Sally had used a garden-based mugwort poison. You used a synthetic cyanide, which you tried to hide in the piano hence the third glass."

The mention of the piano made Sally glance toward it; the Christmas sheet music was still open there, "Silent Night" on one page, "In the Bleak Midwinter" on the other. A spray of holly berries in a silver vase gleamed dully beside it. For a moment, the whole scene looked almost peaceful if one could forget the accusations circling in the air.

"At first," Catherine continued, "the poison was found, oh yes. Seeing all these glasses especially the one in Carla's hand made me realise that she was still alive."

Philip's eyes narrowed. "If she was dead already," he said, "how did I kill her?"

The room held its breath. Outside, the snow fell heavier, muffling the world. A branch tapped against the window like an impatient finger.

Philip tried to shift his weight as though to step away, but Catherine's voice stopped him cold. "You tried to get away with it in the first instance," she said. "But I found the part of the notebook you ripped out of Carla's notebook in your bedroom. It proves that you did it."

Philip's mouth opened, but no sound came out.

For a moment, no one spoke. The only sounds were the crackle of the fire and the slow, steady tick of the clock. Tulip gave a low, soft whine and laid her chin on her paws.

Then David spoke, his voice quiet but firm. "You knew," he said to Philip. "You knew exactly what you were doing."

Philip didn't look at him. "I... I thought she would ruin everything. It was all invested I never saw the money myself" Everything Reginald built. Everything I..." He broke off.

"You ruined it yourself, taking the eight million." Catherine said. Her tone wasn't harsh now, but cold and precise, like frost forming on a windowpane. "You ruined it the moment you decided to silence her instead of facing what you'd done."

David let out a shaky breath. "All this over money," he whispered. "All this at Christmas."

Catherine turned to her. "No," she said quietly. "Not all this at Christmas. All this because people chose lies over truth. Christmas only shows the cracks more clearly."

Enid spoke again, her voice steadier now. "I always said," she murmured, "that what's done in the dark will come to light." She looked at the tree, at the tiny wooden angels swinging gently. "Even here."

The fire hissed softly, the scent of pine and wax mingling with the faint tang of cold air leaking through the window frames. Someone shifted; the bells on a garland of silver stars jingled faintly.

Chapter 36: Get Rid of Her

Catherine stood at the centre of the room, her hands clasped in front of her, her expression calm but resolute. David was beside her. Around them, the others sat scattered on armchairs and sofas, the remnants of a once-cheerful gathering now replaced by a courtroom-like stillness. The scent of pine needles and burnt candle wax lingered in the air.

Peter broke the silence first. His voice was quiet, unsure. "Catherine," he said, "well, how does Simon fit into all of this? You've spoken about Martin, Philip, and Sally... but Simon?"

He leaned forward, elbows on his knees, his eyes searching hers. There was something boyish in his confusion, something that made Catherine soften for a moment.

She nodded slowly. "Then we get on to Simon," she said. Her voice carried across the room low, deliberate, every word measured. "Poor Simon. All he said was that he 'wanted to get rid of her.'" She turned her gaze toward Sally, who sat pale and trembling by the window. "And in saying that," Catherine continued, "he sealed his death. Didn't he, Sally?"

Sally's lips parted, but no words came out. Her hands were clasped tightly around a crumpled handkerchief, and her chest rose and fell in shallow breaths. "I saved you all," she muttered, barely audible. "I saved you all. They were coming for us. Peter, Martin, Simon they were all coming for us."

"No," Catherine said, her tone firm but not cruel. "They weren't."

The words hung in the air, final and heavy. Even the fire seemed to pause its crackle.

David moved slightly closer to Catherine, he knew that after all this, when the house was quiet again, she'd let it break through the weariness, the sadness of it all. But for now, she stood unshakable.

"Simon saw you," Catherine went on, her voice softening. "He saw you that morning, out in the garden, building the snowman. He thought nothing of it thought you were simply enjoying the morning frost, the way people do at Christmas. In his delight, he didn't see the dagger in your hand."

Sally let out a short, broken sound half sob, half gasp. "It wasn't meant to be like that," she whispered. "I thought I thought he was going to…"

Catherine took a step forward. "You stabbed him in the stomach, Sally," she said, her voice trembling slightly now. "You killed a young man because you perceived danger. You were wrong."

Sally's head dropped. "I was trying to protect us, I needed to protect me, I needed the Kitchen knife for protection." she murmured. "I heard them talking. I heard Martin and Simon, I heard them planning something in the study. I thought it was about me. About all of us."

David spoke then, gently but firmly. "Fear can twist things, Sally. It can make us see shadows where there are none."

The clock ticked again, louder this time, marking the silence that followed. Somewhere, a log cracked in the fire, sending a faint spray of sparks up the chimney.

"I've called the police," Catherine said finally. "When the snow has melted enough for the roads to clear, they'll be here." She paused, her eyes sweeping the room Peter, Martin, Enid, Holly, Philip. "So that concludes it. There were two killers at work here. Both didn't want to start it, but they definitely finished it. Sally, out of fear. Philip, out of opportunity."

Philip shifted in his seat, his jaw tightening, but said nothing. Catherine turned her gaze to him.
"You saw someone who was already dead and thought, 'Well, if I kill her, it'll mean everything will be plain sailing in the future.' You couldn't resist, could you? One small act to tidy the mess only it wasn't small at all. It was murder."

Her words cut through the air like the edge of ice.

"It's just sad," she went on, her voice quiet now, "that it had to happen in my house. And at Christmas."

A deep silence followed. Even Tulip, lying by the hearth, lifted her head briefly before settling again, as though sensing the solemnity of the moment.

Outside, a church bell tolled the hour slow and mournful, echoing through the cold night. The sound made Peter look toward the window, where frost traced delicate patterns across the glass. The snow beyond glowed faintly under the lamplight, untouched and cruelly peaceful.

Peter sighed. "Simon was always the cheerful one," he said softly. "Always laughing at something, always with that ridiculous scarf of his." He gave a weak smile at the memory. "He didn't deserve that."

"No one did," said Catherine. Her eyes softened again, and she sat down beside David on the sofa. "That's what makes this worse. Every one of you has been driven by fear, greed, or guilt. And for what? Money? Safety? Pride? None of it will bring back the people we've lost."

Holly, who had been silent until now, wiped her eyes with the back of her sleeve. "I was only supposed to be writing a story," she said in a trembling voice. "I thought this would be the perfect Christmas feature the mansion, the snow, the family reunion." She gave a shaky laugh. "Now I look at it and think only that I will miss Simon greatly."

"You've done what you came to do," David said said quietly. "It's over now."

Catherine nodded slowly but didn't speak. She was staring into the fire, watching the embers shift and fall. "Is it ever really over?" she murmured. "The people who die don't leave us, not truly. They linger in rooms, in memories, in regrets. Especially when Christmas lights are burning and everyone pretends to be happy."

Catherine takes a present out of her pocket from Enid. She opens it, it is a letter. "Philip killed Carla, Sally killed Aunt Frances. Simon??? Yours Enid. "Thank you, Enid, and in ten words" she said raising the letter in Enid's direction.

Peter rose from his seat and walked toward the window. "The snow's clearing," he said. "By morning, the police will be able to make it through."

"Good," said Catherine. She stood and straightened her jacket. "The sooner this is over, the better."

Sally was still staring at her lap, her handkerchief clutched so tightly that her knuckles were white. "Do you think," she whispered, "that they'll understand? The police, I mean. That I didn't mean to... that it was fear?"

Catherine hesitated. "They'll listen," she said at last. "And I'll tell them what I've seen. But the truth is the truth, Sally. It doesn't vanish just because we're sorry for it."

Sally nodded, a tear slipping down her cheek. "He looked so surprised," she said quietly. "When I when it happened. He just looked at me, like he couldn't believe it. I'll never forget that face."

David stood up and crossed to the window, resting his hand on the frame beside Peter's. "The snow's beautiful tonight," he said softly. "It hides everything the tracks, the blood, the mistakes. Tomorrow, when it melts, the truth will be visible again."

Catherine joined him "That's how it always is," she said. "The snow covers what we don't want to see, but it never lasts."

The fire gave one last crack before sinking into a quiet, steady glow. Enid stirred, her voice surprisingly clear. "You've done well, Catherine," she said. "Better than most of the inspectors I've known. You've got a sharp mind and a good heart."

Catherine gave her a faint smile. "Thank you, Enid. Though I'd trade both for a peaceful Christmas."

"Peaceful Christmases are overrated," Enid said, a touch of her usual humour slipping back in. "It's the messy ones that stay in the memory."

Peter turned and looked at Catherine. "You think they'll all make it through this?" he asked. "After everything?"

Catherine took a deep breath. "Some will. Some won't. But Christmas is about forgiveness, even when it's hardest. That's the part everyone forgets."

David slipped his arm around her waist and gave her a gentle squeeze. "You need rest, love," he murmured. "You've been holding this whole house together for days."

"I will," she said, leaning briefly against him. "Just not yet."

Outside, the moonlight glimmered on the frosted lawns, and the snowman still stood in the garden silent, watchful, its shadow stretching long and thin across the ground. The dagger was gone now, but its absence seemed to speak louder than its presence ever had.

Sally looked up suddenly. "I keep thinking of the carols," she said, almost to herself. "The ones we used to sing as children. *'Peace on Earth, goodwill to all men.'* It feels so far from that now."

Catherine walked back toward her and knelt down, her voice quiet but steady. "That's why we sing them," she said. "Not because the world is peaceful, but because we hope it could be."

Sally nodded, fresh tears falling. "You really called the police?"

"Yes," Catherine said. "It's the only way this can end properly."

David put another log on the fire, the flames leaping back to life. The warmth spread slowly through the room again, chasing away some of the chill that had crept in through the windowpanes.

"Do you remember," Peter said suddenly, "that Christmas when Simon fell into the pond? He insisted it was frozen solid, said he could skate across it in his boots."

Catherine smiled faintly. "He came back dripping wet, furious that no one had warned him."

"He was always like that," Peter said. "Wouldn't listen until he'd learned the hard way."

Silence fell again, but it was softer this time not empty, just reflective. The firelight flickered over their faces, casting long shadows across the walls. In the corner, the tree lights blinked gently, their rhythm slow and tired.

After a while, Catherine rose. "We should all try to sleep," she said. "It'll be morning soon enough."

Peter nodded, glancing once more at the window. "You think they'll take her and Philip tonight?" he asked quietly.

Catherine shook her head. "No. The roads are still too dangerous. She'll stay here until morning. I've told them that."

David looked strongly at Philip "We don't want you leaving so I am afraid we are going to have to lock you in your rooms until morning."

"I was so close to pulling it off" said Philip as he walked in the direction of his room.

Sally looked up at her with gratitude and fear mixed in her eyes. "Thank you," she whispered.

"Don't thank me yet," Catherine said softly. "Just rest."

David and Peter escorted them to their rooms and locked the doors.

David dimmed the lamps, leaving only the glow from the hearth. The room seemed to exhale the tension easing, though not gone entirely. Tulip gave a small sigh in her sleep.

Catherine lingered a moment longer, looking around the room at the people, the decorations, the faded holly garland drooping over the mantel. The house had seen so many Christmases, so many memories. It would see more, though this one would never be forgotten.

As she and David stepped into the hallway. "You did what you had to," he said.

"I know," she replied. "But that doesn't make it easier."

They walked slowly toward the staircase, their footsteps echoing softly on the polished wood. The hallway smelled faintly of cinnamon. At the landing, Catherine paused and looked back down at the hall below the flicker of the fire still visible through the drawing-room door, the faint hum of wind against the windows.

"Tomorrow," she said quietly, "the police will come and we'll tell them everything. Then maybe we can have some peace."

David smiled faintly. "We will. And maybe we'll even get a proper festive dinner if the cook hasn't fled by then."

Catherine laughed softly, the sound weary but real. "We'll see."

Chapter 37: The Visitor

There was a sudden knock, firm, deliberate, echoing through the long hallway of Price Mansion. The sound carried through the drawing room, where the fire crackled low and the scent of pine and beeswax hung in the air. Outside, the snow was still falling, soft flakes tapping gently against the windows, dulling the winter light.

Catherine lifted her head. "There's somebody at the door" she said, her tone calm but edged with curiosity. Tulip gave a single bark from her place by the hearth, then settled again with her nose tucked under her paws.

Henshaw, the butler, appeared a few moments later, brushing a trace of snow from his shoulders. His manner was as precise as ever, though his cheeks were flushed from the cold.

"I must announce," he said, bowing slightly, "that we have a Mr Keane who has just arrived."

Catherine frowned, exchanging a quick glance with David, who was sitting beside her on the old Chesterfield sofa. The holly garlands above the mantel trembled slightly in the draught as the front door closed in the distance.

"Oh," Catherine murmured, her eyes narrowing. "That must be the police. They've come a day early."

She squeezed his fingers, and the warmth of his touch steadied her. The firelight caught the gold in her hair as she stood. "Very well," she said to Henshaw, straightening her jacket. "Let them in."

Moments later, the door opened again. A gust of cold air entered with the visitor, carrying with it the sharp smell of wet wool and the faint metallic tang of frost.

The man who stepped into the room was tall, broad-shouldered, and travel worn. His dark coat was dusted white at the shoulders, and in his gloved hand he held a leather briefcase and one of Reginald Price's old brown folders. His eyes were a clear, steel-grey, and though his smile was polite, it did not reach them.

"I'm sorry to disturb you," he said, his voice clipped but not unkind. "It's taken a little while for me to get here. I tried to make it for Christmas Eve, but the snow…" He gave a small, weary shrug. "Too much snow."

He glanced around the room, taking in the Christmas tree that stood proudly in the corner tall and fragrant, its branches heavy with glass baubles and small, flickering candles. The light caught on the brass ornaments and the ribboned pinecones, casting reflections across the dark wood panelling.

"I take it," he went on, "that you're all friends and relatives of Reginald Price."

There was a pause, the air shifting uneasily. Catherine stepped forward first, her chin lifted. "I am Catherine Forrester, Reginald's daughter. And this is my husband, David. You have me at a disadvantage, Mr Keane."

The man inclined his head slightly, his gaze steady. "My name is James Keane," he said, setting the folder on the table between them. "I was… acquainted with your father, though not in the usual sense."

Peter, who had been leaning against the window frame, arms folded, straightened up. "Acquainted?" he repeated, his voice sceptical. "That's a curious word to use."

Keane smiled faintly. "Perhaps not curious at all, once you've heard me out."

He laid a gloved hand on the folder and drew in a breath. "You see, there is this new thing a development they've been talking about in scientific circles. DNA testing, they call it. A way of finding out who your parents are, through blood samples and genetic markers."

David frowned slightly, exchanging a glance with Catherine. "I've heard of it," he said. "Mostly in medical research not something you'd expect to hear about in a country house at Christmas."

Keane's eyes didn't waver. "Quite so. But it has its uses outside laboratories too. And in this case," he tapped the folder lightly, "it has revealed something rather remarkable."

He paused deliberately, letting the weight of silence fill the room. The only sound was the faint ticking of the clock on the mantel and the soft crackle of the logs.

"It turns out," Keane said at last, "that I am a half-brother to Reginald Price's children. To you, Catherine, and to Peter. It would seem that your father had another family once. Or at least, another… arrangement."

The words hung there like frost in the air. Catherine did not move. She simply looked at him, eyes unflinching, searching his face for some trace of mockery or deceit.

Peter let out a low whistle and turned towards the fire. "Well, Merry Christmas," he muttered. "That's quite the gift to unwrap."

Keane gave a short, humourless laugh. "Indeed. I wish it had come under better circumstances. But my mother kept certain letters, and now with this new testing, the truth is… undeniable."

He looked directly at Catherine again. "I presume you are Catherine Price, Forrester now, of course?"

"I am," she said quietly. "And you claim to be my father's son."

"I don't claim," he replied smoothly. "The evidence does."

He reached into the folder and produced a sheaf of typed papers, each stamped and dated, along with a few photographs, one of Reginald as a younger man, smiling beside a dark-haired woman Catherine did not recognise.

The firelight flickered across the photographs, catching the edge of the glossy paper. Catherine felt a coldness settle in her chest. She had spent years believing she knew her father, his flaws, his pride, his temper but this stranger's arrival seemed to rewrite the past in one cruel stroke.

David rose quietly and joined her side, his hand brushing hers in a silent gesture of reassurance. She felt his strength in that simple touch and found her own voice again.

"And what exactly do you want, Mr Keane?" she asked, the steel back in her tone.

Keane straightened. "I think it's only fair to say it plainly. I will be expecting a third of the estate, a third of this place and its holdings. My solicitor will be in touch to arrange matters formally after Christmas."

Peter gave a sharp laugh. "You'll be lucky," he said. "You turn up uninvited, announce yourself as family, and think we'll just hand over a third of everything?"

Keane looked at him with a calm, level expression. "You don't need to hand anything over yourselves. The courts will see to it. I've already filed my claim."

There was a beat of silence. The Christmas tree lights seemed to flicker lower, as though the room itself had absorbed the tension. Even the scent of mulled wine on the sideboard had turned faintly sour.

Catherine drew in a slow breath. "This is not the time, nor the place, for arguments," she said. "It's Boxing Day, and we've had more than our share of tragedy this week. You may leave your paperwork with me, Mr Keane. We will, of course, have our lawyer look at it."

Keane inclined his head. "Very good. I can see you've inherited your father's manner."

David's eyes hardened. "You've said what you came to say. I think that's quite enough for one visit."

Keane nodded once more, collecting his gloves and adjusting his scarf. "It was lovely to meet you all," he said, his voice polite again, almost rehearsed. "I will see you in court."

And with that, he turned and strode out of the room, the door closing softly behind him. Henshaw followed to see him out, and the sound of footsteps echoed away into the hall until there was only silence again.

For a long moment, no one spoke. Catherine stood staring at the folder on the table, its brown edges catching the firelight. Outside, the snow thickened, the world beyond the windows fading into white.

At last, Catherine turned to David. "We can't afford to keep this place if we have to pay him out," she said quietly.

David ran a hand through his hair, sighing. "I think today is hard enough as it is," he said. "Let's not think about money now. We'll talk to the lawyer in the new year see what can be done. There might be loopholes, or… settlements."

She looked at him then, her eyes weary but soft. "It's strange," she murmured, "how quickly peace turns to chaos. We had barely started to breathe again."

He smiled faintly. "That's life with the Prices, isn't it? Or the Forresters, depending which side of the mantel you're on."

She gave a short, rueful laugh and sat down beside him once more. "I used to think this house would bring comfort," she said. "That it would feel like a home again. But sometimes it feels more like a mausoleum, full of ghosts, old arguments, unfinished stories."

David reached out, taking her hand in both of his. "Then perhaps it's time to stop letting them rule us," he said softly. "We can sell, move somewhere smaller. Start fresh. You've got enough spirit for that, Catherine, more than anyone I know."

She looked at him, her lips curving into the smallest smile. "You always know how to say the right thing."

"I try," he said, brushing a strand of hair from her cheek. "Even if I rarely get it right the first time."

Tulip stirred then, stretching and yawning, before hopping up onto Catherine's lap as if sensing the tension needed softening. Catherine stroked the dog's fur absently, her thoughts drifting between past and future.

Peter poured himself a drink from the decanter on the sideboard, the amber liquid catching the light. "If he thinks he's getting a third of this place," he muttered, "he's mad. Let him have a slice of the leaky roof if he's that determined."

Catherine smiled faintly. "You always did have a gift for perspective, Peter."

He turned towards her, glass in hand. "You're not really thinking of fighting him in court, are you?"

"I'll do what's necessary," she replied. "But not tonight."

Peter nodded, glancing towards the window. "Hard to believe it's still Boxing Day. Feels like the world's moved on without us."

David rose, walking to the mantel. He adjusted one of the candles that had burned low, relighting it with a match. "We've had enough darkness," he said. "Let's have some light, even if it's only for a while."

The flame flickered back to life, reflecting off the tinsel and glass baubles. The soft glow spread across the room, catching on Catherine's features and softening them.

"Do you remember last Christmas?" she asked quietly. "We were in London, freezing in that tiny flat, and you insisted on cooking the turkey yourself."

He chuckled. "And burned it, if memory serves."

"Completely," she said, laughing gently. "We had sandwiches instead."

"And it was still the best day of the year," he said. "Because we were together."

Her eyes warmed, and for a moment the strain of the day melted away. She leaned against him, resting her head on his shoulder. "Perhaps that's all that matters," she whispered. "Not the house, not the name, not the money. Just this."

In her head she knew she had would do anything to keep her lifestyle her way of life with David.

The fire popped softly, a log collapsing into embers. Outside, the church bells in the village began to ring faintly through the snow, slow, measured tones marking the end of Boxing Day. Catherine listened; her fingers intertwined with David's.

Peter sighed and set down his glass. "Well, I suppose we'll have to face it sooner or later," he said. "But I'll take later, if no one objects."

"No objections," David said lightly. "Not from me."

"Nor me," Catherine added. "Tonight, we keep Christmas, what little remains of it."

They sat together in the warmth of the fire, the tree lights twinkling softly, the snow beyond the windows still falling in slow, deliberate sheets. The house creaked now and then, settling under the weight of the storm. Somewhere upstairs, the old grandfather clock chimed nine.

For a time, there was peace the kind that came not from absence of trouble, but from quiet defiance of it. Catherine rested her head against David's arm, eyes half-closed, her thoughts turning not to courts or estates but to the simpler hopes of the season: peace, truth, and endurance.

And though the future loomed uncertain, for that brief moment, the Price Mansion was still, a flicker of calm in a world of snow. But the snow was melting.

Chapter 38: The Million Pound Chat

The study smelled of fir, an old house's particular cologne of dust, leather and the faint sweetness of brandy. A wreath of holly and ivy, studded with red berries, was looped over the heavy oak mantel; a small carved nativity sat in the centre, its figures lit by a single, guttering candle.

Peter stood by the tall window, his breath fogging the pane as he looked out at the frozen formal gardens. The study's lamplight picked out the white of his hair and the pale tiredness about his eyes. He had the look of a man who had been awake too many nights in succession, counting sums in his head and refusing to let the numbers settle. A neat leather wallet lay open on the desk; a bundle of notes, rolled and secured with a cheap band peeked from it like some sordid confession.

David sat in the armchair by the hearth, one booted foot on the fender, his hands wrapped around a mug of something warm. He was still in his coat; one could tell he'd come in from the cold only minutes before, the collar damp. He watched Peter with a mixture of patience and steel, a man used to calming storms rather than stirring them.

"We have that two million," Peter said at last, as if the money were something solid, placed on the rug between them. The words landed in the room and seemed to vibrate against the woodwork. "We took it from Reginald. The ledger, you know, the extra accounts, we kept that portion. It was a foolish, stupid thing, but it's there. We could use that to pay off Keane. It'll scarcely cover him, but it's near enough."

David let the warmth of his mug seep into his palms and didn't answer immediately. He watched the candlelight on the nativity, on the tiny faces of Mary and the child, and something like the old church bells chimed distantly, perhaps from St. Michael's, perhaps imagined by the house itself. Christmas had a way of making right and wrong feel larger, the moral lines sharper, or else more blurred, depending on the light you were in.

"We can't use that," David said finally. His voice was low, practical as a ledger entry. "If Catherine finds out, it will put us both in prison. She'll tell the police. You know what she's like. She won't stand for it. We can only spend a little at a time, carefully. It's annoying. If we could buy Mr. Keane out straight away, we could close this chapter. But that would mean telling Catherine the whole truth. And if the police find out…"

"You always say that" Peter cut in; guilt and a sort of stubbornness mixed in his tone. "I'm sorry, David. I don't own this place any longer, but I still have the cash from the sale. I could pay Keane outright. Yes, it'd be a big hit, but I could live with that. You, though… you'd have to lose the house. You'd lose everything."

Peter shifted under the lamplight and for a moment looked older than his years. "Then what do you expect of me?" he asked. "To let you be crushed? To stand and watch you lose everything we grew up with? I can't do that. Not when I have it when I have something to give."

David stared at him. The fire cracked, a gust of heat lifting the thin smoke; the nativity's candle flared then steadied. "It's not simply about what you can buy, Peter. It's about how you bought it, and what it would mean to keep it. Putting the money into circulation, however carefully, is one thing; Getting out in one go, quite another. And telling Catherine telling her that we took it would be to force her into a choice she should never have to make. She hates lies the way some people hate liars. You know that."

Peter's mouth thinned. "She's always right, isn't she? Always righteous. That's what frightens me most. Not the law, Catherine. She would judge us more harshly than any magistrate."

"That could be my marriage over." David countered. His voice wasn't angry; it was weary. "She'll see the theft for what it was. She'll want it returned. She'll want us to make it right. She's Catherine she cannot bear the thought of injustice left unamended. You know that. That's who she is."

Outside, the church bells struck the hour, a clear, resonant peal that rose up through the snow. They were the kind of bells that seemed to peel away small sins and soft regrets; for a moment, the house felt like a chapel, the conversation a confession.

Peter looked down at his hands, and they were small and pale in the lamplight. "We didn't think," he said simply. "I thought of the banks and the ledgers and the way Reginald had kept everything under seals. I thought foolishly it was only right for us to take a cut. He'd been squeezing us for years. I convinced myself of that." He gave a brittle, embarrassed laugh. "And then it became easier not to look back."

David watched him like a surgeon watching a wound. "We both did it Peter, I felt the same." he said. "But theft is not the same as murder. It's not... we don't need to hide in perpetuity for it. There are ways to make restitution without losing everything. We just can't pay out the money in one go and draw attention to us."

Peter's voice fell to a whisper. "If only Catherine would not see. We can't face her accusing us. I can't bear her disappointment. You always had that the look of someone who forgives where others condemn."

At that, David's expression softened, the lines about his mouth changing as if a warm hand had smoothed them. He set the cup on the side table and rose, crossing the thick rug in two long strides. He came to stand behind Peter and, without preamble, laid his hand on his shoulder. It was a small gesture, almost casual, but there was an intimacy in it that belied its simplicity. Peter blinked like a man awakened.

"We will find a way," David said. "We'll talk to the solicitor discreetly. We'll map out options. We'll make sure Keane can't hurt us. We might have to sell the house. If the worst comes, if we are forced into a corner, we will face it together. Not with quick fixes and secret payments, but with our eyes open."

Peter took a breath that looked like the beginning of an apology and the end of a long-held fear. "You say together," he murmured. "That's what I want. That's why I came to you."

In the doorway, a soft shuffle; the study's door opened and Catherine stepped in. She had been in the library arranging a small pile of Christmas cards, straightening a miniature evergreen on the table. She wore a dress of deep green that went well with the darkness of her hair; a sprig of holly was pinned at her throat. She moved with her usual assuredness, the kind of woman who took up a room by simply entering it. For a breath, the sight of her at the threshold seemed to steady both men.

"Peter, David," she said, voice bright enough to be a chime yet carrying that familiar sheriff's edge beneath. "I hope I haven't intruded."

Peter's face went flush. He turned and forced a smile that didn't reach his eyes. "No, no. We were just… talking."

Catherine closed the door behind her, dusting imaginary snow from her skirt. She crossed to the mantel and touched the nativity, straightening one of the tiny shepherds. The movement was small, domestic, and it revealed nothing. "It's almost time for the choir," she said, glancing at the clock. "They'll be here for Ten. I had to tell the vicar he could use the drawing-room for the carol practice. I insisted on the old hymns this year. 'Hark! The Herald Angels Sing' I can't abide anything too modern."

David gave a short laugh. "You have a fondness for the old ways."

"I have a fondness for good music," she corrected, turning to him. Her eyes softened when they met his. "And for good company." She came to stand beside him, and he reached automatically for her hand, threading his fingers through hers with a familiarity that spoke of years and small, steady affection. She leaned in, pressing her shoulder into his, the single, unostentatious gesture of two people who had weathered storms together.

The contact seemed to anchor the room. Catherine's expression sharpened, and she looked at Peter. "You look pale," she said not unkindly, but with the bluntness of someone who would not let things hide. "Have you been ill?"

Peter swallowed. "No, just… this weather. I went for a walk to get the air; I can tell you the air is bitter cold"

"Let's go and sit with the others in the drawing room." Commanded Catherine.

As they crossed the threshold, the house seemed to breathe with them, the fire's glow retreating into the room. The nativity looked on from the mantel, small figures carved in wood, humble and unadorned. Outside, the snow muffled the world into a soft hush, and for one small breath of time a household in winter, three people bound by history and by love, the moral calculus of two million pounds could wait until morning.

Chapter 39: The Police

Catherine woke early on the morning of the 27th of December. A weak light seeped through the curtains, and for the first time in days she heard the steady drip of thawing snow from the gutters. The world outside looked washed and tired, like a party guest who had stayed too long. The snowman in the front garden, once proud and round, had lost his shape entirely his coal eyes sliding, his carrot nose half buried in the softening drift.

She pulled the curtains back and stood for a moment, arms folded, looking out. The lawns were patched green again, the gravel path dark and wet. A robin hopped along the low wall, its red breast bright against the dull morning. Somewhere in the distance, the church bell tolled eight times.

David stirred behind her, his voice thick with sleep. "Well," he murmured, rubbing his eyes, "another Christmas over. Just like that."

Catherine smiled faintly. "Yes. And a memorable one, for better or worse."

He sat up, leaning against the headboard, his hair ruffled. "It's been another good one," he said, and there was genuine warmth in it. "In its own peculiar way. Though I wouldn't say no to a quiet New Year. Just the two of us. No murders, no guests, no detectives. What do you think?"

Catherine turned back to him, the morning light catching her dark hair. "I think," she said softly, "that sounds perfect." She leaned over and kissed him lightly, her hand resting on his shoulder for a moment longer than necessary the kind of touch that spoke of years of shared storms and steady comfort.

They dressed in companionable silence, David humming "In the Bleak Midwinter" under his breath while Catherine gathered her papers from the dressing table and tucked them neatly into a folder. Downstairs, the house was waking slowly, the faint clang of breakfast dishes, the creak of old pipes, the smell of frying sausages and toast drifting from the kitchen.

When they entered the dining room, the Christmas decorations still hung but had lost their sparkle. The garland over the mantel had begun to shed needles, the candles were half burnt, and the last of the mince pies sat on a plate by the sideboard. A cold draught whispered through the half-open window, carrying the scent of wet pine and smoke.

Catherine paused, looking around. "It always feels like this after Christmas," she said. "As if the house itself has sighed and decided to rest."

David poured coffee from the pot on the table. "And so, it should. It's earned it."

But as they sat, Catherine's sharp eyes noticed two empty places. Peter's chair, pushed neatly under the table, and the absence of Martin's coffee cup. She frowned slightly. "Where are Peter and Martin?"

Henshaw, coming in with the toast rack, shook his head. "I haven't seen them since last night, ma'am. I believe Mr. Peter's car left the drive sometime after midnight. I heard the engine."

Catherine nodded slowly. "I thought as much. When I looked out of the window earlier, I saw the car was gone." She exchanged a look with David, not of alarm, exactly, but of weary understanding. "They probably left in the night. Perhaps they wanted to avoid the police visit today."

David raised an eyebrow but said nothing. The two of them knew that silence could hold more truth than argument.

At the table sat Enid, wrapped in a wool shawl the colour of holly leaves, her eyes bright and cheerful despite the hour. Beside her was Holly, pen already in hand, scribbling in her notebook as if inspiration had struck over breakfast. Tulip lay by the fire, tail thumping occasionally against the rug.

Sally and Philip, of course, were absent, locked in their rooms by Catherine's order and given trays for breakfast. There was no need for public confrontations this morning.

"Good morning, my dears!" Enid declared, cutting into her sausage with surprising energy. "I must say, I've enjoyed myself immensely. Far more excitement than my usual Christmas in that poky little cottage. I'm not looking forward to going back, truth be told. My little old life will seem frightfully dull after this."

Catherine smiled at her, pouring milk into her coffee. "You'll manage, Enid. You always do."

"Oh, I'll manage," Enid said, sighing. "But it will be strange not waking up in a house full of people, even if half of them turned out to be murderers." She chuckled softly to herself.

Before Catherine could reply, a sudden movement by the doorway caught everyone's attention. A black-and-white cat strolled confidently into the dining hall, tail held high like a banner of victory. Its fur glistened, sleek from the warmth of the kitchen, and its green eyes gleamed with mischief.

Enid gasped, setting down her fork. "Oh, Mr Whittaker!" she cried, half rising from her chair. "Where have you been, you naughty thing?"

Tulip gave a startled bark and bounded forward, tail wagging furiously. The cat arched its back but stood its ground, staring the dog down with regal disdain.

David laughed. "Well, that's a face-off for the ages."

Enid bent to scoop up the cat, who tolerated the embrace with an indignant meow. "He's a good size, isn't he? Have you been catching mice, my boy? I expect he's been enjoying himself in the pantry."

She broke off a bit of sausage and offered it. Mr Whittaker accepted it delicately, then licked his paws with royal approval. Tulip whined, ears drooping, until Catherine relented and cut a small piece of sausage for her as well.

"Fair's fair," Catherine said, smiling as she handed it down. "We can't have jealousy before nine o'clock."

Enid chuckled, stroking the cat's head. "You know, he reminds me of my old headmaster's cat. Used to sit on his desk during assemblies. Terrified the children into good behaviour."

Holly laughed. "Maybe that's what schools need now, more cats, fewer rules."

David glanced at Catherine with a grin. "I can just see you, darling, running an investigation with a cat perched on your shoulder."

Catherine smirked. "Better company than some of the constables I've known."

The room warmed with the sound of gentle laughter, the sort that comes when tension finally begins to thaw. Outside, the sun rose weakly over the thinning snow, throwing pale gold across the windowpanes.

Holly looked up from her notebook, her eyes bright with excitement. "I've been speaking to my publisher," she announced. "They're keen on my book idea, all this, the murders, the mystery, the snow, the family drama. They think it could sell."

Enid clapped her hands. "Oh, wonderful! And will I be in it?"

"Of course," Holly said with a smile. "You'll be everyone's favourite character, the wise old observer with the sharp tongue."

Enid giggled. "Good heavens, I'd better start practising my modesty."

Catherine leaned back slightly, sipping her coffee. "Just make sure you change the names, Holly. We don't need libel suits as a Christmas encore."

"I'll disguise everyone," Holly promised, twirling her pen. "Though I might make you taller, Catherine. More dramatic."

David chuckled. "Good luck with that. She's dramatic enough as she is."

Catherine reached under the table and nudged him lightly with her foot. "Careful, or I'll have your character killed off by chapter two."

Their eyes met a brief spark of affection and amusement that spoke of everything they'd endured together. For all the darkness of the past week, there was still light here, and love that had survived far worse than scandal.

At that moment, the door opened, and Henshaw stepped in, his expression as formal as ever though there was a flicker of curiosity behind his professional calm. "There is a Mr Strong to see you, madam."

Catherine set down her cup. "Ah," she said. "That will be the police, this time."

David rose with her, but she put a hand on his arm. "Let me speak to them first," she said quietly. "You know how these things go."

He nodded, brushing his thumb over her fingers. "All right. But I'll be close by."

Catherine straightened her jacket, smoothed her skirt, and followed Henshaw out into the hall. Her footsteps echoed on the polished floorboards. The Christmas tree in the foyer still twinkled faintly, though several of its candles had burned down to nubs. A faint scent of pine hung in the air, mingled with something more domestic, toast, coffee, and the faint musk of dogs and old wood.

Outside the front door, a police car sat in the drive, its tyres cutting slush into the gravel. The uniformed officer standing beside it stamped his feet against the cold.

Mr Strong was waiting in the entrance hall, cap in hand, his expression polite but businesslike. He was a tall man with the ruddy complexion of someone who had spent his life outdoors.

"Mrs Forrester?" he asked. "Detective Inspector Strong, Maidstone Division. I understand there's been... some incident."

Catherine met his gaze squarely. "You could say that," she replied. "In fact, there's been three."

Strong blinked, his brows lifting slightly. "Three murders?"

"Indeed." She gestured for him to follow. "Come into the drawing room. I'll explain."

As they walked through the hall, she spoke calmly, her tone that of someone presenting a report rather than a confession. "You'll find this a rather tangled case, Inspector. But the short version is, Sally killed my aunt, Frances, and a young man named Simon. Philip killed Clara. I've solved it, though I'm sure you'll want to confirm the details in your own way."

Strong's face was unreadable. "You've... solved it yourself?"

"I have," Catherine said simply. "And I believe you'll find both culprits still here in the house. They've been confined to their rooms since last night."

"I see." He cleared his throat, clearly recalibrating. "And what led you to these conclusions?"

Catherine gave a small, knowing smile. "I'll fill in the details later, Inspector. For now, I'd appreciate it if you could take them into custody before they have an opportunity to vanish into the snow."

Strong hesitated only a moment before nodding. "Very well, Mrs Forrester. I'll see to it."

"Thank you." She turned slightly, glancing toward the dining room. "But first, I need to say goodbye to my guests. They've been through enough."

Strong inclined his head. "Of course."

Catherine returned to the dining hall, her composure perfectly intact, though there was a faint colour in her cheeks now, the look of a woman who has finally laid down a heavy burden. David stood as she entered, concern flickering in his eyes.

"Well?" he asked quietly.

"It's done," she said. "Mr Strong will see to the arrests. I've given him the outline, he'll want a full statement later. For now, I'd rather let the others have their breakfast in peace."

Enid looked up from feeding the cat the last of her sausage. "Arrests, dear? Oh, it's all coming to a close, then?"

"Yes," Catherine said gently. "At last."

Holly closed her notebook and exhaled. "So, it's really over."

Catherine glanced toward the window, where the snow continued to melt in soft rivulets down the glass. "As over as these holidays, I think." She managed a small smile. "We'll have a quiet New Year after all."

David moved to her side. "You deserve it," he murmured.

She looked up at him, her eyes softening. "We both do."

For a long moment they stood there, side by side, watching the snowman collapse into a lopsided heap. Tulip gave a quiet bark, and somewhere down the corridor the clock struck Ten, its chime echoing through the old house.

Christmas was over, the truth had been spoken, and though the snow was fading, the light through the window felt a little stronger, a little warmer, than it had for days.

Chapter 40: Hollow Marrow

The morning air had that particular stillness that follows a snowfall, the hush before the world fully wakes again. The drive of Price Mansion was damp and glistening, edged with thin ribbons of ice that cracked softly underfoot. The snow that had blanketed the lawns all week was finally surrendering to the thaw, leaving behind wet patches of earth and the occasional stubborn drift that sparkled faintly in the pale December sun.

Catherine and David stood together outside the front steps, their coats pulled tight against the lingering chill. Behind them, the great house loomed, festive still but a little weary now, the garlands slightly drooping, the wreath on the door dusted with frost, the coloured lights in the windows dim in the watery daylight. Somewhere within, a clock struck ten.

Enid Bascombe stood beside them, wrapped in a fur-trimmed coat that looked far too grand for her age and size. A tartan scarf was knotted under her chin, and in one gloved hand she clutched a battered carpet bag; the other held the wicker cat carrier, from which a faint, imperious meow sounded every now and then.

A single cab was due to collect her, one of the old Austin models from Maidstone, still with its worn black paint and the smell of petrol. Henshaw had gone to the gate to flag it down, and now the three of them waited in the cold forecourt.

"Thank you again for saving my life, Enid," Catherine said, her breath curling in the air. "And for all of your input into the case. I wouldn't have been able to solve it without you."

Enid gave a modest shrug, the sort that managed to be both self-deprecating and proud. "Oh, that's no problem, dear. I've really enjoyed it. Loved every bit of it, truth be told, listening, picking up hints, helping each other. I may be old, but the mind still works when it's fed something juicy."

David smiled faintly. "You've certainly kept us all on our toes."

Enid chuckled, rummaging in her coat pocket until she produced a small jar wrapped in paper. "Pickled onions," she announced. "Made them myself before Christmas. I keep a jar in my pocket for moments like this." She unscrewed the lid, plucked one out, and popped it into her mouth with a small crunch. "I'm sorry I led you astray a few times," she said between bites, "by not telling you everything. But that's how I work. I like to know what's what before I spill the beans."

Catherine laughed softly. "That's exactly what I've learned about you. You never reveal all at once."

"Of course not," Enid said, smiling slyly. "Where would be the fun in that?"

Tulip trotted up beside them, tail wagging, her breath clouding in the cold. She sniffed curiously at the edge of Enid's bag, earning a tolerant glance from Mr Whittaker's carrier.

"You see," Enid went on, "you and I are not so different, Catherine. We both like our mysteries properly arranged before the final act. You've got the sharper instincts, mind you I'll grant you that. But I've the patience of age on my side."

David, amused, put an arm lightly around Catherine's shoulders. "And yet," he said, "you two together seem to make quite a formidable team. I'm not sure the county is ready for a repeat performance."

"Oh, nonsense," Enid said, waving her hand dismissively. "They'll get used to us. Besides, I'm feeling rather weary of all this excitement." Her expression softened. "You know, I'm in my eightieth year now, and I can feel it. The bones ache, the mornings come slower, and all this travelling tires me more than it used to."

Catherine's face grew tender. "Don't say that. You've got plenty of life left in you yet."

Enid smiled wistfully. "Perhaps. But there are days I feel as though I'm carrying a hundred years instead of eighty. I suppose it's natural to grow weary of life after a while, not sad, just… ready for quieter things."

A gentle silence fell between them, filled only by the distant caw of crows and the steady drip from the roof. The Christmas decorations still clung to the eaves, red bows faded slightly by frost, silver tinsel dulling in the pale light. It was beautiful in its way, like a stage set waiting for the curtain to fall.

After a pause, Enid spoke again, her tone brightening. "We never did discuss the missing in my village; you know Hollow Marrow. That was part of the reason for my coming, after all."

Catherine nodded slowly. "Yes, I've been thinking about that this week. Between everything else." She smiled. "And I believe I've solved it."

Enid's eyes twinkled. "So, do I. I have all the evidence in my spare room." She patted her bag knowingly. "Come and see me next week and we'll go through it together."

Catherine tilted her head, amused. "You won't mind if I bring my own tea, then?"

"I will insist upon it," Enid said firmly. "I drink mine strong enough to strip paint. You'll do better to bring your own pot."

They all laughed the kind of soft laughter that warms the space between people more than any fire.

Tulip barked suddenly, tail wagging as she trotted toward the gate. The distant rumble of an engine grew louder; a black cab appeared through the thin veil of mist at the end of the drive, its headlights cutting through the pale morning.

As the taxi drew up, the driver climbed out a man in his fifties with a cheerful, ruddy face and a flat cap pulled low against the cold. He tipped his hat politely. "Morning, missus. Bit of slush on the lanes, but we'll get you home right enough."

"Thank you, dear," Enid said. "I've survived murders, I'll survive your driving."

The driver grinned. "Fair enough."

While he loaded her bag into the boot, Enid crouched to give Tulip her farewell. The little dog wagged and whined, pressing close to her. Enid fished the last sausage from her coat pocket and held it out. "Here, my darling. This is my last one. You've earned it, after all the excitement."

Tulip took it delicately, tail sweeping the slush.

"There," Enid said, standing with a small groan. "All debts paid."

David stepped forward to take her arm as she balanced herself. "Careful there," he said. "Mind the ice."

"Thank you, young man." She looked up at him, her expression suddenly fond. "You're good for her, you know."

David blinked. "For Catherine?"

"Yes. You steady her. A woman like her needs a man who can keep pace but never stand in her way. You've done that beautifully."

Catherine smiled, a faint colour touching her cheeks. "That's the highest compliment you'll ever receive, David."

He squeezed her hand. "I'll treasure it."

Enid turned back to Catherine. "Now, dear, I mean what I said. Come to Hollow Marrow next week. We'll sort through the business of the missing, and I'll show you what I've been keeping in the back room. You'll find it rather shocking, I think."

Catherine nodded, curious but not pressing. "I'll hold you to that."

"You'd better." Enid's eyes softened. "And don't leave it too long. I've a feeling time is nipping at my heels."

The driver held the door open for her. "All set, missus?"

Enid nodded. She turned back one last time, taking in the sight of the great old house behind them the ivy on its walls, the wreath still hanging proudly on the door, and the two figures standing close together on the steps.

"Well, until next week, Catherine," she said. "And thank you both for everything. It's been a Christmas to remember, hasn't it?"

"It certainly has," Catherine said warmly. "Safe journey, Enid."

Enid bundled herself into the cab, adjusting the carrier on her lap. Mr Whittaker gave a disapproving meow as if to say he'd had enough of adventures. Enid chuckled, whispering to him, "Oh, hush, we're nearly home."

The driver closed the door, climbed into his seat, and with a small cough of the engine the taxi began to roll down the drive. Its tyres hissed on the melting snow.

Catherine and David stood together watching until it turned out of sight beyond the fir trees. The sound of the engine faded, leaving only the drip of thaw and the distant call of a wood pigeon.

For a moment neither of them spoke. The air felt oddly still the calm that follows both endings and beginnings.

"She's quite remarkable," David said quietly.

Catherine nodded. "She is. A strange woman, but wise in her own way." She tucked her gloved hand into his. "I'll miss her chatter echoing through the halls. It'll feel very empty without her."

David smiled. "Perhaps that's not such a bad thing, after the week we've had."

Catherine gave a small laugh. "True enough. But I do admire her spirit. Eighty years old, and still able to see through everyone in the room."

They began to walk slowly back toward the house. The gravel crunched beneath their shoes, the damp air curling around them like breath.

"She was right about you, you know," Catherine said softly.

"Oh?"

"You do steady me."

He stopped, turning to face her. "And you remind me that life should be lived with purpose," he said. "I think we're even."

Catherine smiled, that rare open smile that reached her eyes. She leaned closer, resting her head briefly against his shoulder. "I don't know what I'd do without you, David."

"You'll never have to find out," he said simply.

They stood there a moment longer, framed by the faint glitter of melting frost and the last echo of Christmas bells from the village beyond the hill. Behind them, the mansion seemed to breathe again quieter, lighter, the ghosts of the past few days slowly dispersing.

Inside, Henshaw had already begun to clear away the remnants of breakfast. The scent of coffee lingered in the corridor, mingling with pine and polish. Somewhere in the drawing room, the radio played softly a choir singing *The Holly and the Ivy*.

Catherine glanced back once more down the drive. The cab was gone now, leaving only tyre tracks in the slush and a faint curl of exhaust in the air. She sighed gently. "Do you know, I almost envy her," she said. "Going home to her quiet little life, her cat, her spare room full of secrets. There's something peaceful in that."

David chuckled. "You wouldn't last a week without a mystery to chase."

She smiled. "Perhaps not. But for a few days, I'd like to pretend I could."

They reached the door. David opened it for her, and she stepped inside, brushing the cold from her coat. The warmth of the hall wrapped around them like a blanket. The Christmas tree twinkled faintly in the corner, its baubles reflecting the golden light.

Chapter 41: Book Deal

Catherine stood by the landing window, a mug of tea warming her hands, watching the slow drip of thawing icicles. She felt that curious blend of relief and emptiness that always followed a storm the silence after the orchestra stops. Behind her, David was buttoning his shirt, humming a few bars of "God Rest Ye Merry Gentlemen," his voice low and pleasant.

"Well," he said, straightening his tie, "we're nearly back to normal. The house feels so much bigger when everyone's gone."

Catherine turned, smiling faintly. "Bigger and quieter. I'd forgotten what that sounds like."

"Until next Christmas," he teased.

"Let's not think about that yet," she said, coming to stand beside him. She reached to fix his collar, fingers brushing his neck with absent fondness. "I'm still recovering from this one."

He grinned, catching her hand and pressing it briefly. "You say that every year."

"I mean it every year."

They shared a smile, the kind that comes from years of knowing exactly when to tease and when to hold one's tongue. Downstairs, Tulip barked once, the sound echoing faintly through the hall, and Catherine took that as her cue to begin the day.

The Christmas tree, tall and noble even in retreat had begun to shed its needles, scattering green over the rug like confetti. A few wrapped gifts lingered under the branches, leftovers from guests too distracted to take them home. A half-burnt candle stood beside the nativity scene; its wax dripped into a frozen wave.

Holly was there already, bustling about, her bright red jumper and matching scarf adding colour to the greying morning. Her suitcase lay open on the armchair, and a scatter of notebooks, pens, and cassette tapes covered the nearby table.

"I can't believe it," she was saying, folding a jumper into the case. "Philip Marsh of all people. He seemed so… well, dull."

David raised an eyebrow. "That's often the way, isn't it? The dull ones surprise you."

Holly shook her head. "To think he'd stoop to murder all to cover up the millions he stole." She paused, looking from one to the other, as if the enormity of it still refused to settle. "I keep going over it in my mind, and it just doesn't fit with the man who offered me brandy and asked about my writing."

"People are put into difficult situations," David said quietly, "and you never really know how they'll react until they're there."

Catherine poured herself a coffee and sat down opposite Holly, her tone measured but thoughtful. "Greed and desperation make a potent mix. Once someone starts down that road, they'll do anything to protect what they think is theirs. Murder often starts with a very small lie."

Holly nodded, still dazed. "It's such a strange world you live in, Catherine. People killing for money, secrets, or pride. I write about it, but you… you really see it."

Catherine smiled faintly. "Yes, but don't envy me. There's little glamour in it. Only paperwork, sleepless nights, and an endless stream of questions that don't always have good answers."

David leaned against the mantel, his hands in his pockets. "She says that" he said lightly, "but she'd go mad without a mystery to solve. She thrives on them."

Catherine gave him a mock glare. "I thrive on order, not chaos."

He grinned. "If you say so."

"Sally got herself into so much of a tizz she really believed your guests were going to kill her I feel sorry for her." Holly looked down.

"I do think she thought she was doing good at the time, but Murder is murder and I am going to miss Aunt Frances" Catherine said with sadness.

The mood softened into gentle laughter, the sort that helped shake off the heaviness of the past few days. Outside, a light drizzle began to fall, tapping against the window.

Holly zipped up her bag, pausing a moment as if reluctant to close the chapter entirely. "I don't know how you both stay so calm through all of this. I barely slept last night. Every creak in the corridor made me jump."

"You'll sleep tonight," David said. "When you're back in your own bed and it's all behind you."

"I hope so." Holly smiled, a little wistful. "It's been… an unforgettable Christmas."

Catherine chuckled softly. "That's one way of putting it." She took a sip of tea, then added, "Talking of difficult situations, though we're going to need a million pounds to pay off Mr. Keene."

David looked over sharply, his calm expression tightening a little. "Yes. I've been thinking about that. We can't just hand over money; it would be admitting fault. We need to take legal action first see what cards he's actually holding."

"Always the pragmatist," Catherine said, approvingly. "That's what I love about you. You think in lines and columns, not panic."

He smiled. "One of us has to."

Holly hesitated, her expression shifting as if she'd been holding something back. "Actually," she began, "I didn't want to say anything before I didn't want to distract you while the police were still here but…"

Catherine looked up. "But what?"

"The book," Holly said quickly. "The one I've been planning. The publisher has seen my notes. With your name attached to it, Catherine with your involvement they're predicting it'll make a fortune. Millions."

David blinked. "Millions?"

She nodded, almost shyly. "I didn't want to make assumptions, but the market's crying out for real detective stories. Not fiction, not fantasy *real* cases. You've solved three murders in a week, Catherine. The world will want to hear about it. And if we time it right after the court case, once everything's public record it will be enormous."

Catherine regarded her quietly for a moment, the steam from her tea rising between them. "I see," she said finally. "And what exactly would you call this masterpiece?"

Holly grinned. "I was thinking *Murder at Christmas*. Simple, classic, unforgettable."

David laughed. "You might want to change a few names."

"Oh, of course," Holly said. "No one wants a lawsuit for New Year's. But with your permission, Catherine, I'd like to use you as the central figure the investigator. Not officially, of course. Just... inspired by you."

Catherine leaned back, her eyes narrowing in amusement. "I can imagine it now: a stern but brilliant woman with impeccable taste in coats and an unruly dog."

"Exactly," Holly said, laughing. "And a long-suffering husband who brews perfect tea and tolerates her genius."

David mock bowed. "I'll take it."

For a moment, the room filled with gentle warmth again laughter, the faint hiss of the fire, the comfortable shuffle of normal life returning.

"Seriously, though," Holly said, her voice softening, "the deal could really change things. You might not have to worry about this Mr. Keene at all. The advance alone will be substantial. My agent's drawing up the details."

Catherine tilted her head, still calm. "That's kind of you, Holly. But money earned honestly takes time. And court cases... have a way of swallowing it whole."

"I know," Holly said, "but it's something, isn't it? A way forward."

"It is," Catherine admitted. "And I appreciate it."

Tulip, sensing the lull in conversation, padded over and rested her head on Catherine's knee. Catherine scratched her ears absently, smiling down at her. "Even Tulip looks relieved that things are over."

"She's had quite the adventure," David said. "I half expect her to start writing her own memoirs next."

Holly laughed. "I'd read it." She bent to give the dog a farewell pat. "Goodbye, Tulip. You've been a very brave girl."

Tulip's tail thumped once against the rug.

Henshaw appeared briefly at the doorway. "Miss Holly's car is ready, ma'am. The drive's a bit slushy, but she should manage."

"Thank you, Henshaw," Catherine said.

Holly snapped her suitcase shut and slung her scarf around her neck. "Well," she said brightly, though her eyes were a little misty, "I suppose that's that. Thank you both for letting me stay for Christmas. You didn't have to, especially with everything going on."

Catherine stood and came around the table. "You're always welcome here, Holly. Even if you do turn our misfortunes into chapters."

Holly smiled. "I'll write kindly, I promise."

David offered to carry her bag, and the three of them stepped out onto the front steps. The air smelled of damp earth and pine, and from somewhere in the distance came the faint sound of church bells St. Michael's again, marking eleven.

Holly's little 2CV stood waiting near the gate, its bright red paint gleaming against the dull sky. She turned back for one last look at the mansion, its high windows glinting faintly.

"It's strange," she said. "I feel like I've just stepped out of a storybook."

"You'll turn it into one soon enough," David said.

She smiled, brushing a strand of hair from her face. "I will. And when it's published, I'll make sure you're the first to read it."

"Just promise me one thing," Catherine said. "Don't romanticise it. Tell it as it was cold, complicated, and human."

"I'll try," Holly said softly. "But you have a way of making even the darkest moments seem extraordinary."

Catherine looked at her for a moment, then nodded, accepting the compliment. "Drive safely, Holly. And call when you get home."

Holly gave a playful salute. "Yes, ma'am."

She climbed into her little car, started the engine which sputtered once, coughed, then caught and rolled slowly down the drive, tyres splashing through the slush. She waved through the window as she went, and Catherine lifted her hand in return.

They watched until the red car disappeared around the bend, the sound of its engine fading into the distance.

David slipped his arm around Catherine's waist, drawing her close against the cold. "And then there were two," he said quietly.

Catherine leaned into him, resting her head briefly on his shoulder. "Just how I like it," she murmured. "No noise, no guests, no chaos. Just peace."

"Peace and paperwork," he said dryly.

She laughed softly. "Always the realist."

They stood there for a moment longer, watching the empty lane where the car had gone, until the church bells faded and the only sound left was the slow drip of thawing snow from the eaves.

Inside, the Christmas tree still glowed faintly, and the scent of pine lingered in the air a reminder of the season that was slipping quietly away, leaving behind its stories, its scars, and a strange kind of hope.

Chapter 42: Happy New Year

The house was quieter than it had been in weeks. The great fire in the drawing room still glowed, fed now and then by David, who insisted on using up the last of the Yule logs before the year was out. Outside, the wind carried a chill, though the snow had mostly melted into slick patches of frost on the gravel drive.

A few candles burned low in brass holders, their flames trembling in the draught. The old clock on the mantel ticked with reassuring rhythm, its pendulum gleaming in the light. Tulip snored gently in her basket by the hearth, occasionally twitching her paws in some small dream.

David sat on the arm of the sofa, a glass of brandy in his hand, his other arm draped casually around Catherine's shoulders. She leaned against him, her hair brushing the fabric of his shirt. On the table beside them were the remnants of their supper a cold goose, a plate of pickles, and the last wedge of Christmas pudding that neither had quite the appetite to finish.

"Well," David said at last, breaking the comfortable silence. "That's the end of the year and what a year it's been."

Catherine smiled faintly. "I'll say. Sometimes I think we've lived ten years in one."

He took a sip of his drink, the amber liquid catching the firelight. "Do you realise, this time last year we'd only just solved our third case? We were in that little terrace in Maidstone, remember? With the broken boiler and that dreadful wallpaper."

Catherine laughed softly. "I remember. You said it looked like a migraine waiting to happen."

"It was true," he said, smiling. "And the rent was high, and the neighbours fought every night."

"And money was tight," Catherine added. "We'd just about managed to pay for Christmas dinner, and I remember saying that if another case didn't come in soon, we'd have to start selling the good china."

David chuckled. "Yes. And then came that strange telephone call the one from the art dealer with the missing manuscripts."

Catherine nodded. "And after that, everything changed. The cases got bigger. The clients wealthier. And somehow, we found ourselves here in this house."

David looked around at the high ceilings, the heavy curtains, the glow of the fire reflected in the dark wood panelling. "Sometimes I still can't quite believe it's ours."

Catherine smiled. "Nor can I." She paused, thoughtful. "You know, it was that case in Greece that really turned the tide. The one where Adrian wrote that piece for me the article in *The Times*."

David's eyes lit with memory. "Ah yes, the island of Thasos. I can still smell the sea air and hear those infernal cicadas."

She laughed. "You complained about them every day."

"They were louder than church bells," he said with mock indignation. "But that was the beginning of everything, wasn't it? That's where we met Sally and Matthew now Martin."

Catherine nodded slowly. "Yes. And when that story was published, the letters started pouring in. All those people wanting the clever lady detective from the newspaper to solve their family troubles. That's when the money really began to flow."

David smiled, setting down his glass. "And then we bought Peter out of this place. That was the best decision we made."

Catherine hesitated, her gaze flicking to the window where faint reflections of the Christmas lights shimmered. "I know Mr Keane's managed to put a spanner in the works," she said finally. "But I believe things will come right. This book that Holly's writing it'll show the world who we really are. I'll be seen as the number one sleuth. And with that recognition, more money will come in, more cases, more success. Eventually, we'll rise again."

David turned toward her, smiling with quiet affection. "In the meantime," he said, "I get to relax with my beautiful wife."

Catherine rolled her eyes slightly but smiled, resting her hand on his knee. "Flattery will get you everywhere."

He leaned closer and kissed her, slow and tender, the kind of kiss that held years of understanding. "Happy almost New Year," he murmured.

She smiled against his lips. "Not quite yet. Ten minutes to go."

"Ten minutes to 1990," he said, looking toward the clock. "A new decade. Can you believe it?"

"It's strange to think of it," Catherine said. "A whole new decade. I wonder what it will bring."

"Hopefully less murder," he said lightly, rising to his feet. "And more evenings like this."

He stretched, glancing toward the hall. "I just need to visit the little boys' room before midnight. Don't start the singing without me."

"I'll try to resist," Catherine said dryly.

As he left the room, Tulip stirred, blinking sleepily. The fire crackled softly. Catherine leaned forward to top up her drink and then noticed a faint rustling sound. She looked down.

Tulip was now lying beside the hearth, licking a grease off of some paper. Catherine frowned. "Tulip, honestly. You're going on a diet tomorrow," she said affectionately. "You'll make yourself sick."

The dog wagged her tail guiltily but continued her feast. Catherine bent down, reaching to pull the paper away. "And you're not eating that paper either," she scolded gently. "Goodness knows what you've found this time."

But as she picked up the scrap, she saw it wasn't just rubbish. The paper was folded, faintly stained with goose fat, but covered in writing neat, slanted handwriting she recognised instantly.

Catherine's eyes narrowed. "What on earth…?"

She unfolded it carefully. It was a letter.

Her heart gave a small, uneasy lurch as she began to read:

Dear Sally,

You are right. Martin is Matthew Askew. Martin, Simon and Peter are going to kill us, as I've discussed with you. It is a shame Carla and Frances drank the poison but you had to try, it was them or us. We both heard what Simon said last night. I lured him out by making a snowman. I stabbed him. It was for us. You keep this letter. It's the guarantee that I'll give you half the money for the book. And in return, you should do the time for me in prison for Simon's death as you are doing time for Carlas and Aunt Frances murder already. Remember, we saved them all.

Yours, Holly.

For a long moment Catherine just stared at the page. The room seemed to contract around her; the sound of the fire faded, replaced by the steady, dreadful rhythm of her own heartbeat.

"So, it was Holly," she whispered. "It was Holly all along."

She sank slowly into the armchair, the letter trembling in her hand. "So that's how Sally was drawn into it. Manipulated. Fed on fear and lies."

Her mind worked rapidly the way it always did when faced with new evidence but there was a different weight to it this time. The discovery didn't fill her with triumph, only weariness.

Did Holly truly want the story that badly? Catherine wondered. Did she kill for fame? For money? Or was it something more immediate self-defence, panic, lust turned sour?

She stared into the flames, the letter glowing faintly in the orange light. "I wonder," she murmured to herself, "if Simon came on too strong. He was impulsive. Maybe she struck out of fear. Holly, eager one minute, cold the next. She always played emotions like cards. Perhaps he misread her. Perhaps she felt cornered."

The fire popped softly. Tulip gave a small sigh and shifted in her basket.

"Come to think of it, Holly orchestrated it all. She wanted murder at Christmas. She wanted this book written. She needed Murder, winding up Sally to such a degree, maybe she even gave her the Mugwart. Philip wouldn't have murdered Carla if everyone knew she was alive. All Holly could see was the pound signs and the fame, Enid was right she would do anything to have my fame. There would have been no murder without her."

"If I hand this in," Catherine said aloud, her voice barely above a whisper, "the book will never come out. The story will be twisted. I'll be the sleuth who missed the real killer. The newspapers will tear me apart."

Her eyes drifted toward the window, where her reflection stared back at her calm, poised, but haunted. "We'll lose everything," she went on quietly. "The house, the reputation…maybe even David. And yet..."

She held the letter tighter, the paper crackling between her fingers. "The right thing to do," she said softly, "is to hand it to the police. To tell David. To make it right."

For a long time, she sat there, the weight of her decision pressing down like the cold outside the windows. The minutes ticked by. The clock chimed faintly in the hall, reminding her that the year was drawing to its final seconds.

She could hear David's footsteps returning.

"Catherine?" he called cheerfully from the corridor. "Are you ready to sing *Auld Lang Syne*?"

She looked at the letter once more, the ink shimmering faintly in the firelight. Then she folded it slowly, carefully. Her hand hovered over the desk then moved toward the small bin beside it.

"Nearly," she said quietly, as David entered the room.

He crossed to her, smiling, holding two glasses of champagne. "You look miles away," he said, handing her one.

She accepted it, her expression composed. "Just thinking of the year gone by."

He raised his glass. "And of the one ahead."

She nodded, forcing a small smile. "To new beginnings."

The clock began its slow, solemn chime. Midnight.

David leaned in and kissed her, his hand warm against her cheek. "Happy New Year, my love."

"Happy New Year," she whispered.

As he turned to fetch the record player for the music, Catherine's gaze dropped to the letter, she scrunched it up and thew it into the bin, it rested half-hidden beneath a crumpled napkin.

The firelight flickered across it, and for a moment she thought she saw the ink glimmer again, as though the words were alive a confession waiting to be found.

But she looked away.

Outside, fireworks burst faintly in the distance. Bells rang across the valley, carried on the winter wind. The new decade was about to begin.

Catherine lifted her glass again, her expression unreadable, her fingers brushing David's as the first notes of *Auld Lang Syne* filled the room.

About the Author

Alan Moody has always loved a good murder mystery. For him, it's not just about solving the puzzle of whodunit, but also exploring the emotional depth and tangled relationships that lie beneath the surface.

He lives with his wife, their mad dog, Tinker and Silver the cat, in a semi-rural village in Kent, where the quiet surroundings offer the perfect setting for plotting fictional crimes. By day, Alan is a teacher; by night (and early mornings), he escapes into the world of mystery writing.

Murder at Christmas fourth novel with Catherine Forrester — a sharp, determined investigator and the kind of strong female lead Alan has always admired.

If you enjoyed this book, please consider leaving a positive review on Amazon. Reviews make a real difference and help authors like Alan continue sharing stories.

I have even used reviews to edit this story in a better way. He is currently working on his fifth book, **Murder in the Village**, which is set for release in February.